MISS JULIA SPEAKS HER MIND

MISS JULIA
—
SPEAKS
—
HER
—
MIND

A NOVEL BY

ANN B. ROSS

BOOKSPAN LARGE PRINT EDITION

WILLIAM MORROW AND COMPANY, INC.
New York

This Large Print Edition, prepared especially for Bookspan, contains the complete, unabridged text of the original Publisher's Edition.

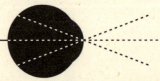

This Large Print Book carries the
Seal of Approval of N.A.V.H.

FOR ALICE, CHARLES, AND JOHN MICHAEL

ACKNOWLEDGMENTS

—

My thanks to all the Wordwrights, but especially to Elizabeth, Katie, Susan, Sally, and our fearless leader, Ted; to Boyd B. Massagee, Jr., Charles Waters, and Sharon Alexander, attorneys-at-law, all of whom proffered advice not always taken (so don't blame them); to Marion for his forebearance; and to Marian, Claudia, and John for never failing in their encouragement and support. My thanks also to the friend whose name I confiscated and, most especially, to Jennifer Robinson, Delin Cormeny, and Katharine Cluverius.

Miss Julia Speaks Her Mind

CHAPTER ONE

—

I'd just caught my breath after the shock of my husband's sudden passing when his last legacy showed up on my front porch. We'd buried Wesley Lloyd Springer some few months before that hot, still morning in August, and I hoped I was through signing forms and meeting with lawyers and shuffling through various and sundry legal papers. I declare, this business of dying has more legal aspects to it than you would think. The deceased never knows what you have to go through to get his affairs in order, and Wesley Lloyd's were in as much order as they could get. I thought.

Lord, it was hot that morning, and I recalled again how Wesley Lloyd had always put his foot down about air-conditioning the house, even when the Conovers had theirs done. Central air, too. Wesley Lloyd said it was a waste of money and, besides, fresh air was good for us. He felt that way only at home, though, because his office at the bank was kept cool enough for the three-piece suits he wore day in and day out. But I don't believe in speaking ill of the dead, even when it's the truth.

So I was sitting in my living room trying to get my mind off the heat by looking through a stack of mail-order catalogs. Making a list of the items I intended to call in for and having a good time doing it, since Binkie Enloe'd said I needed to spend some money. Sam Murdoch had agreed, and he ought've known since he was the executor of the will that had put me in my present more-than-comfortable position. Lord, there was more money than I ever knew Wesley Lloyd had, and it all belonged to me, his grieving widow. But a proud widow, too, and justly so, because I'd made such a fine and fortunate choice of husbands.

But I tell you, I thought I'd never get over the shock of finding Wesley Lloyd dead as a doornail, slumped over the steering wheel of his new Buick Park Avenue. Steel gray with plush upholstery, parked right out there in the driveway.

But I did, laying him to rest in a properly ordered Presbyterian ceremony as he would've expected. Then I had to suffer another shock when I found out how well-off Wesley Lloyd had been. Why, besides the bank his daddy'd left him, he owned half the county, seemed like, plus stocks and bonds and tax-deferred annuities, all of it making more and more money every day of the week. When the extent of his estate was laid out for me, all I could think of was how he used to hand me a housekeeping allowance every Friday, saying, "Make it last, Julia. Money doesn't grow on trees, you know." And all the time he was cultivating a whole grove! Well, a lot of good it did him, because I ended up with every penny.

Now, after forty-four years in blissful ignorance of Wesley Lloyd's activities, financial and otherwise, I had settled down to enjoy the benefits of widowhood and a full checkbook, both of which I was mastering with hardly any problems to speak of.

I looked out the window as a few cars passed by on Polk Street, headed down to

Main. I declare, everybody and his brother seemed to have a telephone glued to his ear, though this town's not big enough to need BellSouth whenever you drive to the grocery store. Across the street the parking lot spread from Polk to the back of the First Presbyterian Church of Abbotsville, my church and the one Wesley Lloyd and his father, before him, had supported with their presence, tithes, offerings, and over-and-above donations. Advice, too, which was always taken but not always appreciated. Heat waves shimmered up from the asphalt lot as I took note of whose cars were parked over there. It was my custom to keep up with what went on around me and, since Mondays were Pastor Ledbetter's days off, I couldn't be blamed for wondering why he was meeting with several men on the session at the church. But far be it from me to be nosy.

I could hear Lillian humming along with the radio above the occasional clatter of pans out in the kitchen as she prepared my lunch. That was another thing that was different, now that Wesley Lloyd wouldn't be home for meals anymore. He'd liked a quiet house, meals served on time, and everything done right on schedule. I had already begun to enjoy a little freedom from that schedule, telling Lillian that we'd eat whenever either of us got hungry or she got the urge to put something on the table.

I licked a finger and turned a page in the Neiman Marcus Christmas catalog, wondering what Sam and Binkie would say if I ordered a few trinkets from it. I declare, some of the offerings were for people with more money than sense, a condition that didn't apply to me, I'm happy to say. I expect, though, that any number of people would've said it did if they'd known the full extent of Wesley Lloyd's prudence and foresight.

However. His prudence and foresight hadn't taken heart attacks into account. I knew as sure as I was sitting there he never intended to leave me in charge of everything he owned. I knew it as soon as Pastor Ledbetter came sidling up to me not two days after laying Wesley Lloyd to rest, telling me he knew I'd want to honor Mr. Springer's last wishes even if they'd never gotten written down. That was the first I'd heard that Wesley Lloyd had planned to make the First Presbyterian Church his main beneficiary, with Pastor Ledbetter and a member of the session as trustees who'd dole me out an allowance every month.

And speaking of which, you wouldn't believe the phone calls and circulars and brochures and letters on embossed stationery that had come to me from investment counselors, financial advisors, estate planners, and you name it, wanting me to turn my assets over to them. It didn't matter if it was a church, a college, a charity, or a businessman in an office, they all knew what was in my best interests. If I'd just let them take care of everything, I would be assured of an allowance dribbled out every quarter throughout my lifetime. Well, I'd been on an allowance for forty-four years, thank you, and having it all was better.

I reached over to close my wine velvet drapes against the morning sun streaming through the window—you have to watch that the sun doesn't fade your Orientals— and shifted in my chair to move out of the glare. A hairpin slid down my neck and, as I tucked it back in, I recalled how Velma had started talking during my last appointment, paying no attention to the business at hand, which was giving me a permanent.

It'd just made me sick when I saw what she'd done. She said the curl would loosen up when it was washed, and besides, my hair was real fine, and I ought to know that hair texture changes with age, and was I taking any medication that would react with the solution. I declare, I wish just once in her life the woman would admit to a mistake and not blame me or my hair for coming out looking like a Brillo pad.

But some things you just have to live with. Like frizzy hair. And no children to comfort you in your old age, both of which can make you want to bury your head and cry.

But to look on the bright side, hair can grow out and children can grow up to squabble over inheritances, so I couldn't feel too sorry for myself. Not that I would ever deny a child of mine what was rightfully his. Or hers, but they might fuss among themselves. As it was, I was spared the shameful spectacle of a family split apart over who got what. I know what I'm talking about, because I've seen it happen too many times, more's the pity. I expect there's never been a will in the world that satisfied all the beneficiaries, so I couldn't feel too sad about being the sole survivor.

I sighed and turned another page, my attention so taken with the glitter of the catalogs that I nearly jumped out of my skin when the doorbell rang.

I went to the front door and looked through the screen at a woman standing there in heels too high, dress too short, and hair too yellow. All of it too young for the hard-living lines around her eyes and slick, red lips. A skinny little boy stood behind her hanging his head, and I thought she was selling something. Door-to-door salespeople do that, don't you know, take a child with them to make you feel guilty about turning them down. I opened my mouth to say "No, thank you," but she was already talking.

"I'm sorry to bother you," she said, hefting up the strap of her shoulder bag. I could see the sheen of perspiration oozing out from under her makeup as she took a deep breath and let the words pour out. "I wouldn't do this if I could come up with anything else. But I can't, and he didn't leave me no choice, and I got to make a livin'. You know how it is; well, maybe not. But I'm on my way to beauty school down in Raleigh. Learning nails? You know, acrylics and all? There's money in nails, and I just don't know what else to do."

I kept opening my mouth to tell her she had the wrong house, I didn't know her from Adam, but she didn't give me a chance. She pulled the child in front of her and gave him a little push toward the screen door. Sorry-looking little thing, scrawny and pale, standing there with a hangdog look to him and holding a brown Winn-Dixie grocery sack in both hands.

"This here's Wesley Lloyd Junior, though I guess," she said with a nervous laugh, "his name's not too legal, as nobody'd know better'n you. Wesley Lloyd Junior Springer is what I call him, it don't matter what's on his birth certificate, though his daddy's name's on it as the father. See, his name's right here." And she held out a piece of paper with the words "Certificate of Live Birth" across the top.

I could've been sleepwalking the way I opened the screen, took the paper, and read my husband's name on it. "Father: Wesley Lloyd Springer. Mother: Hazel Marie Puckett."

"I got to leave him with you," Hazel Marie Puckett said, pushing the little runt closer.

"I got to depend on your Christian charity, 'cause Wesley Lloyd didn't leave me a red cent. I talked to that lawyer of yours, and she said not even the house I been livin' in some twelve years now. I'm broke, Miz Springer, and I'm not asking you for nothing but to look after my boy while I go get some trainin'. There's nobody else I can leave him with and, I mean, it's kinda like he's your stepson, idn't it? I'll be back to get him, six weeks, max, and I really hate to do it, but. Be a good boy, now," she said, patting him on the back, and using a foot to shove a pasteboard suitcase over beside him.

"Mind Miz Springer, now, you hear?" She gave him a quick kiss on the top of his head and tripped down the steps to a rumbling maroon-and-white car parked in front of my house. Burning oil so bad that thick fumes curled around my boxwoods.

"Miss! Miss!" I called, finally gaining my voice and hurrying out on the porch. "Come back here! You can't do this! I can't take this child! Miss! I'm calling the sheriff, you better get back here!"

But she hopped into the passenger seat, and the car sped off before she hardly had time to slam the door. Passenger seat, it came to me. Somebody else driving.

"What's all this yellin' about?" Lillian was at the door, her white uniform glowing through the screen mesh. You could mistake her for a heavyset nurse or waitress unless you noticed the run-over heels of her shoes that flapped with every step she took. She looked at me, and then we both looked at the boy.

I'd never seen such a pitiful-looking specimen. About nine or ten, I guessed, with lank brown hair hanging in his eyes, big horn-rimmed glasses down on his nose, pale skin dotted with freckles, shifty eyes that wouldn't look at either of us. He stood there with his shoulders slumped, the clip-on bow tie crooked on his thin cotton shirt and his shiny pants gathered high above his waist with a brown stretch belt. Wal-Mart special, no doubt. I looked him over good, ignoring Lillian standing there with her mouth open. I lifted his chin and studied his face, confirming what was as plain as day. My heart sank like an elevator as I gazed at Wesley Lloyd Springer, minus sixty-some-odd years. Looked just like him, but without Wesley Lloyd's self-confidence and leadership qualities.

I took a deep breath. "Lillian, look what else Mr. Springer left me."

CHAPTER TWO

—

"Go call the sheriff," I told her as I turned back to the porch railing. I should've thought to get the tag number, but by then the car had roared down the street and turned right on Lincoln. A pall of black smoke drifted down in its wake.

Not hearing any movement behind me, I turned to see Lillian's arms around the little bastard, his head against her white nylon uniform. He turned loose of the grocery sack long enough to wipe the sleeve of one arm across his running nose, smearing his glasses even more. It was enough to turn your stomach.

Lillian looked at me like I'd lost my mind. "You can't call the sheriff on this pore little chile. What he done to you?"

"*He's* not done anything to me. Except be here. But I mean to report his mama." I crossed my arms against my chest and climbed on my high horse. "She can't just go abandoning a child on somebody's doorstep. I'll report her to the sheriff and the district attorney and anybody else I can think of. The idea of just dropping him off on me and leaving town. You're mighty right I'm calling the sheriff. If they hurry, they can catch her on the interstate and bring her back. This child's her responsibility, not mine!"

This tirade brought forth another wet snuffle from the little stray and another squinty-eyed glare from Lillian.

"Yessum, and I guess you want this whole thing on the front page of the *Abbotsville Press,* too, don't you? You thought of that? You thought what all this town gon' be talkin' and whisperin' and specalatin' about? You thought about what yo' preacher gon' say? An' all yo' church people? An' Miz Conover?"

Well no, I hadn't. Lillian had been giving me good advice for as long as she'd been with me, some twenty years now. We knew each other inside and out, and neither of us hesitated to say what we thought. Even so, we both knew how far to go without over-stepping ourselves, so I guess that made us friends as well. LuAnne Conover accused me of being too friendly with the help, said I'd encourage thieving, which would lead to back talk and then, if I wasn't careful, to downright laziness. She said it's better to have a businesslike arrangement and keep my distance. But LuAnne had never been able to keep help more than six months at a time, so I didn't see her advice as all that sound.

Besides, Lillian was a capable, self-as-sured woman, unlike me, who had to ask Wesley Lloyd what I thought about most every subject. She had a lot of common sense, too, in spite of that gold tooth she had put in a few years back. In fact, I put more stock in what Lillian thought than I did LuAnne Conover, who had to tell anybody who'd listen how important her husband was. Leonard, a slump-shouldered, paunchy man who Wesley Lloyd never had much use for, was big in county politics. He had to run for half a dozen offices before he finally won one. Leonard's name on the ballot got to be such a joke around town that we all felt sorry for him and elected him a few years ago to some clerical office in the courthouse annex just to get him out of sight. When Wesley Lloyd told me to vote for Leonard, he'd said the clerk of court didn't have to be a lawyer or college educated or even acquainted with the law. So since Leonard qualified on all counts, I'd cast my ballot for him and now I had to put up with listening to LuAnne tell how lawyers and judges depended on him, and how influential his decisions were. To hear her tell it, the county's business wouldn't get done without Leonard being there to keep everybody straight. I didn't have the heart to tell her that Wesley Lloyd had also said that Leonard couldn't do much damage clerking in the courthouse, because he knew how to take instruction. LuAnne loved to bask in the glow of Leonard's job and, even though I'd been guilty of the same thing with Wesley Lloyd's position, I was now trying to get over it.

Lillian, however, had more sense than either of us. I studied what she'd said a few minutes, walking back to the railing and clenching it as my knees began to tremble.

I knew she'd looked farther ahead than I'd been able to in my state of shock.

"All right," I said. "Go wake up Deputy Bates."

"I ain't gon' disturb that man's sleep. He work all night an' he need his rest."

I heaved a dramatic sigh and went into the house myself. "Well, at least do one thing without an argument," I said as I headed for the stairs. "Get that child inside before the whole town sees him."

Deputy Coleman Bates was my boarder, one that Sam Murdoch had strongly urged me to take in after Wesley Lloyd's demise. Not because I needed the money, because I didn't. But because Sam had said he'd sleep better knowing I had a man in the house. "There're a lot of wicked people out there, Julia," he'd said. "And a woman alone, especially one with your assets, would be an attraction to every thief, and worse, in this town." And he went on to point out that a deputy sheriff's car parked in my driveway would be a deterrent that no alarm system could match. So I'd fixed up the back upstairs bedroom, the one that opens onto the sleeping porch, which connects to the back staircase, and taken in a boarder. There was some comment about it at first, some speculation that Wesley Lloyd hadn't left me as well off as people had assumed. But soon after this young man moved in, I traded in Wesley Lloyd's Park Avenue, not wanting to be driving around in his deathbed, so to speak, for one of those little foreign coupes. Then I had the trim on the house touched up, and the drapes replaced in the living room, and on top of that, I made a sizable contribution to the church organ fund. That stopped the tongues wagging about my financial position.

I banged on Deputy Bates's door and called to him to get up, we had some bad trouble downstairs. I had no qualms about disturbing his rest, for he'd been in my house for a full six weeks and this was the first time I'd had to call on him. He'd told me that he left the Atlanta police force for a quieter, less stressful job here in Abbotsville, but I figured a little stress now and then wouldn't hurt him. So I banged on the door again.

I heard his feet hit the floor and a drawer crash open. The door sprang back, and Deputy Bates stood there in his boxer shorts, red and white stripes, with bleary eyes in his head and a dull gray pistol in his hand.

"What?" he asked, his eyes darting from side to side. "What's the trouble?"

"It's not that bad," I said, pointing at the gun. "You probably won't need to shoot anybody." The one who needed it was already dead.

He blinked at me, then shook his head. "Let me get some clothes on," he said.

I went back downstairs and out into the kitchen, where I heard Lillian bustling around. She had that abandoned child seated at the table with a huge slice of chocolate cake and a glass of milk in front of him. I took a deep breath and felt my mouth tighten into a sharp line.

"We're not entertaining company, Lillian," I said. "This child's moving on just as soon as I find somewhere to move him on to."

"Chil'ren get hungry," she said as she checked a pot on the stove. She wouldn't look at me, so I knew she didn't like the attitude I was taking. Too bad.

I ignored her and walked over to the table. I stood there, tapping my foot and looking at him as the anger in my heart turned my hands into fists. He slumped lower and lower in his chair until his face was about level with the second layer of the cake. The Winn-Dixie grocery bag was on the floor beside his chair.

"What do they call you, boy?" I demanded.

Tears flowed like a gushing stream out from under the smeared glasses, but he made no attempt to wipe them away. He held his hands in his lap and just sat there bawling without making a sound.

"Oh, for goodness' sake!" I said. "I asked you a simple question, so sit up straight and answer it."

His scrawny shoulders started heaving then, though he made an effort to pull himself up in the chair. Lillian decided to intervene then, though the Lord knows it didn't take much for her to make that decision.

"Junior," she said to me, and sharply, too. "They calls him Junior an' that ain't no way to talk to no baby."

I rolled my eyes at the thought of a nine-year-old baby. I knew I shouldn't be talking so hatefully, but every time I looked at that child I wanted to do some damage to somebody, and I couldn't reach the one who deserved it.

"Well, he won't be called Junior around here," I announced. "Not in this house, he won't. It's illegal, and as long as you're in my house," I said, turning back to the little sniveler, "which won't be for long, you'll be called Lloyd."

"Yes'm," he mumbled, sounding like he was underwater. Which he was.

"Okay, Miss Julia," Deputy Bates said, coming into the kitchen. As he walked through the sunshine streaming in the window, his gold-filled watch and the fine blond hair on his arms put me in mind of a Pawley's Island lifeguard, suntanned and sparkling with light, I'd once taken notice of. He'd put on a pair of blue jeans over the boxer shorts I'd previously been greeted with, and he was wearing cowboy boots, for the Lord's sake. Still, he made a fine figure of a man to be so young, with all those muscles filling out his white T-shirt. Nothing in his hands, I was happy to note. "What's the problem?"

"This," I said, pointing a finger at the child, whose blotched face screwed up again and overflowed with another torrent.

"How you doin', Bud," he said, nodding to the child, ignoring the river of tears and turning to Lillian with a grin. "Got any left-over coffee?"

"Pourin' right now," she said, her face beaming like it did whenever a man was around to feed. This one, in particular. She'd taken to Deputy Bates from the first minute he'd walked into the house in his dark blue uniform complete with badge, nightstick, pistol, walkie-talkie, and I-don't-know-what-all. You know how some women are.

I rolled my eyes again and sat down across the table from Deputy Bates. "If everybody's been served," I said after Lillian had set a steaming cup in front of him and put a fork in the child's hand, "I need some help here."

"Tell me," Deputy Bates said, and I did.

"That's some story," he said as I finished with an indignant shake of my head. "You didn't know anything about this?" He indicated Little Lloyd with a lift of his eyebrows.

"Nobody did! Not one soul. Did they, Lillian?"

"No'm," she mumbled, stirring a pan of corn like it needed all her attention.

"Did you know anything, Lillian?" I demanded, half rising from the chair. "Did you?" Fear and shame rushed over me like an ocean wave. I felt rolled over, turned around, and left with the gritty taste of sand in my mouth.

"Jus' talk, you know how peoples talk." She wouldn't look at me as she busied herself with moving pots around on the stove.

"You mean," I croaked, my hand on my heart, "that people *knew* what Wesley Lloyd was doing all this time, while I . . . I had no idea?"

I couldn't take it in, the thought that I'd been walking around town, going to church, the hairdresser's, the Winn-Dixie, holding my head up in oblivious pride while everybody else had known my husband—the banker, the church elder, the moneymaker, the leader of men—was philandering with a floozie. Faces of my friends, neighbors, church members, merchants—the paperboy, for the Lord's sake—flashed through my mind, all whispering, watching, tittering, and gloating. Some of them laughing at me, others feeling sorry for me. I didn't know which was worse.

CHAPTER THREE

—

I sank back in my chair with a sinking feeling in my soul. "What in the world am I going to do?" I whispered.

"Let's think this out," Deputy Bates said. "First of all, the Department of Social Services can take Bud here. They'll look after him for a few days while we try to get a line on his mother. If we can't locate her, they'll find a foster home for him." He stopped and ran a finger across his mouth as he thought. "I guess there'd be a hearing when they do locate her. She could be declared unfit, maybe, and then he'd be a ward of the state. You'd have to testify, you know."

The child was watching him as closely as he could out of those glasses, taking tiny bites of the cake between hiccups. But when Deputy Bates said "ward of the state," Little Lloyd put his fork down and hung his head again. Lillian walked over to the table, the heels of her shoes flopping on the linoleum. She stood there with her hands on her hips as she looked me straight in the eye.

"You do all that, Miss Julia," she said, "an' ever'body know what they been 'spectin' be the gospel truth. You get the law an' the courts an' all in this, and it'll come out in the public, ever' bit of it!"

She was right. I could see myself telling a judge just how Wesley Lloyd Junior Springer had been sprung on me. The whole town would be slapping their knees. Wesley Lloyd had been too sharp a businessman for people not to enjoy his fall from grace. Even if he was dead and buried. As for me, I'd been too proud of him, and of myself, to be able to escape the eyes cutting in my direction as I passed, or the small, knowing smiles as people put up a pretense of the respect I was accustomed to.

"What am I going to do?" I whispered again.

"Well," Deputy Bates said, "I can put out

some unofficial feelers, see if we can locate her that way. If she'll take him back, then that'll be the end of it. If she won't, or I can't find her, you can decide then whether to get social services involved. Not much you can do about it going public then, 'cause reporters watch the docket for interesting cases. And this would be interesting."

"You could look for her unofficially?" I asked, feeling some hope. "I mean, so nobody'd know why you were looking?"

He rubbed his hand over his hair and twisted his mouth. "I can try, but I can't promise much. I could do this, though," he said, sitting up in his chair. "I could sure nose around here, check arrest records, voting lists, run her name through DMV, see if there're any other, I mean, any relatives at all in town. Just do a general background check to be sure what she's claiming is true."

"Oh, it be true," Lillian said, looking directly at Wesley Lloyd's spitting image. " 'Less Mr. Springer had a brother don't nobody know about."

"Lillian, please," I moaned. Then with a sudden thought, the answer came to me. "That's it!" I said. "We'll say this child is Mr.

Springer's nephew! We'll say he's his brother's, or his sister's, son, come to visit me. That'll do it, and it'd explain the resemblance, too." I laughed at the simplicity of it.

"Uh-uh." Lillian pursed her mouth, shaking her head. "That ain't gon' work. Ever'body knowed the Springer fam'ly ever since before Mr. Springer's gran'daddy give the land for that church 'cross the street. Mr. Springer growed up in this town and never left it 'cept for the time he went to that Davisum Collidge. Nobody'd believe he had a brother nor a sister, 'less they figure it was his daddy what had hisself a yard chile."

I hung my head and moaned again, knowing she was right. Wesley Lloyd had no cousins, either. He'd been a loner since the day he was born, and in this town that kept up with kinships going back a hundred years or more, the old men in the barbershop and on the bank corner would be telling and retelling any attempt to make a lie jump a generation.

"I don't want this whole town whispering about me, making things even worse than they are," I started, as humiliation bowed my head again. "Right now, I don't much care what they say about Mr. Springer, but anything they say about him makes me a laughingstock. I won't be able to hold my head up in this town again."

I felt my throat close up as tears blurred my eyes. I pulled a handkerchief from my pocket and covered my face, trying to get myself back under control. Every time I closed my eyes, that child's image flickered in my mind. And when I opened them, there he was in the flesh staring at me out of those fishbowl glasses. Breathing through his mouth, too. What had I done to deserve this?

"Miss Julia," Deputy Bates said, "it won't be that bad. Seems to me you're to be commended if you decide to keep this little boy until we find his mother. Besides, you haven't done anything to be ashamed of."

He was trying to be kind, so I managed a quavery smile at his innocence. "That's not the way it works, Deputy Bates," I said. "Don't you know it's always the wife's fault if a man strays? Or drinks too much? Or gambles? Or goes bankrupt? There's always something the wife's doing, or not doing, that pushes a man over the brink. That's just the way it is."

"Oh, surely not."

"It's the truth, and not much to be done about it, either. Especially now that Pastor Ledbetter is doing a series on how the welfare of the family hinges on the wife and mother." I took in a deep breath and occupied my hands with folding my handkerchief in pleats. "So. I might as well get used to the fact that all the telephone lines will be buzzing with gossip and rumors. Everybody'll be dredging up anything they can think of to excuse Wesley Lloyd and blame me."

"Womens be the worst when it comes to 'scusin' a man," Lillian said.

"That's right," I agreed, "and it's because they think if they're good enough, their husbands won't do anything wrong. As if that had anything to do with it. They can't admit that a man'll do whatever he wants, regardless of what kind of wife he has." I sniffed and dabbed at my eyes, the injustice of it all cutting to the quick. That child's watery eyes, so like Wesley Lloyd's, watched every move I made. Warily, as befitted his situation, I thought.

I made one last swipe at my eyes and squared my shoulders, self-pity giving way to a flood of anger. "And I'm living proof of it, because none of this is my fault! I haven't done one blessed thing wrong, because I did everything, I mean everything, just the way Wesley Lloyd wanted me to. Why, I didn't walk out of this house without his approval. I didn't express an opinion or even ask a question without looking to him first. The Bible says, 'Wives, submit yourselves unto your husbands,' and that's what I did, and this is the thanks I get for it! This whole mess is his fault, and he's the one who ought to suffer for it."

I could feel strength and determination coursing through me as I spoke. My back got straighter and I didn't feel like crying anymore. Lillian was squinting at me as the spoon she was holding dripped creamed corn on the floor. Little Lloyd stared at me, his mouth gaping open, and Deputy Bates smiled a little uncertainly.

"I know what I'm going to do," I said.

"Uh-oh," Lillian said.

"I can't wait to hear it," Deputy Bates said.

Little Lloyd sniffed and wiped his nose with his napkin.

"Lillian, get this child a Kleenex," I said.

"Here's what I'm going to do," I went on, feeling my way as I talked. "The first thing I'm *not* going to do is call any of those child welfare agencies. Keeping this child is my cross to bear, even though I don't deserve it, and it's the only way to get back at Wesley Lloyd. He hid this child for a decade, but I'm not hiding him. And I'm not going to hide my face, either. None of this is my fault, so why should I act like it is? There's not a reason in the world. They're going to talk no matter what I do, so I'm going to give them something to talk about. I'm going to hold my head up if it kills me, and I'm not going to protect Wesley Lloyd Springer from the consequences. This is his son, and everybody's going to know it, without any guessing. I'm going to flaunt this child before the whole town, so let the cookies crumble!"

"Uh, Miss Julia," Deputy Bates said, "how's that going to affect Mr. Springer?"

"Why, Deputy Bates, don't you believe in eternal life? You must not be a Presbyterian, because we believe the dead live on in one place or the other. And, believe me, Wesley Lloyd Springer's suffering now wherever he is. Nothing was more important to him than his good name, and I've lived my whole life trying to come up to his high standards. Well, I'm through doing that. I'm taking this child with me everywhere I go, and I'm going to make sure they know who his father was. Let them make what they will of it!"

"You thinkin' that's a good idea?" Lillian asked with more than her usual skepticism.

"You might ought to consider how that'll affect this little boy," Deputy Bates suggested. "I don't mean to tell you what to do, but it might be pretty hard on him." He shrugged. "Just something to think about."

The child's head had been swiveling from one to the other of us as we talked, and I wondered how much he knew or understood about his precarious situation. Not much, I decided, as I noted the dazed or addled or, have mercy, half-witted expression on his face.

I looked at him long and hard, taking in the streaked and splotched face, the crooked bow tie and glasses, the scrawniness of him, and felt my stomach churn.

"I've thought about it," I said. "And he has some choices. He can stand up for himself and face them down alongside of me. Or he can hide in a closet until his mother comes back. Or maybe he'd prefer to be turned over to the sheriff and social services." I leaned across the table to catch the child's eye. "You don't want to go to an orphanage, do you, boy? Answer me that."

"No'm." His shoulders shook with the effort to keep from crying.

"See there, he knows what's good for him," I said, feeling a sense of triumph now that I'd decided on a course of action.

"Miss Julia, quit scarin' that chile," Lillian rebuked me. "Eat yo' cake, honey, an' don't pay her no mind."

"And you quit undermining me," I told her. "Here's what we're going to do. Deputy Bates, you find out everything you can about this boy and his mother, but keep it quiet or some do-gooder official'll be on my doorstep wanting to take over. Lillian'll be helping me here with the child, and Little Lloyd!" He jumped as I turned to him. "You are Mr. Springer's only surviving child— Lord, I hope—and you're proud of who you are. You understand that?"

He nodded his head miserably, but I didn't have time for pity.

"I hope you know what you doin', 'cause

you makin' trouble for yo'self and ever'body else, now," Lillian accused. "Mr. Springer didn't have no legal chil'ren, an' you might be makin' a bigger mess than you already got."

"He didn't have two legal wives, either," I snapped back. "But I'm stuck with what he did have, and I have to make what I can of it. This child is Mr. Springer's son, and sooner or later, credit will come to me for going above and beyond my Christian duty, and a few extra stars in my crown wouldn't surprise me, either!"

"Well, maybe," Lillian allowed, wiping her hands on a dish towel and trying not to roll her eyes. She knows how I feel about that.

"You're a pistol, Miss Julia," Deputy Bates said with a wide grin. "I thought Atlanta was hairy, but this'll be something to see."

CHAPTER FOUR

—

I'd about paced a rut in my hardwood floors before I was able to reach Sam that afternoon. I knew where he was, of course, but that didn't make the wait any easier. Sam had retired not long after Wesley Lloyd passed, right when I needed him the most, *to fish!* for the Lord's sake. He'd turned my routine affairs over to Binkie Enloe, so now I had two lawyers, one a young woman whose ability I'd doubted at first and the other that old man who'd rather fish than eat.

"One more call," I said to myself, "and if he's still not home, I'm going over there and sit on his porch till he gets there."

I looked out the window and saw Deputy Bates with the boy out in the backyard. He was supposed to be conducting an investigation, questioning the child and trying to get some details as to the Puckett woman's plans. Looked more like they were playing, though, than treating the situation with the seriousness it warranted.

As I stood there watching that unlovely child—I declare, only a mother could love him and, Lord, even she had taken off—I felt a twinge of pity for him before I could stop myself. It got even worse when I saw the child bend over in a fit of crying. Deputy Bates pulled him close and let him cry on his shoulder. I gripped the side of the sink and bowed my head, overcome with too many feelings that didn't make sense. Of course, I am tenderhearted when it comes to children.

Even though I intended to parade that child before the town, I was glad for the hemlock hedge around the yard that hid him from curious eyes. I knew I had to get myself together before going public with the pretense that he hadn't been the shock of my life. I looked out the window again and saw him take off those cockeyed glasses and wipe his eyes with the handkerchief Deputy Bates gave him. The child needed distraction and entertainment or he'd be dripping tears all over Main Street and everywhere else. There wasn't one thing around my house to play with, though, since Wesley Lloyd and I had never been blessed. Well, obviously, Wesley Lloyd had been. I'd just have to write some checks for swings and play toys so everybody would know how happy I was to have the little visitor.

I turned loose of the sink, sighing, and dialed the phone again.

"Sam!" I said when he finally answered. "Get yourself over here. I need to talk to you."

"Nice to hear from you, Julia," Sam Murdoch said in that smiling way of his that I didn't appreciate much at any time, and certainly not at this one. He'd gotten worse about it since Wesley Lloyd had passed. "What's got you so stirred up?"

"I'll tell you when you get here, so put up that fishing rod or whatever you're piddling with, and get over here. I've got more trouble than I can handle."

"Then it must be a doozy. I'm on my way."

I sat down on my Duncan Phyfe sofa in the living room to wait for Sam, who in spite of laughing at me half the time was a man I trusted. I used to think he'd been Wesley Lloyd's closest friend, but I was beginning to think that my husband hadn't had any close friends. Wesley Lloyd had played everything close to his chest, an admirable quality in a sharp businessman but likely to cause unexpected heart attacks, as he'd found out to his sorrow.

I'd known Sam Murdoch ever since I'd come to Abbotsville as a bride, and considered him and Mildred my friends. They used to come by on Sunday afternoons and we'd go for a drive together, Sam and Wesley Lloyd in the front seat, and Mildred and me in the back. That was before Mildred went to her reward some years back. The men had talked business and church—they were both elders—and we'd talked housekeeping and church, with a little whispered gossip to spice things up. Wesley Lloyd didn't approve of gossip.

Sam always ended the drive with a stop at the Dairy Queen for a chocolate-dipped vanilla soft cone. We all got one, except Wesley Lloyd, who had his in a cup with a spoon. Didn't want to drip on his three-piece suit. He was careful in everything he did, and at the time I took quiet pride in all his neat peculiarities. Like, for instance, he always stirred his iced tea seventeen exact times—I counted—each time with seventeen little tinks on the bottom of the glass.

The thing you had to know about Sam Murdoch, though, was not to trust his rumpled appearance and slow-moving ways. There were stories about him around town, like how he'd tell other attorneys from over in Charlotte or Raleigh, "I'm just a country lawyer up here in a country town," he'd say. And they'd come to Abbotsville for a court case, all patronizing and sure of themselves, until Sam took them on in open court. They'd leave town not knowing what hit them.

When Sam showed up at my door, his sweat-stained panama in his hands, I knew he'd walked the four blocks from his house. And in August heat, too.

"Get in here and cool off, Sam," I said, opening the screen for him. "I declare, it's foolish to be walking in this heat. It must be ninety degrees out there."

"Pretty warm, Julia," he said, coming into the living room. "Reckon Lillian's got any ice tea around?"

"Yes, and chocolate cake, too, which I don't suppose you'd refuse. Come on back to the kitchen; I want you to see something out there, anyway."

He followed me down the hall and out into the kitchen, settling himself at the table where Lillian and I'd had many a cup of coffee together. It struck me how natural it seemed to ask Sam back there, when it had never occurred to me to sit at that table with Wesley Lloyd. Wesley Lloyd had not been a kitchen kind of man. He'd had his meals in the dining room—"A place for everything, Julia," he used to tell me, "and everything in its place."

Since Lillian was nowhere around, I glanced out the window and saw her outside with Deputy Bates and that child. So I got Sam his iced tea and a slice of cake. Then I sat down across from him and told him about the heavy burden that had been laid upon me that morning.

He ate and nodded, frowned a few times, and then said, "I'm sorry you had to find out this way, Julia."

That took the wind out of my sails. Any lingering hope that Wesley Lloyd's nefarious activities weren't widely known went with that wind.

"Why didn't you tell me?" I said, wavering between screaming my head off and crying myself sick.

"That's not exactly the kind of story to take to a wife," he said. The pity I heard in his voice nearly broke me in two. "And besides," he went on, "I didn't know it for a fact; I just strongly suspected it. Nobody with any sense would come to you with a story based on rumor."

"There're a lot of people in this town without much sense," I said. "That's why I'm surprised no one told me, or even hinted at it."

"People're afraid of you, Julia," he said, his eyes beginning to smile again.

"Afraid, my foot. How can anybody be afraid of me?"

"You're a woman with a strong sense of right and wrong, and you don't mind telling the difference to anybody who'll listen."

"It's all a sham," I whispered, digging out my damp handkerchief. "All I've ever done was parrot Wesley Lloyd. I've never had a thought or opinion of my own, I realize that now. Maybe if I'd had enough sense to think for myself, I'd have found out about him long before this.

"I need to know something, Sam. Why in the world didn't he provide for that woman and her child in some way before he passed? Didn't he care about them? How did he think she was going to get along, raising the child by herself? It's just not like him to be unprepared for a contingency."

"I tried, Julia," he said. "I kept after him for years to get his affairs in order. I don't mean specifically for the woman, although like most everybody I'd heard the stories. But all he had was that standard will that you and he made out, what, twenty years or so ago. Remember that? He came in wanting a will for himself and one for you, each leaving the other everything. Just your basic kind of will until, he told me, he could plan one out in detail."

I could feel my face turning white and my eyes getting bigger. "Do I remember it? Like it was yesterday! That was right after Papa died and left me twenty-five thousand dollars, my share from the sale of the home place. Sam," I said, as a hot pain shot through me, "those wills were for his benefit! He wanted to make sure he got everything I had if I went before he did. That's the truth, isn't it? He didn't count on dying first, did he? And, Lord help me, I didn't think twice about signing whatever he put in front of me." The pain in my chest stopped the flow of angry words. I closed my eyes and took a deep breath. "I know he didn't intend for it all to come to me. He never trusted me with anything financial, so I don't understand why he didn't change his will later on."

"I don't understand it either, Julia. When I stopped practicing law, that was one of the things I told Binkie to get on to. See if she'd have more luck in getting old W.L. to update his will."

"W.L.," I said with a rueful smile. "He never did appreciate you calling him that."

"Too uptight for his own good. You know, it's crossed my mind that one reason he kept putting off making another will was that he'd have to admit to this woman. Maybe he couldn't bring himself to tell me why he would include her and the child. That's why I thought Binkie might be able to do it."

"Binkie'd never have had a chance with Wesley Lloyd," I said, waving that consideration away. "He wouldn't've confided in anybody who, in his opinion, was untried, much less a woman, no matter how capable. But, Sam, he wouldn't have had to admit to anything if he'd made some provision for them outside of a will. You know, bought her a house and set up some kind of fund for the child. Why couldn't he have done that?"

"Julia," Sam sighed, "I hate to speak ill of the dead, but here's my opinion. I think W.L. just couldn't turn it loose. He had to control it all, and that's a failing of a lot of successful men. But," he went on, "tell me this. Why're you so worried about them? You aren't feeling guilty about it all coming to you, are you? Or feeling sorry for that litte boy out there?"

"Neither one!" I said, pushing back my chair and getting to my feet. "The idea! I'm not feeling guilty about the one nor sorry for the other. No, I'm just mad as thunder, because if he'd provided for them outside of the will, I'd never have known about them. Since I never knew how much he had in the first place, I wouldn't've missed what he did for them. I tell you, Sam, if he had to get involved with that woman, it seems the least

he could've done was to've kept them out
of my life. Now here I am stuck with that illegitimate, illegal, and . . . and unwanted
child out there!"

CHAPTER FIVE

—

I paced back and forth, wringing my handkerchief until I calmed myself enough to sit
back down. Sam put his hand over mine,
but I was too exercised to be so easily
comforted.

"And here's another thing, Sam," I said,
intent on learning as much as I could about
the man I'd spent forty-some-odd years
with. "Do you know anything about him
planning to leave anything to the church?"

Sam put both hands on the edge of the
table and leaned back in his chair, tipping it
off the floor. He smiled and shook his head.
"Not from him. Never a word of any intention like that. But I heard plenty about it
while I was on the session. Seems W.L.
hinted around about it to Larry Ledbetter,

and Ledbetter took it to heart. He's been planning how to spend that windfall for years and, since W.L.'s death, the whole session's been discussing new building plans. That's one reason I resigned."

"You what?" I couldn't believe I'd heard right. "You can't resign from the session! You were elected, Sam. How could you resign?"

"Easy," he said. "I just did it. I thought things would change when the church began to rotate elders, but they haven't. Bunch of old coots on there now who haven't had an idea of their own since nineteen-fifty. I got tired of fightin' 'em."

"Well," I said, not quite able to take it in. I'd never heard of anybody resigning from the session except for a terminal disease or a move out of town. "Well," I said again, "I guess I shouldn't be surprised at anything you do, Sam Murdoch."

I got up and walked to the window, maybe hoping my problem out there had disappeared. But there he was, sitting on a garden bench with his head down and that grocery sack hugged to his chest. Deputy Bates was leaning over, his elbows on his knees, talking to him. I watched as the boy shook his head, then a bit later nodded at something Deputy Bates said. The child hadn't been raised right, which didn't come as any surprise.

"What am I going to do, Sam?" I turned away from the window as I realized how much I wanted Sam to approve any course of action I took.

"I take it you're planning to keep the boy?"

"I don't have much choice, though Deputy Bates is going to do everything he can to find that woman." I fumbled for my handkerchief as the injustice of it all flew through me again. "I ought to sue her! And I just may do it, if he ever finds her."

"Careful with that kind of talk, Julia," Sam said, very carefully himself. "The last session meeting I attended, there was some discussion of suing you."

"Me! What on earth for?"

"Money. Some on the session, a good many, in fact, think there's a better than even chance of laying claim to some of W.L.'s estate, based on what Larry Ledbetter calls verbal commitments to him. He seems to think that a promise made to a member of the clergy ought to carry more weight than a twenty-year-old will." Sam paused, studied his empty plate, then looked me straight in the eye. "I'll tell you this, Julia, when a preacher and his session decide the Lord needs a new building, there's very little that can stop them. Except how to pay for it, and that's where they figure you come in. So I want you to watch yourself. Don't imply anything, don't promise anything, and, above all, don't sign anything."

Well, that really took my breath away, but at the same time a reassuring thought entered my mind. "That's why you resigned, Sam, isn't it?"

"Since I'm the executor of the will, I couldn't very well be party to an effort to have it set aside. I won't deny that money's important, but the idea of a church suing one of its own members to get it is more than I can stomach. Especially if that member is a helpless widow woman." He grinned until I had to smile back.

"Huh," I snorted, "I'll show them a helpless widow woman, and I'll show them a few Scripture verses, too. 'Ye shall not afflict any widow or fatherless child,' Exodus twenty-two, twenty-two, and that's just one. So with you and Binkie Enloe on my side, to say nothing of the Lord, I'm surprised they'd even consider such a thing."

"Oh, they'll try to get some big firm out of Raleigh or Atlanta, but they won't have any luck. The only way they could overturn that will is to come up with a later one."

"They're a bunch of fools," I pronounced, "and I can't worry about them now. I've got too much else on my mind."

"I know you have, Julia, and I'm sorry for it. I don't want to add to your worries, but it does surprise me a little that this Puckett woman hasn't thought of suing. She'd have a better chance than the church at a share of the estate. If she can document what she claims."

"She told me she'd talked to Binkie, so maybe she has thought of it."

"Well, you'd better talk to Binkie, too, and let her know what's going on. For all we know, she's not left town to study nails but to consult an attorney. Leaving the boy with you might be her way of getting on your soft side, make you recognize him or feel sorry for him. In case the suit doesn't turn out so well for her."

"That's the most foolish thing I ever

heard," I said. "How in the world could anybody think I'd give a flip for a child like that? That's beyond my comprehension. No. No danger of that, but, Sam, this whole situation's a pure tribulation to me. Tell me what I ought to do."

"Seems to me you've already thought it out pretty well. Let's hope Coleman can find his mother, and she can make better arrangements. If she can't"—he shrugged his shoulders—"well, you're doing the only decent thing you can do. I hate to see any child get put into the system. But, Julia, be careful, people don't like too much flaunting. You may not care what they say about W.L., or you, but they could hurt that little boy out there."

"Just let them try," I said, wringing my handkerchief until it was stretched out on the bias. "If I take that child under my wing, they'll have to deal with me first!"

"Well, I sure wouldn't want to tangle with you," Sam said. Then, rising from his chair, he added, "Unless it was on my terms."

I never spent such a miserable night as I did the first night that child was in my house. I was so edgy and shaky that I couldn't bring myself to do anything for him.

"Lillian," I said, "would you please stay a little longer and get that child to bed for me? I just don't think I can touch him or anything that belongs to him."

"You better get over that," she told me. "If you gonna do like you said and put on a good show, you got to make out like you glad to have him. And that means takin' care of that baby."

"I know it. I know it. You don't have to tell me. I declare, my mind is so jumbled, all I can think of is how bad that child needs a haircut. Now, with all I have to worry about, you'd think something besides a shaggy head of hair would be weighing on my mind." Appearances are important, I've always thought, but to tell the truth, it was my appearance with that child in tow that was bothering me.

"Huh," she said, heading back to the kitchen, where the boy was waiting. "Jus' get him one, and that be it. Another worry'll pop up to take its place."

There were plenty of worries waiting in line, I thought, as I heard the two of them go up the stairs. Lillian put fresh sheets on the bed in the room across the hall from mine, tucked the child in along with his paper sack, and, before leaving for her own house, told me to go to bed and quit worrying.

Easy to say, for it was the worst night of my life, and I'm including the night I found Wesley Lloyd draped over his steering wheel, his eyes and mouth wide open as if he'd had the surprise of his life.

I'd been sleeping the sleep of the just when I heard his car pull in the driveway about midnight, no different from any other Thursday night for ten years or more. Wesley Lloyd believed in routine, and his never changed from sunup to sundown. Except on Thursdays, when I thought he worked late to prepare for the Friday morning meetings in the boardroom of the Springer Bank and Trust. I'd turned over and waited to hear the car door slam, the jingle of his keys, and his heels clicking on the cement walk. But I'd heard nothing.

After some little while of lying there wondering what was keeping him, I'd put on a robe and gone downstairs to see about him. I tell you, when Wesley Lloyd's routine changed, it had to be for a good reason.

And it was, because he was dead as a doornail. Right in our driveway. In his new Buick Park Avenue. Steel gray with . . . but I've already told that.

It was awful and I never wanted to go through another experience like it. I didn't intend to, either, since I didn't plan to marry or bury another husband. Well, the burying part hadn't been so hard, what with the way this town and my church comfort the bereaved. They came with piles of food and flowers and donations to my favorite charity, and somebody sat with me every minute of the day ready to fulfill my every wish. I felt like the star of Wesley Lloyd's funeral. Queen for a day or two, until they figured it was time for me to manage on my own. And I'd done that with Lillian's help, and Binkie's. Sam's, too. In fact, it'd been so easy that I didn't know why in the world a widow woman would ever remarry. You might find out what kind of man you were yoked to after it was too late to do anything about it, like I had.

Not that I'd've known what to do if I'd known what Wesley Lloyd was up to before he passed on. But all through that long night as I stared in the dark on my lonely bed, thinking about that child across the hall, I kept telling myself I'd have done *something.*

But you have to know about something before you can do anything about it. And I didn't know a blessed thing until the results of it showed up on my doorstep. Blindest woman in North Carolina. Believed everything anybody'd ever told me, especially if it was a man doing the telling. That's the way I was raised, Southern and Presbyterian. But no, I take that back. I only believed it was gospel truth if it came from Larry T. Ledbetter, my preacher, or Sam Murdoch, my lawyer, or Wesley Lloyd Springer, the man I'd been married to for forty-four years.

I'd been proud of that. Proud that I was married to a man of means and position, one of the few men left in the state who owned his own bank, and solid as a rock, too. Both him and the bank. People trusted him with their money and, I gave him credit, their money was always safe in the Springer Bank and Trust.

We had a good marriage. I thought. He'd found me at my papa's home down in

South Carolina, when he was looking at some new ways of running the bank his daddy had left him. Wesley Lloyd was a progressive thinker even then. He was a churchgoer, too, and that's where I met him—after Sunday services at my home church. He was always in church whenever Sunday rolled around, didn't matter where he was or what he was doing. "Sunday's the Lord's day, Julia," he told me. "And the Lord's house is where we ought to be on it." So there he was, shaking hands with the preacher, and then with me, as soon as the benediction and the seven-fold amen was over that Sunday so many years ago.

I was the oldest girl in the family, the last one left. My two sisters had already married, and everybody figured I'd be a spinster the rest of my life. Twenty-three years old, unmarried, and no prospects. Sounds pitiful today, doesn't it? Why in the world I didn't think of going out on my own and making a life for myself, I don't know. But that was another small town, choked to the gills with the traditions of the past. I'd gone a while to the teacher's college at Winthrop, but when Papa needed help at home, guess who was picked? When Papa said,

"Jump," I was always the first one in the air. I knew he'd have preferred one of my sisters—have you ever noticed how the one who wants to please never does?—but he was stuck with me. Until Wesley Lloyd Springer showed up.

Sounds like a love story, doesn't it? Well, it wasn't much of one, but I was grateful for it. Wesley Lloyd never was one for romance and sentiment and all the things you read about. He was a businessman, knew what he wanted and how to get it. That's the way he proposed to me. Everybody thought it was a whirlwind romance because it all came about so fast. But Wesley Lloyd, being some years older than me, always had his head on his shoulders.

"I need a wife of a certain character and background," he'd said to me. We were sitting in the front parlor of Papa's house, and I was studying the half-carat solitaire in its blue velvet box that he'd handed to me. "I have a position to maintain," he went on as he pulled his gold watch from his vest and glanced at it. That was a habit that never left him. Time is money, he always said. "And I need a wife who'll keep my house and be a helpmate in my town. I'm not what some would call wealthy, but you'll never want for anything."

I took the ring out of the box and turned it round and round. Then I tried it on, and the fact that it fit seemed a sign to me. I was always on the lookout for signs so I'd know the right things to do. I accepted Wesley Lloyd's proposal without any of the bells and music I'd heard at the picture show on Saturday afternoons. And I didn't miss it. My sisters had married with stars in their eyes, and after only a few years their eyes had dimmed with the despair of niggling over every penny. I prided myself on making my choice based on sensible grounds and figured, on the basis of our mutual levelheadedness, that Wesley Lloyd and I made a good match. I wanted my own household with a man who could afford it, and I got exactly that.

He brought me to this house forty-four years ago, and I guess I'll live here till I die. But I'll be blamed if I'll die hanging over the steering wheel of a Buick Park Avenue. The house was new then. Brick, two stories with a front veranda that provided an unhampered view of all the comings and goings at the First Presbyterian Church. Only a couple of blocks from Main Street, so I've been situated in the middle of everything. Wesley Lloyd said he built the house for his bride, and I remember being so pleased and proud. It took a while for me to realize he'd built it before he ever met me. But that was Wesley Lloyd for you, always thinking ahead, always prepared. I thought.

I fit into this town like I'd been born to it. Wesley Lloyd Springer's wife had a built-in place, and I slid into it like butter on a biscuit. I learned right quick that everybody in Abbotsville had the same respect and high esteem for Wesley Lloyd that I had. It didn't matter that other men towered over him or that they had deeper voices and stronger muscles. When Wesley Lloyd studied a loan application, there wasn't a bigger man in town. People listened to him and heeded his advice, and not just in his office at the bank. Town commissioners consulted him, lawyers telephoned him, businessmen pleaded with him, and the First Presbyterian Church of Abbotsville didn't spend a penny without his approval. He was a leader of men, and everybody knew it.

And, oh, I'd been so proud of who I was. Julia DeWitt Springer. Wesley Lloyd Springer's wife.

Dumbest woman in town.

CHAPTER SIX

—

It's a wonder I slept a wink that night. How could I with my husband's bastard child in my guest room right across the hall? I'd never been so torn up in my life. The idea of Wesley Lloyd betraying me, breaking his vows, living a life of hypocrisy, fornicating not once but, I now realized, every Thursday night for years upon years.

And who knew if the Puckett woman was the first, or even the only, one? My whole life, everything I'd relied on and believed in, was like dust under my feet. I told myself that there was not one thing I could do about the past, that I had to clear the fog I'd been living in and face everything clear-eyed and levelheaded. I had to call a spade a spade and let the chips fall.

When daylight finally came, I got out of bed with my mind made up and my resolve thoroughly firmed.

There was one thing I could and would do—flatly refuse to sugarcoat or whitewash what that man had done to me. Wesley Lloyd had been a hypocrite of the first order, but there was no reason for me to be. A whited sepulchre was what he'd been, clean on the outside but rotten to the core. Oh, I was mad at him, mad at what he'd done to me and mad that he didn't have to live with the disgrace. During that long night, I had come to an understanding of how easy it would be to wring a husband's neck.

Now if you think those boiling feelings came from love and jealousy, you'd be wrong. I always thought I loved Wesley Lloyd; after all, I was married to him, wasn't I? But I didn't give a lick about that. I raged at him, not out of love or because of his betrayal of the marriage bed, but because he'd demanded such a high level of conduct from me, lecturing, criticizing, and quoting Scripture at me, and all the while he was jumping weekly into another woman's bed.

Don't get me wrong; there was no other bed I wanted to jump into, Lord, no. Too old for it, for one thing. But it was the *principle* of the thing.

I moved from ranting and raving at him to cringing in humiliation at what the town was going to do with this juicy item. It was going to take everything I had to hold my head up and ignore their smirking faces. I just wished Wesley Lloyd could be there to see how strong I was going to be. I'd show him a thing or two about strength of character. After all, I was already doing things he'd never credited me with the ability to do. Like keeping records. And writing checks. And balancing my checkbook.

Binkie Enloe, at that first meeting I'd had with her, could hardly believe how Wesley Lloyd had protected me from the harsh realities. I was sitting there in her law office in my gray crepe, my Red Cross shoes, white because Labor Day was still a while away, clutching my pocketbook in my lap while Binkie explained the facts of finance to me. She'd looked at me over the gold-rimmed glasses she used only for close work and said, "Miss Julia, I didn't know there was a woman in the world who didn't know how to write a check." "Yes," I'd said with a prideful smile, "Mr. Springer always took good care of me." Binkie blew out a breath, then commenced to show me how to write checks and keep records, and it was ever so easy. I don't know why Wesley Lloyd thought I didn't have a head for figures.

By six-thirty that morning I was dressed and ready to march downtown to Binkie's office. It was going to be a long wait until eight when she was usually behind her desk. I started downstairs and found the boy sitting on the stairs, dressed in the same chintzy clothes he'd had on the day before, including the clip-on bow tie. I hadn't heard a peep out of him all through that long night, now here he was, up and dressed, with his suitcase and Winn-Dixie grocery sack beside him.

I stood two steps above him and looked him over as he hunched against the wall. He slid the grocery sack closer to clear the stair, and glanced quickly up at me. The sack looked flat and half empty, rolled down the way he had it, but he seemed to like having it close by. I'd heard about little boys' treasures, so I didn't want to think what might be in it.

"Up pretty early, aren't you?" I asked. What do you say to a nine-year-old first thing in the morning?

"Is my mama coming back today?" he asked.

I took a deep breath, not knowing exactly how to answer him. But the truth is always the best. "Not likely," I said. "Now come on to the kitchen. Lillian'll be here soon and we'll have breakfast. Leave your things here."

He followed me down the stairs and into the kitchen, scrunching his shoulders so that he reminded me of a little old man. He looked like Wesley Lloyd, but he didn't act like him. Wesley Lloyd had not been a tall man, but he stood as straight as a poker and walked with purpose, shoulders back and heels clicking.

I pointed Little Lloyd to a chair while I started the coffee. The day looked to be a fine one, sun shining, birds singing in the backyard, impatiens heavy-headed with a sprinkling of dew. The world was going on as if the earth hadn't shifted under my feet since I'd stood at that same window yesterday morning.

I poured two cups of coffee and set one before the boy. He looked quickly up at me and then down again. Lillian needed to get out the Windex and clean those glasses. I shoved the cream and sugar beside his cup and said, "Fix it the way you like it."

He poured cream to the top of the cup and stirred in two spoonfuls of sugar. Leaning over, he tasted the coffee with the cup still in the saucer, screwed up his face, and put in two more spoonfuls. Not much of a coffee drinker, I thought as I sat down across from him and occupied myself with my own cup.

I couldn't look at him except out of the corner of my eye and then I realized he was watching me the same way. We had little to say to each other, and I wished I'd turned the radio on while I'd been up. I racked my brain to come up with something to talk about, believing that ease of conversation is the mark of a cultured person.

I put down my cup and said, "Have you had a movement since you've been here?"

Coffee sloshed over into his saucer. "Ma'am?"

"Your bowels. Have they moved yet?"

His eyes veered wildly behind his glasses as he looked from one side of the kitchen to another. "Yessum. A little."

"Well, you need to have a good one today. I've always found that you can handle problems better if you have regular movements on a daily basis. I have some Ex-Lax if you need it."

"No'm, I don't need it."

He kept his head down over his coffee, and that was the end of the conversation. I gave up trying to draw him out. A little later he ventured to ask where Deputy Bates was. I told him Deputy Bates worked nights and would be home in a little while to go to bed, so we couldn't be running and jumping and making a lot of noise. That seemed to satisfy him, but it was a relief when Lillian came in the back door. She put the *Abbotsville Press* on the table, then looked sternly at me.

"You givin' that chile coffee?"

"And why not? He could use a little perking up."

She shook her head, then began pulling out bacon and eggs. The boy turned out to be a picky eater, which I'd noticed the night

before at supper. He tried everything without complaining, but it was plain that he
didn't have much appetite. I made a mental
note to get him a tonic from the drugstore.
And a haircut at Buddy's.

At seven-forty-five, I stood before the hall
mirror and adjusted my hat. Then, taking
my pocketbook, I left the house for Binkie's
office. I got to the sidewalk, then turned
back. Might as well face the music from the
start.

"Little Lloyd!" I called from the front door.
"I want you to go with me."

He came, carrying his grocery sack, but
he looked more like he was headed for a
dentist's office than a lawyer's. Miserable
looking, if you want my opinion, but it
wasn't my fault.

"You want to leave that sack here?" I
asked, thinking he'd look a lot less trashy
without it.

"No'm." He clutched it to his chest, so I
rolled my eyes and started off again.

"Stay right with me, now," I said. "We've
got business downtown."

He walked by my side, but a half step behind, those shoulders hunched over so bad
that I was beginning to worry about his

posture as a grown man. You can freeze in unattractive ways, you know.

It was too early to meet anybody on the sidewalk, but several people in cars waved to me. I could see them adjust their rearview mirrors to get a better look as they passed.

Binkie took us right in, with hardly any waiting. If you have enough assets, a lawyer will make time for you without fiddling around with appointments and such like. Binkie Enloe kept a severe expression on her face, but it was still mighty young looking, which was no surprise since she *was* young. She made up for it with those glasses that she'd snatch off when she wanted to make a point. She wore dark suits with plain linen blouses, and tried to tame her curly hair with a severe cut. It didn't work. By midday her head would be a tangled mess of curls. I expect that flyaway hair was one reason for her serious demeanor. I've always found that you have to compensate in other ways when your hair won't behave. But Binkie was all business, and I don't know what I would've done without her those past few months. In spite of having felt she didn't know enough to get in out of the rain when Sam first sent me to her.

"You know who this is, don't you?" I asked before I got sat down good. "His mama said she'd talked to you."

"Well, yes, she did," she said, cool as a cucumber. Not much flustered Binkie Enloe. "How did you end up with him?"

When I told her how the Puckett woman just left him and took off, she raised her eyebrows. Totally shocked.

"Well," she commented. "I see. You plan to keep him until she's found?"

"What else can I do?" I demanded. "Don't swing your legs, Little Lloyd." He was sitting in one of Binkie's big chairs, his legs dangling in the air.

"Well, you could—"

"No, I couldn't," I said, interrupting her. "I know you're going to say that I could turn him over to social services, but all that'll do is look like I'm trying to hide from the truth. And the talk will be just that much worse. No, I'm going to face the town with the facts. And if it hurts Mr. Springer's reputation, then so be it.

"Now. Sam Murdoch told me to tell you what's going on, so that's what I'm doing.

And I want to know how many people are planning to sue me. This boy's mother? My own church? Who else?"

"Nobody, at this point," she said. "I'm getting inklings about the church, but you don't need to worry about them. Promises and/or intentions don't mean anything. Mr. Springer's will names you as the sole beneficiary, and that's that. The church can't do anything but threaten and gnash its teeth." She smiled a little at the thought. Little Lloyd sniffed wetly from his chair behind me. I reached in my pocketbook and handed him a Kleenex. "As for Ms. Puckett," Binkie went on, "she gave no indication she was thinking along those lines. But I'll have to tell you, Miss Julia, she might have a good case with the proper documentation of her claims."

"My Lord, she's got a birth certificate with Mr. Springer's name on it, big as life! What else does she need?"

"Birth certificate information is usually taken by a nurse from the mother. That information is as good as the mother's word. But if she can show with receipts and so forth that Mr. Springer supported the child as his own, then she's in a pretty strong position."

"But she didn't say a word about laying any claims! In fact, she said she wasn't asking for anything but for me to take care of him until she got some training so she could support him herself. Binkie, I'll tell you this, I don't want to be sued. Mr. Springer, regardless of his *intentions,* left everything to me, and I intend to keep it."

"All right," she said, nodding like she agreed with me, and I knew she did. Fair is fair, after all. "There's not much we can do, unless and until somebody serves you with notice of a suit. Now on to other business while you're here. You've got First Union and Wachovia banks putting out feelers to buy the Springer Bank and Trust. They're interested, but not willing to commit at this point. They're hoping you'll come down on the price, but the Springer Bank is worth every penny we're asking. I'm going to approach one or two others, and see if that won't stir them up a little. I'll make as good a deal as I can for you. You don't want too much cash, for tax reasons, but we'll want a good stock exchange. Does that still suit you?"

"As long as the bank we deal with is in good shape, it does. I don't want a lockbox full of worthless stock if one of them pulls a savings-and-loan stunt."

She smiled that quick smile of hers, and studied her papers. Then she studied Little Lloyd for a minute. Finally she shook her head at this living testimony of a hypocrite. "Keep me informed," she said. "If you hear from Ms. Puckett, I want to know about it."

I thanked her and left, Little Lloyd tagging behind. I got to the door of the reception area, then turned around to Mary Alice McKinnon, behind the desk. Pleasant young woman who always put me right through to Binkie whenever I called.

"Mary Alice," I said, turning the child by his shoulders, "I want you to meet Mr. Springer's son. This is Lloyd Springer. Say hello to Miss McKinnon, Lloyd."

He ducked his head, while Mary Alice gasped and turned red. She managed a word or two of greeting, because she's from a good family, but it was clear she was impressed with my truthfulness.

Out on the sidewalk, I said, "Now, see, that wasn't so hard. Let's go get a fountain Coke at the drugstore."

Chapter Seven

—

When we were through with the pause that refreshes, I marched the child down the block to Buddy's Barber & Expert Depilatory Shop. Buddy Whitesides had two chairs in the front where he and Arlo Turner wielded razors, scissors, and electric clippers. And flung around clouds of talcum powder with their little whisk brooms. In the back, separated by a gray flannel curtain, Alva, Buddy's wife, had a chair where she ministered to those with hair in unsightly places. You couldn't've paid me to go back there.

Both Buddy and Arlo were working on two men I didn't know, farmer types, when we walked in. And sitting in one of the maroon Naugahyde and rusted-chrome chairs was Leonard Conover, of all people, waiting his turn. He looked up from his magazine when the bell over the door tinkled, then he slammed the magazine shut and shoved it under a stack on the table beside him.

"Why, Julia," he said, his face turning an unappetizing red. "I didn't expect to see you here."

"I didn't expect to be here, either. But here I am because this boy needs a haircut. Buddy," I said, turning to the owner, "which one of you does the best haircut for a child?"

"Oh, we're both good," he said, clippers suspended as he looked from me to the boy. "Either one of us will do you a fine job. That a little friend of yours?" He nodded toward the boy.

"You could say that," I said, sitting down by Leonard and motioning Little Lloyd to take a seat, too. "How are you, Leonard? How're things down at the courthouse?"

"Good, good, I stay busy." He kept looking across me to the boy, curious as a cat. I should've said something right then, because if you want something to get around town, just tell it in a beauty or barbershop. But I held my peace for the time being.

"Yes," Leonard went on, his fair complexion gradually returning to its natural state, "besides all I have to do at the courthouse, church business is taking up a lot of my time. Lots of plans. Yes, lots of plans. Takes a lot of work." He nodded his head for emphasis.

"I don't doubt it," I said. Leonard had never been known as a ball of fire even before he became a civil servant. I rested my hands on my pocketbook in my lap and fixed a steady gaze on Buddy so he'd hurry up and get to us.

"You know, Julia," Leonard said, half turning in his chair to get my attention. I noted the fine graying hair that barely covered his scalp, the soft weight of his shoulders, and how he spread out in the chair, and wondered if LuAnne minded. But then, once married, you take whatever the results turn out to be. "I'm not supposed to say anything about this," he told me in a confidential whisper, "because it's just in the planning stage. But the church has grown so much that we've just got to consider a building program. I've been thinking, and it's just my idea, but now, with Wesley Lloyd gone and all, you might be ready to move to a smaller place. You ought to think about donating your house to the church. We could sure use the space, even if it's just for parking."

I turned and looked at him. I clamped my teeth together and said, "You want to tear down my house so you can park cars over there for one hour each week? Leonard Conover, not in a million years."

He raised and lowered a shoulder, then slumped back in his chair. Leonard was used to having his ideas shot down. "It was just a thought for, you know, well, when the house gets to be too much for you."

Arlo was shaving his customer's neck while Buddy snipped around his client's ears, their attention on us more than on their work. It made me cringe to think of a slip. Contrary to what I'd always heard about conversation in a barbershop, there was very little going on in this one. Too busy trying to hear Leonard and me, and trying to figure out what I was doing with a child who looked awfully familiar.

"Don't plan on that happening anytime soon. Buddy," I said, "I don't mean to hurry you, but some people have things to do." He nodded and snipped faster as I added,

"We don't all work at the courthouse, you know."

"Now, Julia," Leonard said, heaving himself up in his chair for another approach, "you don't have any idea what I do at the courthouse, and I hope you never have to find out. But you ought to consider that Wesley Lloyd never wanted you to be burdened with responsibility. What he left is too much for one person, 'specially for somebody who's never had experience handling estates and such like. Believe me, I know what I'm talking about. I sure wouldn't want LuAnne to be burdened like you are."

I stared at him. LuAnne was as likely to be burdened with Leonard's estate as she was with the Publishers' Clearing House Sweepstakes grand prize.

"You don't think I'm capable?"

"Well," Leonard said, and exchanged knowing smiles with Buddy and Arlo. Three barbershop tycoons. "You're not getting any younger, Julia."

There was a bulletin for you.

Buddy flipped the cape off his customer and started flicking talcum powder around the poor man's neck.

"Come on, Little Lloyd," I said, taking his hand. "Mr. Buddy will take you next."

I helped Little Lloyd up in the chair and onto the board that Buddy put across the arms to raise him to the right height. "Take your glasses off," I said, and then to Buddy, "I don't want it shaved, buzzed, or styled. I want a decent haircut that gets the hair out of his eyes and off his neck. In fact, you can give him one just like you used to give his daddy."

Recognition of the boy and confirmation of their suspicions froze every man in the place. Arlo's eyes bugged out as his jaw dropped. His customer frowned, trying to make sense of what was going on. Leonard sat in his chair like he was paralyzed with shock. He kept opening and closing his mouth, his lips making a smacking noise each time they met. The voice of some country music singer on the radio yearning for commitment did little to fill the embarrassed silence.

"Well, get on with it," I said to Buddy, who stood with his hands held up in the air like a surgeon.

"Yes, ma'am, okay, we'll give this boy a fine haircut." He jerked around, picked up a comb, dropped it on the floor, fumbled for another one, and gave me a sick grin as he finally got started on the boy's head.

Some people don't know how to act when the truth stares them in the face.

By the time we started home, after meeting any number of people downtown, I was drained to a fare-thee-well. Telling the truth, which I'd forced myself to do after nearly falling down on the job in the barbershop, can really take the starch out of you. Little Lloyd felt the same way, because he scuffed his feet all the way home and I had to speak to him about it.

"Pick up your feet, Little Lloyd," I said as we walked down the sidewalk on our way home. "Here, let me have your hand, and smile so everybody'll see how happy you are."

He gave me his hand and said, "I don't much think I am."

"Well, of course not, what with your mother gone and all. But you have to put up a good front so people won't know your personal business and talk about you. And that reminds me, we should've gotten you something to play with. What do you enjoy doing?"

He thought for a minute, then said, "I like to put puzzles together. And I like to listen to music."

"I used to like puzzles myself. We'll have to get us some and work them together. What kind of music do you like?"

"All kinds, but I like Tim McGraw and Sawyer Brown best. My mama, she likes Dwight Yoakam. She likes to watch his videos."

"Do tell," I murmured, not having an idea in the world of what he was talking about. "Here we are," I said, turning into the front walk. "I declare, we've had a time of it. And the day not half over yet."

There was still a long day in front of me, because LuAnne Conover was sitting there ensconced in one of my wine velvet Victorian chairs. She hopped up as soon as we got in the door, flapping and waving her hands with the thrill of it all.

"Julia, oh, Julia," she said, running to my side like I needed help to get in the door. "Oh, I just heard this terrible news; I just can't believe it; tell me it isn't true! Oh, Julia, I just feel for you so much, I don't know

how you're bearing up. How are you, anyway?" She was speaking to me, but her
eyes, bright with curiosity, were fastened
on the boy.

"Sit down, LuAnne," I said, trying to get
my hat off my head. "I'm all right, but it
looks like you need some help. Didn't Lillian
offer you anything?"

"Oh, I couldn't eat a thing. I'm just too upset by all this, and *suffering* with you, Julia.
Tell me now," she said, sitting beside me on
the sofa and leaning practically in my face,
"just what all happened. You wouldn't believe all the stories I've heard this morning!"

"Oh, I probably would," I said, sighing. I
knew the town about as well as it could be
known, and Mary Alice, along with everybody else we'd met, except maybe
Leonard, who'd never been able to put two
and two together, would've been on the
phone as soon as my back was turned. "By
the way, this is the subject of all you've
heard." I looked over at Little Lloyd, who
was still standing by the door. "Say hello to
Miz Conover, Lloyd, then run on in the
kitchen and ask Lillian for your lunch. If you
didn't spoil your appetite with that cherry
Coke."

He ducked his head and mumbled something at LuAnne before scurrying out of the room. I would've corrected his manners, but LuAnne's were worse. She just stared at him with her mouth open.

"I wouldn't have believed it if I hadn't seen it!" she gasped. "Somebody told me you had that boy, but I told them, 'No, Julia wouldn't do that.' What in the world are you thinking of, Julia? How can you stand to have that child in your house? I tell you, if Leonard pulled a stunt like that, I wouldn't take in his"—she paused, looked around, and whispered—*"bastard."*

"You do what you have to do, LuAnne," I said, "which is what I'm doing. Now, I want to ask you something. Did you know Wesley Lloyd was keeping that woman?"

"Oh, Julia, *everybody* knew it. Well, I mean," she corrected herself, "it's been talked about for years. You know how these stories get around."

"Why didn't you tell me?"

"Why, you know, I just didn't believe it." She laughed a little nervous laugh and quickly cut it off when she saw the look I gave her. "And nobody did, believe me, they really didn't. Or maybe they thought you knew and didn't care. Ann Landers says the wife always knows, and everybody should MYOB."

"My Lord," I moaned, holding my head in my hands.

I heard the telephone ring and Lillian's voice as she answered it. I didn't want to talk to anybody, including LuAnne. But on she went.

"Julia, everybody's upset over what you're doing and, I have to tell you, they're wondering if maybe you're not thinking too clearly.

"Oh, I mean," she said as I lifted my head and glared at her, "we all know you've been under a strain, what with Wesley Lloyd's passing and all. It's just been too much for you, and you need to sit back and let your friends take over for you. Leonard was saying just the other day that there are legal remedies."

"Legal remedies? What are you talking about, LuAnne?"

"Why, all your problems, of course. Leonard sees this type of a problem every week or so, and the decisions he has to make just tear him up."

I leaned my head back against the sofa

and closed my eyes. "Have mercy," I prayed just loud enough for LuAnne to hear, as well as the One addressed. If I were fool enough to let Leonard Conover make decisions for me, I'd need not only mercy but shock treatments, too.

"Now, Julia," LuAnne went on, "I'm here to do anything I can for you. You just go up and lie down, and I'll answer the door and keep a record for you. People are going to want to come by or call to see how you're doing."

"Nobody's died here, LuAnne! And I don't need to receive people who just want to satisfy their curiosity. I'm too busy to see anybody anyway, so you can run on home and look after Leonard."

"Well," she said, and I could see her feelings were hurt. Too bad, because mine were, too. "I just thought you'd want a friend beside you in your time of trouble."

"My time of trouble was all those years when Wesley Lloyd was gallivanting with that woman. I could've used a friend then, but I didn't have a one in this town."

"I can see you're upset, Julia, and I don't fault you for it." She got up and stood by me, her hand on my shoulder. "I'm praying for you, and so is the whole prayer chain. I started it right before I came over here."

"Thank you," I whispered. What else could I say? The Presbyterian Women's Prayer Chain transmitted news of sickness, accident, death, divorce, pregnancy, teenage problems, bankruptcy, and anything else you could name, and did it faster than a streak of summer lightning. Well, it was no more than I expected, having activated the prayer chain myself any number of times when I'd heard something that needed to be prayed over and passed on.

When LuAnne left, Lillian came into the living room where I still sat trying to collect myself.

"I made you some soup," she said, setting a tray on my lap. "I'm feeding that little boy in the kitchen, then he gon' help me peel apples for a pie. Eat somethin' now. You gon' need it, 'cause that was yo' preacher callin'. He want to know can you walk over to the church. He want to counsel with you."

"I guess I could use some counseling," I said. "Thank you, Lillian. I'll eat this and go on over there."

I'd been a Christian all my life and a Presbyterian for most of it. The way I was raised and who I married hadn't offered much choice in either matter. Not that I'd ever expected or wanted a choice. Still, neither Wesley Lloyd nor I had ever been the type of person who needed counseling. Now I found myself hoping that my preacher could comfort my hurting heart and help me accept the burden laid on me by Wesley Lloyd.

We'd had this preacher four, no, about five years now, and he'd settled in fairly well. Larry Ledbetter was his name; not Lawrence, but Larry. Have you ever noticed how many preachers and evangelists have little-boy names? Just open up the Abbotsville Press most any day and you'll find Jimmys and Johnnys, Billy Earls and Ronnies advertising their services at some local church, usually with somebody named Dawn or Tammy or Debbie singing and playing the piano or the saxophone or some such thing. You'd think grown men would put aside childish things, including childish names.

That's why I liked the Presbyterian church; we believed in doing things decently and in order. When you went to church, you knew exactly what you were going to get. We didn't want to be surprised or entertained. And, Lord knows, we didn't want anything changed.

Take that time we had an interim pastor who changed the order of worship so that the offering plates were passed right after the sermon instead of beforehand during the anthem. You'd have thought he'd instituted something indecent. It upset a lot of people who'd been accustomed to digging out a dollar bill or their pledge envelopes as soon as the choir director stood up. I didn't think it was a good idea, either, but not because I was against change. I just thought the pastor was taking a big chance in passing the plates right after he'd finished preaching. I mean, what if he'd had an off day and his sermon hadn't been too good? I wouldn't risk it myself.

Wesley Lloyd spoke to him about it, and pretty soon the order of worship went back to the way we'd always done it.

But as soon as Pastor Ledbetter accepted our call, he saw the lay of the land right away and didn't make a false move. He was a quick study when it came to latching onto the men of power and agreeing with them. Contrary to most of the new breed coming out of our seminaries, he was a dyed-in-the-wool Calvinist, which meant he was as good as Wesley Lloyd at finding Scripture verses to support his opinions. He and Wesley Lloyd saw eye to eye on just about everything, and if they didn't, why, you'd never know it from Pastor Ledbetter. He picked up right away that Wesley Lloyd didn't like confrontations or arguments about the way the church was run.

I'd noticed recently, though, that Pastor Ledbetter had a freer look about him, both as a pastor and as a pulpiteer. More expansive, maybe, in the way he moved and sermonized, the last of which he'd do at the drop of a hat or a greeting on the street. I thought I knew what he was feeling—something close to being loosened from the ties that bound.

Chapter Eight

—

After walking across the parking lot, I found it a relief to step inside the air-conditioned church. I went through the fellowship hall and on into the preacher's office suite. Norma Cantrell, Pastor Ledbetter's secretary, always acted like she was doing me a favor whenever I wanted to talk to him. As I walked into her office, she glanced behind me and tried to crane her neck to see out in the hall. She was looking for Little Lloyd, I knew, and I was glad I'd left him at home. She liked to make out like she was so professional, but she was the biggest gossip I knew. That's why she liked her job, since every Presbyterian in trouble sooner or later ended up talking to the preacher. I'd warned Pastor Ledbetter about her talkative tendencies, but he'd just patted my shoulder and told me he'd take care of it. Ever since then she'd flounced herself around anytime I was in her office, not that anybody with all that weight ought to do any flouncing. So I knew the preacher had confided in her, and that's when I stopped confiding in him.

Still, he was my pastor and he'd done a good job burying Wesley Lloyd. The sermon had been all I could ask for, telling all the good deeds Wesley Lloyd had done for the church and the community, and making me feel proud.

But I wasn't feeling proud on this visit, just broken and humble. I longed for some spiritual comfort for the double bereavement that was now my lot.

Norma patted her teased hair with one hand and, with the other, fingered the pearl necklace that was attached to the earpieces of her glasses. "Afternoon, Miss Julia," she said, reaching for a pencil to show me how busy she was. "Are you here to see Pastor Ledbetter? He's pretty busy right now."

"He just called me to come over, Norma, which you know because you probably dialed the phone for him. Tell him I'm here, please."

She aimed a glare at me that was unbecoming in a church setting, lifted the phone receiver, and pushed a button. It wouldn't have taken her two steps to walk to the door of his office, but no, she had to use that push-button phone.

She turned her head away from me and practically whispered, "Mrs. Springer is here. Shall I ask her to wait?"

She must not've gotten the answer she wanted, because she pursed her lips before hanging up. About that time, Pastor Ledbetter opened his door and stood there filling that space and the air around him with his ministerial presence and authority. Charisma, I think it's called, and he'd preached a whole sermon one time on all the meanings of the word. He loved to call on his seminary training to instruct us in the Greek language. He'd made it plain that being charismatic for Christ didn't mean you had to speak in tongues, which is something mainline Presbyterians don't hold with at all.

"Come in, Miss Julia," he said in his hearty voice that aimed to make me feel welcome. "How are you? It's good to see you on a day besides a Sunday."

"I'm over here on Mondays for the Women of the Church meetings and on Wednesday nights for prayer meeting," I reminded him. Did he think I only showed up on Sunday mornings?

"Oh, I know, I know," he said, smiling his wide smile. "Just joshing you, Miss Julia. Have a seat, now. Here, let's sit in these comfortable chairs." He closed the door behind us and indicated the two wing chairs beside a bay window. They were fine chairs, upholstered in cream damask, that were bought instead of a swing set for the children's playground.

I sat down and smoothed out the skirt of my Leslie Fay shirtwaist. I felt edgy, like I always did when a preacher wanted to see me. It was like being called to the principal's office, even though I couldn't think of a thing I'd done wrong. I halfway expected to hear about building plans and my contributions thereto, especially since Leonard Conover had spilled the beans. What I wanted from him was some commiseration and prayer over the intolerable situation

Wesley Lloyd had left me in. I was ready for some pity.

"Now, Miss Julia," he said, templing his hands before him and looking into my eyes with deep concern. He crossed his feet at the ankles and leaned toward me. I could feel that charisma I was telling you about, and I thought again of how powerful a pulpiteer he was. Why, he filled out a pastoral robe to an outstanding degree, and made a commanding figure behind a pulpit. He liked to stretch out his arms and grasp each side of the podium as if he had to keep the thing from flying off above the congregation.

"Now, Miss Julia," he said again, sorrow dripping in his words and pulling his mouth down. "What's this I hear about you?"

I was having queasy feelings that felt strangely like guilt, but for the life of me, I couldn't think why.

"Why, I don't know. What have you heard?"

"Ah," he said, searching my face intently. Then he nodded as if he'd confirmed something. "It's hard to remember things, isn't it? But short-term memory loss is a natural result of aging, just the Lord's way of helping us cut our ties to worldly things."

"There is nothing wrong with my memory, short- or long-term. I asked what you'd heard, because rumors fly so thick in this town I didn't know which one you'd come in contact with."

"Just to remind you, then, I'm concerned about this child, the one you've been introducing around as Mr. Springer's son."

"Oh, Pastor," I said, with some relief that he wasn't going to start in about how the Lord needed more parking spaces. "You don't know how I need your prayers, for I've never had such a shock in my life. You can imagine. It's about broken me in two to learn about Mr. Springer's waywardness. I'm trying to do the Christian thing, even though it's the hardest thing I've ever done."

"I understand," he said in a soft, understanding voice. I felt tears spring to my eyes at the compassion I heard. I could put on a steely face for the curious and the ridiculers, but kindness just about crumpled me up.

"Yes," he said, "I can imagine what you're going through. Emotional turmoil plays havoc with our ability to rightly discern a situation. You must be very careful, Miss Julia. Unscrupulous people can take advantage of your trusting nature, as I am led to believe is happening to you right now, and it's confusing your mental processes. For instance, we don't always know what the Lord's will for us is in unusual circumstances. And what we think is the Christian thing to do may not be at all. That's why I wanted to counsel with you."

My eyes dried up and I felt confused. "I don't understand," I said. "I thought I was doing the Lord's will."

"Well, it's a delicate matter, but I'm sure we can straighten this out and you'll be able to handle things a little better after we talk. You see, Miss Julia, Mr. Springer was highly thought of in this town, indeed, in this whole section of the state. To say nothing of our beloved church. I can't tell you the contributions he made to everything he cared about, and it seems to me that we should be careful about anything that would be a blot on his good name."

"I'm not following you," I said, but my insides were beginning to knot up on me.

"I'm saying that your running around town

proclaiming that child as Mr. Springer's son is unbecoming to a fine Christian woman like yourself." He leaned so close that I could smell the breath mint and hear it click against his teeth. "It helps nothing," he went on, "to besmirch Mr. Springer's reputation, which you're perilously close to doing. Why, you know that the Springer family donated the very land this church is on and contributed greatly to this sanctuary."

"Yes, I know it." My hands twitched on the arms of the chair, and I clasped them in my lap.

"And there's a Sunday school room named for your husband, and all the hymnals have his name stamped in them because he donated them."

"I know that, too." Wesley Lloyd's rings— the ones he'd put on my finger with an oath of fidelity—were cutting into the palm of my hand.

"But, Miss Julia, you may not know that the session is seriously considering a Family Life Center, a building that would strengthen family ties by providing our members with a place for all kinds of activities. We're thinking of a gymnasium, a video arcade room for young people, a

study room, and several other possibilities
to make the church the center of our lives,"
he said, pausing and studying me awhile.
He lowered his voice to a confiding whisper, "And our plan is to name it the Wesley
Lloyd Springer Activities Center."

I couldn't believe it. Little Lloyd's face with
its running nose, smeared glasses, and
open mouth blended with Wesley Lloyd's
as I pictured an oil portrait hanging in their
activities center for all to see. "I don't think
Mr. Springer's name should be associated
with such a thing," I managed to say, "considering the activities he was engaged in."

"Miss Julia, Miss Julia," he said, chiding
me as if I were a child. "See, that's the very
thing I'm talking about. You are not grasp-
ing the essence of what I'm saying here.
And this inability will only get worse as time
goes by. You might consider and earnestly
pray about granting someone trustworthy
your power of attorney so you won't have
to struggle with all these complex matters."

"Sam's taking care of all the complex
matters."

"I know, but as soon as the estate's settled, everything will revert to you. And
frankly, Miss Julia, I don't think you want

that burden. And, if I may speak lovingly, I'm not sure you'd be able to handle it."

He had a point. I wasn't sure I'd be able to handle it, either. I couldn't depend on Sam forever, and Binkie was getting so busy she might not want Wesley Lloyd's affairs dumped in her lap. I probably could've worded that better.

"Who would you suggest, Pastor?"

"Not a lawyer," he said, as if he knew my thoughts. "Lawyers can tie you in knots, giving you first one side of a question and then the other, and letting you make the final decision, and charging you for every minute. You need to consider someone who is, first of all, a Christian, and second, someone who is a strong, stable, family man. One who has proven that he's able to care for those under his protection. I would suggest someone in this church who has proven his ability through consistency and diligence. Someone who would be able to see through these devious attempts to gain access to the Springer estate through guile and subterfuge, as is being done even now by way of that child you've so unthinkingly taken in."

"Maybe I'm still not following you," I said.

"Are you saying that I ought to deny that child's lineage, when anybody who looks at him can tell who his father was? Are you saying that I ought to lie about it?"

"Oh." He laughed and shook his head at my density. "Not lie, Miss Julia. Just not saying anything is not lying. Mr. Springer did so much good in his life, and will do even more in the future, that I think we can afford to overlook some, ah, human foibles. After all, what is a Christian but one whose sins are forgiven?"

My nerves were about to jump out of my skin by this time. I kept thinking that I wasn't hearing him right, but every time he opened his mouth he said something even more unbelievable. "You want me to deny this child's very existence, is that it?"

"Well, we really don't know for sure whose child he is, do we?" He looked at me for a long minute, frowning with concern. "I'm worried about you, Miss Julia, truly worried. I fear that you haven't thought through all the ramifications. It seems to me that you need responsible, spiritual guidance to prevent, shall we say, a rash action on your part. For instance, have you thought that the child could have a claim on

Mr. Springer's estate? And your recognition of him can't do anything but help that claim? Why, it's possible that a good lawyer could take the entire Springer estate away from you and give it to that unknown child. Now what kind of stewardship would that be if you let that happen?"

Now I understood. Anytime a preacher starts talking about stewardship, he's talking about your money and his plans. Especially his building plans. It's hard to fathom the lengths some of them will go to fill the collection plates. Why, not too long ago I heard about a preacher in Chapel Hill who had an ATM installed in his church. But then, as Wesley Lloyd used to say, that's Chapel Hill for you.

"Let me ask you something, Pastor," I said, steering him back to my concerns. "Did you know about Wesley Lloyd's adultery?"

"Well," he said, smiling, as he sat back in his chair and looked off over my head. "I don't think that's a subject for us to be discussing. I'm sure it makes you uncomfortable, and gossip, which is all it was, is beneath us, don't you think?"

"So you did know."

"Let me counsel with you seriously here, Miss Julia." He leaned forward again, resting his arms on his knees and putting an earnest look on his face. "Some men, certain men, carry a heavy burden in life. They have great and terrible responsibilities. We don't understand this, but in many ways they are held to a different standard than the rest of us. Think of David and his many wives and concubines. He was guilty of adultery and even of murder, yet the Lord delighted in him. You see what I'm saying here? We have to overlook and forgive those men who have more to offer than the average person."

I don't know why I'd never noticed how coarse the skin of his face was or how close together his eyes were. "I do see what you're saying," I said. "You're saying that wealthy men can commit sins that would condemn a poor man. And you're saying that you're afraid that little boy will get the money you want for the church. Do I have it right?"

"No, no," he said, still smiling like he was dealing with a half-wit. "You mustn't see it like that. I'm just trying to protect Mr. Springer's name, and yours. And the

church's. Mr. Springer was so closely associated with First Church of Abbotsville that
anything that smears him smears us, too.
We need to work together here, Miss Julia.
I think you'll feel much better when you
learn to accept the Lord's will in this matter.
Now, why don't we have a prayer together?"

He raised his face toward the ceiling and
closed his eyes. When he opened his
mouth to call on the Lord, I stood up and
walked out.

When I stepped into Norma's office, she
quickly stuffed a napkin in her desk drawer
and closed it. Krispy Kreme doughnut
aroma filled the room.

"Through already?" she chirped. "I
thought you'd have a whole lot more to talk
about."

"Don't think, Norma," I said as I traversed
her office to the outside door. "It doesn't
take long to discuss adultery when the pastor's for it."

I glanced back to see her mouth drop
open, so I said, "You've got sugar on the
front of your blouse," and walked on out.

CHAPTER NINE

—

I don't know how I managed to walk across the parking lot and then the street and up the steps to my front porch with my limbs trembling like they were. Somewhere in one part of my mind I was aware of the way the hot asphalt sucked at my shoes with each step I took. And I knew I waited on the curb for a UPS truck to pass before crossing the street, but the roaring in my head kept me from concentrating on anything but getting to the wicker rocking chair on the porch.

I sank down in it, thankful for the wisteria vine that covered one end of the porch. Nobody could see me there, and maybe a few minutes of privacy would settle me down.

My preacher! A man of God saying the things he did. And comparing Wesley Lloyd to David, of all people, who, as everybody knows, had dabbled in somebody else's bed, too. But that didn't excuse Wesley Lloyd. And if it did, then everything I'd ever heard from a pulpit, read in the Bible, and believed in all my life meant absolutely nothing.

I curled my hands on the arms of the rocker and pushed off with a foot. I rocked and thought, and rocked and thought some more, taking stock of my situation. It had never entered my mind that my pastor wouldn't support me in this trying situation. How many times had I heard him preach on how hard it is to do the right thing? Doing the right thing, he'd preached many a time, goes against the natural grain of the sinful heart. So I knew that acknowledging the child was the right thing to do because it was the hardest thing to do. And Pastor Ledbetter should've seen that and encouraged me in it.

That's all right, I told myself, rocking faster. I knew that most of the church members would take whatever position Pastor Ledbetter did. A congregation wasn't called a flock for nothing. So I was going to have to gird my loins to walk into that building for the worship service with Little Lloyd. I had a few more days before Sunday, and I determined to prepare myself for it and not shirk my duty to raise up a child in the way he should go, even if I had only a little while to do it in. The church might abandon me, but it was my church and I'd not abandon it. Preachers came and preachers went, but we Presbyterians continued on.

I got up finally and, with knees still atremble, walked back to the kitchen. Lillian took one look at me and reached for the coffeepot.

"That preacher wadn't no help, was he?" she said, pouring two cups and bringing them to the table.

"Not only no help," I said, easing myself into a chair, "he just made things worse." I told her the gist of the conversation in the preacher's office. "And he had the gall to tell me it was the Lord's will to take his advice!"

"Law, law," Lillian commiserated. "Preachers is sometimes the worst ones for knowing the Lord's will. Seems like they's bad about mixing up their ownselves' will with the good Lord's. I seen it many a time. You 'member me tellin' you about that preacher we had at the Shiloh AME Zion Church? The one what got mixed up with the lead singer in the choir? It was a mess 'fore we got rid of both of them, what with the lead singer's husband wantin' to shoot the preacher, and the preacher sayin' he was bein' led by the Lord." She leaned back and laughed. "All us knowed what he was bein' led by, and it sure wadn't the Lord!"

I smiled, wrapping my hands around the coffee cup. "I'm beginning to think that that's what a lot of men are led by," I said, somewhat embarrassed at talking about such earthy matters.

"Where's that child?" I suddenly asked, not yet used to having another person in the house to account for.

"I sent him upstairs to rest awhile," she said. "He kinda droopy, seem like. I hope he's not gettin' sick on us."

"Oh, me," I said, hanging my head at the thought of another complication in my life. "I'll go call the drugstore right now and have them deliver a tonic. I meant to do it before this, and while I'm at it I might as well call the Western Auto and see if they have a swing set they could put up out in the back."

"That boy too big for a swing set," Lillian informed me. "Besides, Deputy Bates say this morning when he come home that he gonna put a tire swing on that big tree out there, if you don't mind."

"Why, no, I guess I don't," I said, though a few days ago the thought of a tacky tire swing in one of my trees would've struck me as the equivalent of a whitewall planted with red salvia in my front yard. "A tire swing would be fine, if he wants to do it. Lillian, I think I'll go up and lie down for a little. This day's worn me out."

I tiptoed up the stairs, not wanting to disturb the rest of Deputy Bates, who'd worked all night. I got to the head of the stairs and noticed that the guest room door was ajar. Without thinking, I pushed it open, not really intending to check on the boy, because I didn't much care if he was resting or not.

His bed was empty, and my first shocked thought was that he'd run off to find his mother. My second thought was that I'd had about as much trouble from that boy as I could tolerate, and to call the sheriff to

start a search for him was more than I could
face.

I headed toward the back hall to Deputy
Bates's room, not at all reluctant now to
wake him again. But there, right outside
Deputy Bates's door, was Little Lloyd,
sound asleep on the floor, his knees curled
up around that Winn-Dixie sack. I reached
down to wake him but turned around instead and brought a pillow and a summer
blanket from his room. I put the pillow under his head and spread the blanket over
him, and he hardly stirred. Then I went to
my bedroom and closed the door. He could
sleep wherever he wanted to. His daddy
certainly had.

But I couldn't sleep. I couldn't even rest
my eyes. Every time I closed them, I pictured myself walking into church, come
Sunday, with that stray child while everybody craned their necks and whispered behind their hands. I knew what they'd be
saying. They'd be saying that Julia Springer
was finally getting her comeuppance, and
they'd be happy about it. I cringed at the
thought, even though I hadn't done anything to be ashamed of. The Bible says that
children suffer for the sins of their fathers,

but it doesn't say a thing about wives suffering for the sins of their husbands, more's the pity. I lay there, getting more and more nervous and edgy. So I got up and went back downstairs.

"I'm going out for a while," I told Lillian. "I just have to get out of this house and do some thinking."

"Well, you be careful," she said. "You ain't that good a driver to be goin' here, there, and everywhere."

That didn't deserve an answer, so it didn't get one. I took my new car out of the garage and just started driving. It was a new experience for me to drive with no destination in mind and no need to be back before Wesley Lloyd got home. So I drove out of town, taking the two-lane roads throughout the county, searching for those with little traffic. I drove slowly, looking at fields and orchards, finding packinghouses and neat farmhouses along the rolling hills. I drove into areas I'd never been in, discovering small communities along the French Broad River and Briar Creek, inching along behind farm trucks and seeing tractors trailing plumes of red dust out in the fields. I circled the county, avoiding the interstate because in my state of mind I might get on it and never come back. Of course, I hadn't done too much driving on the interstate, since whenever we'd gone anywhere, Wesley Lloyd had always taken the wheel. That was his job. Mine was folding maps.

But that's what I felt like doing now, just getting on that fast track and driving and driving until I'd outrun all my troubles.

I'd not been paying much attention to the details around me, just automatically registering the rows of apple trees, loaded with fruit, and the few cars and trucks that passed me. My mind was heavy with grief and busy weighing the options, the possibilities, the "what-ifs" of the unthinkable mess Wesley Lloyd had left me.

I stopped at a crossroads, where Craven Gap Road intersected with Jessup and, since there was no traffic, let the car idle for a few minutes while I decided which way to go. The sun was edging down behind the mountains in the west, turning them purple and lengthening the shadows of the trees along the road, and I began to feel a little anxious about the lonely countryside. I needed to head toward home.

A deep, rumbling noise suddenly filled my

little car, scaring and confusing me. All I could think of was a crop-dusting airplane about to land on the road, with me in the way.

I looked from one side to the other, trying to determine where it was coming from. Then I glanced in the rearview mirror and nearly had a heart attack. The chrome grill of a huge truck was right behind me, right on my bumper, towering with growling menace over my little car. I stretched to see better, and could hardly see a thing through its darkened windshield. Two figures, maybe. I couldn't be sure, but since I was blocking the road, I quickly pulled out into the intersection, took a right, and headed toward town. The truck followed, staying a few yards behind, where I was able to get a better look at it. It was black with a row of yellow lights on a bar across the cab, but the unnerving thing about it was the over-size wheels that jacked the body of the truck up above everything else on the road. Why in the world would anybody want a thing like that?

I thought the driver would want to pass, so I slowed down. So did he. Then I went a little faster, but still within the speed limit because I didn't want him to think I was afraid. And I wasn't, I just didn't understand the menace I was feeling from him. Night was quickly coming on, so I switched on the headlights. So did he, only his were all yellow, the ones over the cab and the fog lights on the front.

As it got darker, the truck blended into the night and all I could see in the rearview mirrow were those strange yellow lights floating above the road. I didn't like it at all. I felt lonely and scared, although the truck had done nothing but stay right with me at every turn I made.

And it stayed with me until I reached the highway leading into Abbotsville. I pulled into light traffic, relieved to be among other cars on the streets and by gas pumps and at drive-up windows at Hardee's and pulling into Wal-Mart's. I looked back several times, but the truck was gone. I'd been foolish to worry. It had probably been a young man and his date heading for the movie theater, with no thought of me at all. We'd both just been going in the same direction.

Still, I was glad when I finally pulled into the driveway at home. Welcoming light from the windows spilled out onto the yard, and before I could help it, I felt a lifting of my spirits. There was more than a lonely and empty house waiting for me.

Lillian had already fed Deputy Bates and Little Lloyd their suppers, so I had to endure her fussing and complaining while I fixed a plate for myself. She'd been worried about me, which, though aggravating to listen to, gave me comfort that somebody cared.

"I was 'bout to get Deputy Bates to put out one of them pointed bulletums on you," she told me.

"You've been watching too much television, Lillian. Now, where is Deputy Bates? I want to know what he's found out."

"That chile don't need to hear you two talk about his fam'ly like I know you gonna do," she said, taking a carton of ice cream out of the icebox. "He like this chocolate swirl kind." She dipped a hefty spoonful into a bowl and took it to the living room where little Lloyd and Deputy Bates were watching a rerun of *Baywatch*. I would've put a stop to that, for fear those half-naked young women would inflame the boy's senses, but I just couldn't summon the energy.

Deputy Bates came into the kitchen and sat down across from me. "Well, Miss Julia," he said, "I'm not sure I've got anything for you, but I have been asking around. There's nothing on a Hazel Marie Puckett in anything I ran. But a good bit on Pucketts in general. I asked my lieutenant if he knew any Pucketts, and he said everybody in the department knows several of them. Seems they're one of those families that are in and out of trouble all the time. At least, some of them are."

"What kind of trouble are we talking about?"

"Domestic disturbances is a big one. Drunk and disorderlies, DWIs, fights, disturbing the peace, you name it. Years ago, they were into bootlegging, now they're growing marijuana. They all come from down around Benson's Gap in the southwestern part of the county. There're several families down there, all kin to each other, and if they're not fighting with their neighbors, they're beating up on each other. My lieutenant said that if I haven't been called down there yet, I soon will be."

"Lord," I said, "it's worse than I thought."

"Not necessarily," he said, shaking his head. "Remember, I didn't find anything on this woman. There're always some few in families like that who break out of the pattern. And she has no arrest record, at least not in this county."

"I just can't imagine Wesley Lloyd going to the end of the county into a group of people like that every Thursday night. You didn't know him, but I'll tell you that doesn't sound like something he'd do." Even as I said it, I realized that nothing I'd learned that he had done sounded like something he would do. So much for knowing someone.

"Didn't you tell me the Puckett woman mentioned a house she'd been living in?"

"That's right!" I said. "She said he'd not even left her the house she'd been living in for ten years or more. Now, if we could find that, maybe a neighbor or somebody could tell us more."

"Call your lawyer," he said. "If everything came to you, then it should be on a list somewhere. We ought to be able to figure out which property it is with Bud's help. I couldn't get much out of him, though I tried. He just said they lived out in the country and he rode a bus to school. But he ought to be able to identify the house if we get him in the right area."

"You'd think a child would know where he lives," I said.

"I got the feeling that she kept him pretty close to home," Deputy Bates told me. He picked up the salt shaker and turned it around, thinking over the problem. "Seems his mother did most of her shopping over in Delmont, and of course he went to one of the county schools. Looks as if she made an effort to stay out of Abbotsville."

"I just wish Wesley Lloyd had made an effort to stay *in* it." I stirred lima beans around on my plate, not at all hungry, but needing something to occupy my hands. It was humiliating to talk to Deputy Bates, or anybody, about what my husband had done, and how he'd gone to such lengths to keep me from knowing about it. But of course it wasn't just me he'd wanted to keep in the dark, but everybody who'd thought he was a fine, upstanding man.

"I'll get up early tomorrow afternoon," Deputy Bates said, "so if you'll call your lawyer and get a list of the county properties Mr. Springer owned, we'll take Bud and look for the house."

"All right," I said. "I don't know what good it'll do me to find where she lived, but I'll at least see the scene of the crime."

CHAPTER TEN

—

The list I got from Binkie had been win-
nowed down to residential properties in the
county, but it was lengthy enough. Deputy
Bates drove my car, with me beside him
and Little Lloyd in the backseat with his
grocery sack.

"I can't wait to get there," he said, snapping his seat belt on. "You'll like my house.
It's real nice."

"I'm sure it is," I said, and cut my eyes at
Deputy Bates, who was intent on his driving. I didn't want any smirks about who had
bought the house, and why. Not that
Deputy Bates was given to smirking, but
you never know. I craned my neck toward
the backseat and asked, "You sure you
can't give us any directions?"

"No'm, I never been this way before," Little Lloyd said. He was looking out the window as Deputy Bates drove us first toward Benson's Gap and the several small communities along the river. I had to do something about that child, and teach him to look at people when he spoke to them. But maybe it was just me he couldn't face, which was understandable because I could hardly face him.

From the road, we looked at unpainted or peeling farmhouses, an inordinate number of them with sagging sofas on the porches and rusting farm machinery in the yards. Deputy Bates slowed down as we passed each one so Little Lloyd could get a good look.

"That look familiar?" he'd ask, and then, "Think we're getting close?"

Each time the boy shook his head, until we came to a cluster of frame houses around a grocery store and a post office with a dusty flag hanging limply on its pole.

"There it is," he cried, pointing ahead of us.

"Which one, Bud?" Deputy Bates asked.

"There! At the very end. Maybe my mama's there." He hiked himself up to lean on the front seat so he could see through the windshield. He was breathing through his mouth in little gasps, fogging up his glasses.

We turned into a dirt driveway that led to a small white-painted house with a railed front porch. A high hemlock hedge enclosed both the front and back yards, and a huge oak tree shaded most of the house. Right in front of us was a closed two-car garage with a short breezeway connecting it to a side door of the house. Deputy Bates turned off the ignition, and the three of us sat there listening to the tick of the engine as it cooled off. Everything else was quiet, no movement anywhere, no road sounds. My heart hurt as I thought of the many times my husband had pulled into this drive and into that garage, and then slipped, unobserved, into the house where the child who was breathing down my neck was conceived and raised.

"That's my house," he said. "It's real nice, ain't it?"

"Isn't it," I corrected.

"Yessum, it is."

I took a rasping breath and said, "Well, let's see if anybody's home."

We climbed out, Deputy Bates pulling back his seat so Little Lloyd could get out. He ran to the front steps, calling, "Mama, Mama, I'm home!" I hoped she was.

Little Lloyd opened the front door and walked right in, while we followed behind him. As we crossed the porch to the open door, I could hear his feet running through the house and his voice calling his mama becoming more and more shrill. Desperate, maybe, and I couldn't blame him. The house was empty, not a stick of furniture, not a piece of clothing. Nothing.

The boy came back into the front room, his face a picture of despair. I could've felt sorry for him if I hadn't been so put out with that woman for going off and leaving him.

"Come here, Bud," Deputy Bates said, pulling the boy to him. "Your mother said she was going to Raleigh, remember? She's learning a trade and then she'll be back to get you. It makes sense that she'd take her furniture with her, or maybe she's stored it for when you'll be back together. Don't cry, now. This doesn't mean anything."

Well, maybe, I thought. That woman

ought to be strung up for leaving her child with strangers the way she'd done.

"Since we're here, I guess we ought to look around," I said, taking note of the smallness and sparsity of the rooms. No matter how nice Little Lloyd thought it was, his father had certainly not squandered money on his little love nest. I could've felt some shame over his stinginess if I hadn't been busy trying to picture him in it.

The rest of the house was as bare as the front room; not even the kitchen appliances had been left. Deputy Bates looked in all the closets, checked the ceilings for access to an attic, which he didn't find, and then went out through the breezeway to the garage.

"Y'all stay there," he called as the boy and I started to follow him. "Go back out to the car, and I'll be there in a minute."

I wasn't interested in an empty garage any more than I was in an empty house, so it suited me to put my hand on Little Lloyd's back and turn him around. The sooner the child got out of there, the better, it seemed to me.

We sat in the car with the windows rolled down, waiting in the afternoon stillness for

Deputy Bates. It was hot and humid, with butterflies flitting among the shrubs by the porch, insects chirping, and Little Lloyd sniveling in the backseat. I handed him a Kleenex from my pocketbook, but I couldn't think of a thing to say to him. We both had our problems.

"What if my mama don't ever come back?" he said, trying to choke back the tears.

"She will. I wouldn't worry about that." But of course that's what I was doing.

"But I mean"—he stopped, his throat thick with misery—"I mean, what if something's happened to her and she can't come back? I don't know what I'd do."

My land, the child thought I'd turn him out cold on the streets. Where did he get such an idea?

"Well, for goodness' sakes," I said. "If something's happened to your mother, which I very much doubt, you'll stay with me until better arrangements can be made. So you don't need to worry about that."

I hoped I'd reassured him on that score, but I wasn't about to commit myself to any long-term child care, no matter how pitiful the child. I was glad to see Deputy Bates close the front door of the house and walk over to the car. He got in and started it up, his face closed and thoughtful.

"Anything in the garage?" I asked as he backed down the driveway.

"Well, no cars. Just some oil spots and a few odds and ends." He caught his bottom lip in his teeth, and glanced in the rearview mirror at the child, who was scrunched up in the corner of the backseat. "Miss Julia, I'm going to stop at that grocery store down the road and get us all a Coke. It's hot as . . . well," he said with a quick grin, "pretty hot."

"Suits me," I agreed. "I could use a Co-Cola, and I expect Little Lloyd could, too."

Deputy Bates parked in the shade of a tree in the packed dirt parking area in front of the store. Tin signs, weathered and rust-streaked, advertised Winston cigarettes and Peeler's milk. A hand-lettered sign on the screen door announced that fresh farm eggs and homegrown tomatoes were available. While we waited for the drinks, I got out of the car and sat on a bench under the tree, hoping for a breeze to cool me off. Lord, it was hot and heavy. I took last Sunday's bulletin from my pocketbook and fanned myself with it. Little Lloyd stayed in the car, looking with miserable eyes at the front of the store.

Deputy Bates handed him an icy bottle through the window, then came and joined me.

"Miss Julia," he said, in a tone that made me look closely at the frown on his face, "I'm going to let you take that little boy and drive back home. I'll wait here for Sheriff Frady and some of the others, then ride back to town with them."

"What? Why is Earl Frady coming out here?"

"I called him," he told me, turning his steady gaze on me. "I found something besides oil stains in that garage; maybe nothing, but it looked like blood."

It wasn't enough to have that worry on my mind all the way back to town. As soon as we pulled into the driveway at home, I knew something was wrong. Lillian was sitting on the back steps with her hands over her face. She sprang up as soon as she saw us.

"What is it now?" I wondered aloud.

She was at the car window before I got

the keys out of the ignition, and the sight of her face made me forget about blood on a garage floor.

"Oh, Miss Julia!" she cried as I got out of the car. "You not gonna b'lieve . . . I didn't know what to do! I been waitin' for you to get home. Oh, Law, I ain't never!"

"What in the world, Lillian?" I put my arm around her shoulders. "What is wrong with you?"

"I just went to the store, like I always do, an' I locked the doors. You know I always lock the doors. An' I didn't even know it till I got the groceries put up, 'cause the kitchen ain't messed up a bit. But then I went in the front room, an' I couldn't b'lieve it!"

"What are you talking about?"

"Somebody been in the house, that's what I'm talkin' about! Tore it up, too. Least the front room's all tore up, I didn't look no further. I come out on the steps to wait 'cause *Unsolved Mysteries* say don't touch nothing when somebody break in yo' house."

"My Lord," I breathed, feeling dizzy with all the implications. I put my hand on the car to steady myself. "Come here, Little

Lloyd, and hold my hand. We better go see what the damage is." He gave me his hand, and I tried not to think how many times he'd rubbed it across his nose. He held his grocery sack in the other. "Come on, Lillian."

"We ain't s'posed to touch nothing," she warned me.

"I'm not going to touch a thing. But I want to see how much of the house they've been in, and see if anything's been stolen. And I need to get to the telephone to call the sheriff." Except he was at the other end of the county, along with Deputy Bates.

Lillian was right. The house had been ransacked, drawers pulled out of the desk and sideboard, with papers and silver dumped on the floor. The sofa cushions were on the floor, and the chairs tipped over. My needlepoint pillows had been hurled across the room, knocking over a lamp that lay shattered on the floor.

"Oh," I said, holding to the back of a chair. "My *Gone With the Wind* lamp! Who did this? Who in the world is responsible for this?"

We went upstairs, my feeling of trepidation confirmed at the sight of the bedrooms. My dresser drawers had been turned out on the floor and on the bed, with underclothes strung everywhere. Clothes from the closet were piled on the floor, and shoe and hatboxes emptied and discarded. Even the bathroom cabinets and the linen closet had been cleared. It looked like someone had just swept his arm along the shelves, knocking everything to the floor. Soap, bath crystals, talcum powders, cologne, towels, washclothes—everything had been flung to the floor and walked on. A full roll of toilet paper was stuffed into the commode, along with the red rubber bag that had to do with my personal hygiene. The lemon scent of Jean Naté was almost strong enough to mask the putrid smell of the semisoft clump of you-know-what on my white Royal Cannon towels.

"My land," I gasped, holding my hand over my mouth. "This is unbelievable." I pulled Little Lloyd away from the door. He didn't need to witness such an affront to sensitive natures.

"That the worst thing I ever seen," Lillian said. "What kind of person do somethin' like that? We better call the police."

"I'm going to," I said, pulling Little Lloyd

out of the room. "But let's check the other bedrooms first."

They were the same. Little Lloyd's room was worse than mine, if that was possible. The mattress had been pushed off his bed, where it leaned half on the floor. His clothes were on the floor and his cardboard suitcase had been cut and stomped. We stood there surveying this senseless damage, and I could feel Little Lloyd's damp hand closing tighter on mine.

"I'm real scared," he said.

"Don't be," I said. "Let's go to the kitchen, and I'll call the sheriff. Little Lloyd, don't you worry. Somebody sick and evil did all this, but they won't do it again. Don't you be afraid; I'm going to see to it."

CHAPTER ELEVEN

—

While I called the sheriff's office, Lillian paced the kitchen, wringing her hands in her apron. She cried and apologized for going to the store, taking all the blame on herself. Little Lloyd stood next to me, his eyes big with fright.

"They're sending somebody," I said, hanging up the phone and hearing the nervous words pour out of my mouth. "I told them to contact Deputy Bates, too. Now, Lillian, sit down and get yourself together. This was not your fault, and I don't want to hear another word about it. Looks to me like it was either somebody looking for something in particular, or vandals who just like to tear things up for the sake of it. I didn't see a thing missing, did you? Televi-

sion's still here, and so is my silver. I'll have
to go through the papers in the desk, but I
can't imagine anybody'd want canceled
checks, can you? Sit down, Lillian. You're
making me nervous. We've got to think
about who could've done this. Did you see
anything missing? How you reckon they got
in?"

She finally took a seat at the table and
wiped her face with her apron. "I 'spect
they climb up the back stairs. Didn't you
see Deputy Bates's door standing open
with the glass broke out?"

"You're right. I did see it, but I was still
thinking of what was in my bathroom to
make much sense of anything else."

It wasn't long before two sheriff's
deputies arrived to look through the house
and begin making a report. Would you believe they wanted to know my age? As if
that had anything to do with what'd happened. Sheriff Earl Frady drove up soon after with Deputy Bates, and everybody had
to tell their stories all over again. I was
asked a dozen times if anything was missing, but the more I went through the house
with one or the other of them, the more I
was sure that not one thing had been taken.

I was close to the end of my patience, what with uniformed officers trooping in and out, poking here and there and asking one question after another, until I saw one leaving with a large plastic bag held out at arm's length. Deputy Bates asked if I wanted my towels back, but I told him not to bother. I appreciated them taking that calling card out of my bathroom, and I knew Lillian did, too.

By the time they all left, I'd had about as much excitement as I could stand. Lillian called two of her granddaughters to come help her straighten up the mess in the house, and I was grateful for them. Deputy Bates stood in the kitchen with a worried look on his face and a cup of coffee in his hand.

"Little Lloyd," I said, "go out in the yard and play. You've been cooped up in the car or the house all day, and you need to be outside for a while. Here"—I reached into the pantry—"take this bag of Oreos. We may not have much supper tonight."

He looked up at me through those thick glasses in a way that gave me a start. His eyes were so much like Wesley Lloyd's sometimes that it was like looking at my husband before I ever met him.

When he left with his cookies, I turned to Deputy Bates. "What in the world's going on here? First you find blood in that child's house and now this house's been broken into. I'm beginning to feel something bad's going to happen every time I turn around. You don't reckon whoever did this to my house was somebody you arrested, do you?"

"I doubt it, Miss Julia. I haven't been here long enough to make anybody that mad at me. But to catch you up on the other, we had the crime-scene unit down at Bud's house, and preliminary tests confirm that it is blood. Human or not, we won't know until we hear from the SBI lab. There wasn't a lot of it, some spattering and a long smear on the wall. And a little pool on the floor, which was still sticky. That means it got there fairly recently, although the humidity in the closed garage may've had something to do with that. I've got bad news for you, though. If it's human blood, you're going to have to tell Sheriff Frady how you came to have Bud with you. We'll have to track down his mother, using every method we have, to be sure, first of all, that it's not her blood since she was the last known tenant of the house. And as far as we know, you were the last person to see her around here. Tracing her is going to open a whole can of worms for you."

"A can of worms is right," I said. I leaned against the kitchen counter, tired to death of all the complications that Wesley Lloyd had left me. "You know there was somebody with her when she left here. I told you she wasn't driving the car, so I wasn't the last one to see her."

"I know. But we don't know who that was. We don't know if she went straight to Raleigh from here or whether she went back to her house. We don't know if the blood was in the garage before she brought Bud here or if it got there after she left him. We don't know anything, and won't, until we find her. I just want you to be prepared. You're going to have to tell the investigating officers everything that's happened. And be prepared for the possibility that Bud's mother knows something about the blood in her garage. Or that it's hers."

"Oh my Lord," I said, holding on to the counter. "You don't think something's happened to her?" I was ashamed to admit that my first thought was of being stuck with that child forever, in spite of reassuring the child to the contrary not three hours earlier. "That poor woman," I said, quickly getting my mind in the proper frame.

"It's too early to know. But for now I'm going to the hardware store and get some more locks for your doors. And a pane of glass for the broken one upstairs."

"Go to Prince's Hardware," I told him, "and charge it to my account."

I went into the living room to help Lillian and her two grands, but she told me to keep out of their way. So I went outside to the backyard and sat with Little Lloyd in the glider. I folded my hands in my lap and sighed.

"You want some Oreos, lady?" The child held the package out to me.

"Don't mind if I do," I said, taking one. "But call me Mrs. Springer, not lady. That sounds like you don't know who I am."

"No'm. I mean, yes'm." He nibbled a cookie all the way around, then started back at it like a mouse, taking tiny bites until he had only a little nubbin of the center left. Wesley Lloyd had had peculiar eating habits, too.

It made me nervous to watch him, so I said, "Don't you want to play?"

"No'm, I don't much feel like it." He turned his head toward me when he spoke, but still wouldn't look me in the eye.

I didn't feel much like talking, so we ate Oreo cookies and listened to the birds in the trees.

Before long, Lillian stuck her head out the back door and called me in. "You got company," she said. "Miz Conover and Mr. Sam and yo' preacher, they all here to see 'bout you."

I sighed and got up, telling Little Lloyd he'd be better off to stay outside. "If you haven't already learned it," I said, "news gets around fast in this town. I wouldn't be surprised if the nine-one-one line wasn't connected to the Presbyterian Women's Prayer Chain."

I was glad that Lillian and her girls had started with the living room, because it was straightened enough to receive company by now. They were all there: Sam, sitting at his ease in a chair, hat on his knee and a concerned look on his face; LuAnne, chirp-

ing around in her usual excited state; and
Pastor Ledbetter, standing by the front window
like he was daring the burglar to try it
again.

Pastor Ledbetter and LuAnne started toward
me, talking at once, asking how I was,
what was stolen, did I know who'd done it.
Sam stood up when I came into the room,
but he hung back waiting, I guess, to get a
word in edgewise.

"Everybody's fine," I assured them. "Have
a seat now. I appreciate your concern, but
it's nothing. Just vandals, most likely."

"I don't doubt it," Pastor Ledbetter pronounced.
"There're no morals left anymore.
And it's going to get worse before it gets
better, as the Bible tells us. The closer we
get to the millennium, the more of this kind
of thing we can expect. It starts with the
breakdown of the family, Miss Julia, which
is why it's imperative for you to get that
child back with his own family. You don't
want to be standing in the way of a united
family, and my counsel is to get that boy
back with his kin. All this trouble dates from
the time you agreed to take him from his
mother."

Sam frowned, opened his mouth, then

turned away from the pastor like he had to get himself under control. I took a deep breath, not wanting to admit that I, too, had wondered if the break-in had had anything to do with Little Lloyd. But I just shook my head, realizing it was too much trouble to straighten the preacher out on the matter of me taking a child from his mother. I'd hardly had a choice.

So I just said, "I appreciate your concern, Pastor, but please remember that I wasn't the one who had a family to break up in the first place."

"But it's incumbent on all of us," he said, "to put into practice family values. *Biblical* family values."

I couldn't understand why he was blaming me for a break-in at my own house and a breakdown of all families everywhere. I'd had enough of it.

"Which biblical family would you be talking about?" I snapped, having in mind all the adultery, fratricide, incest, murder, multiple wives, envy, and downright meanness displayed by any number of families in the Bible.

"Oh, Julia," LuAnne said, reaching for my hand and patting it. "You're all upset."

"Of course I am, LuAnne," I said, snatching back my hand. "What do you expect after somebody's been through my papers and underclothes and closets and drawers? Sam, have a seat. I don't see anything funny about it." I said that because he was smiling a little, even though his eyes were grave with concern.

"I don't see anything funny, either," he said, but by then I figured he'd seen the humor of somebody going through my underclothes. Drawers, too. That was Sam for you. "What does Coleman say about this, Julia?"

"He's helping with the investigation," I said, "and it's too early to know anything yet. But I want you to know that having a sheriff's deputy boarding in my house sure didn't deter this burglar."

"True enough," Sam said, and got a faraway look in his eyes, so that I knew he was thinking things over. Probably coming to the same conclusion I had, that somebody had wanted something bad enough to risk breaking into and entering this particular house.

After I assured LuAnne and Pastor Ledbetter that everything was under control, I walked out on the front porch to see them off. I wanted them gone so I could talk freely with Sam. LuAnne said Leonard was waiting for her to fix his supper but she could come back later and sit with me.

"No need for that, LuAnne," I said firmly. "I'll be going to bed early. It's been a hectic day, and I'll see you at church tomorrow anyway."

When she realized that Pastor Ledbetter intended to linger, she let herself be persuaded to drive off. The pastor still had something to say to me, even though he knew Sam was waiting in the living room.

"Miss Julia," he said, his voice taking on the tone of a doctor breaking the bad news. "I have to urge you again to give up this plan of keeping that child with you. This terrible occurrence ought to serve as a warning that something's wrong about it all. You don't know what you've got yourself caught up in, and you could be putting yourself in some danger."

I longed to unburden myself to him and be guided by his advice, but I knew his agenda already and it didn't fit with mine. Sometimes, a lot of times, we know what is right without anybody telling us. And I knew it was right that I look out for Little Lloyd whether the blood in his garage or the state of my house had anything to do with him or not.

"Pastor," I said, "that little boy had nothing whatsoever to do with my house getting broken into. It was vandals, plain and simple. Besides, he was with me and Deputy Bates when it happened, and one thing has nothing to do with the other."

"I'm not accusing the child, Miss Julia. All I'm saying is that once we head down the wrong track, we open ourselves up to all kinds of mischief. You're putting yourself between this child and his mother, and that's just wrong. We have to do everything we can to keep families together, not break them up, don't you agree?"

Well, no, I didn't. I'd heard of too many families that needed to be broken up—cruel fathers, drunken mothers, drugged boyfriends, battered wives, and so on and so on. But I'd heard Pastor Ledbetter on all those subjects from the pulpit and, according to him, prayer and a good dose of family values would cure them all. To my way of thinking, about the only thing that would cure them was a baseball bat.

"Sam's waiting for me, Pastor," I said. "He probably needs to discuss some of Wesley Lloyd's business matters. Thank you for coming." I turned and walked back inside.

"Sam," I said, shutting the screen door behind me, "do you think I'm breaking up that child's family?"

He laughed. "Julia, the child's father is dead and his mother's abandoned him. Don't let Ledbetter confuse you. The child has no family, unless it's you and Lillian and Coleman. Use your head, woman."

"I'm trying to, Sam. But I declare, it's swimming by now, and you don't know the half of it." And I told him about the blood in the garage and what Deputy Bates had said about having to tell the sheriff everything. "Now, I reckon the social services will try to put Little Lloyd away somewhere. Busybodies, every one of them, and government interference, too. What would this town say if I let that child be treated like a pauper while I enjoyed Wesley Lloyd's proceeds? I tell you, it's none of their business who's looking after that boy."

"We can probably fix it, if it comes to that," Sam said. "I don't know why you wouldn't qualify as a foster parent, if they insist on following the letter of the law. Let's don't worry about that now. I'll talk to Binkie Monday morning, and we'll see what we can do."

"Well, that'd relieve my mind a good bit. I've got enough to worry about without that on top of everything else. I'm telling everybody it was vandals who broke into the house, Sam, but I don't think it was. And neither does Deputy Bates. We think somebody was looking for something. I just don't know what it could be. Everything I'd consider to be of value was left alone." I leaned my head back on the sofa and stared at the ceiling. "Why now, is what I want to know. What do I have in this house that hasn't been here forever?"

Sam looked at me out from under his eyebrows while he turned his hat around in his hands. "Not a thing, Julia," he said, "but that little boy out there."

CHAPTER TWELVE

—

With that worrisome thought in mind for the rest of the evening, I let Little Lloyd stay up until he was so sleepy he could barely stumble up the stairs. We were all on edge, afraid to walk from one room to another without someone with us. I put up a good front for the child's sake, but to tell the truth, I was still jittery at the thought of some stranger in my house, rummaging through my things looking for who-knew-what.

Lillian offered to stay the night, but I sent her on home. She was too scared to sleep a wink in my house, even though it was unlikely that anything else would happen. Especially after all the official coming and going throughout the afternoon. I'd have felt better, though, if Deputy Bates hadn't had to work, but he told me that he and every other officer on duty would be patrolling the area. And several times during the night I saw the gleam of a spotlight sweep across the house and yard. My tax dollars at work, and I was grateful for it.

As I climbed the stairs after checking the doors half a dozen times, I hoped Little Lloyd wouldn't lie awake listening to every noise in the house, like I knew I would. I left both our doors open so he'd feel safer, but toward morning, when I decided to get on up, I found him curled up in the hall next to my door. The child must've had an affinity for hardwood floors.

I decided against Sunday school that morning, figuring Little Lloyd didn't need to face a dozen nosy nine-year-olds who'd been filled with all their parents' gossip. His week had been hard enough, to say nothing of mine. I knew LuAnne would be in her element without me in the Lula Mae Harding class that morning. She'd be able to tell everybody about the boy and the break-in in every graphic detail. The members of the Lula Mae Harding class were firm on the matter of details, saying that we needed to know every little thing so our prayers would be effective. As if the Lord was sitting up there without a clue, waiting for us to tell Him what was going on. I knew He'd get an earful today.

I laid out Little Lloyd's clothes, some I'd bought for him on Deputy Bates's advice. Khaki pants, white shirt, navy blazer, and a red-and-blue-striped tie. He dressed himself except for the tie, which I took in hand. I tied it and pushed the knot up against his collar, then stepped back to consider my handiwork. One end hung below his belt while the other stopped at his breastbone.

"That won't do," I said, undoing it for another try.

"I could wear the other one," the boy said.

"That clip-on thing? No, you couldn't. When you go to church, you wear the best you have." I stopped myself from saying anything else about his clothes and, by extension, the one who'd selected them. The child wasn't responsible for either.

"Hold your head up, and I'll give it another go," I said, measuring the ends again. "I declare, this thing has a mind of its own."

"It sure is pretty, though," he said, as if to make up for its waywardness.

"Yes, it is, and it looks handsome on you. There!" I said, giving the tie a final tug. "Look in the mirror. I think we've got it."

He studied his reflection some little while, touching and smoothing the tie, with an expression that was solemn as a judge.

"I wish my mama could see it," he finally said. "She likes pretty things. I thank you for it, Miz Springer."

"You're welcome, I'm sure. Now let's go before we're late."

I handed his jacket to him, then stopped to adjust my hat. Wearing a hat to church makes me old-fashioned, I know, but it also makes me obedient, according to Paul and Pastor Ledbetter.

"Before I forget," I went on, "you do know how to act in church, don't you?" For all I knew, the child had never darkened the door of a house of worship.

"Yes'm, I do." He frowned in thought as his glasses slid down his nose. "Sit still. Be quiet. Pay attention. And behave myself."

He looked over his glasses in my general direction, fuzzily searching for confirmation. "Very good," I said. "That's advice to live by." I stopped dead in my tracks. I'd been sitting still, staying quiet, paying attention, and behaving myself all my life, and look where I was now. "On second thought," I said, "one of these days, when you're old enough, I want you to be able to think for yourself. Now, are you ready?"

"Yes'm."

I wasn't sure I was, knowing what we'd be facing. But I'd set my course and was determined to see it through.

"Remember now," I cautioned as we went down the stairs, "be polite to everybody, but don't answer any questions. Let me do the talking."

"Yes'm."

I closed the front door behind us, and we walked across the porch and down the steps.

I brushed a piece of lint from his sleeve and said, "There're a lot of people who just thrive on gossip, don't you know, so don't let them bother you."

"No'm."

With a hand on his shoulder, I stopped him when we reached the street. "Look both ways before you cross."

"Yes'm."

I must say the child was amenable to instruction, but that did little to calm my nerves as we made our way toward the church and two hundred or so pairs of avid eyes.

As we went along the sidewalk, one car after another pulled into the parking lot and people began to stream into the church. A few men, deacons mostly, stood around the back door smoking their last cigarettes before the service. There was a holly bush there that was about dead from all the cigarettes crushed out and buried in the mulch around it.

On Sunday mornings, I always walked around front so I could go in the main door, which was only fitting for a formal service. But when we got to the corner, I almost turned around and went back home. There was that gaudy marquee that Pastor Ledbetter had put up one week exactly after Wesley Lloyd was interred. He'd wanted it for ever so long, but Wesley Lloyd had put his foot down, saying we were Presbyterians, not Baptists, and that a marquee advertising sermon topics was inappropriate and unacceptable. But Wesley Lloyd wasn't around anymore, and there was nobody able or willing to tell the pastor nay. So it was up, blaring forth his name and his topics, changed once a week, and everybody welcome. I declare, it set my teeth on edge, and especially that morning. Pastor Ledbetter's topic for the service was "Woman, the Bedrock of the Family."

But I went into the marble-floored narthex and prepared to lead Little Lloyd to my usual seat, four pews from the front and on the center aisle. I put my hand firmly on his shoulder, just as I used to put it in the crook of Wesley Lloyd's arm. This was partly to keep the child from scuffling along behind me and partly to give him a squeeze if he started to wipe his nose on his sleeve. "Head up, Little Lloyd," I whispered.

We marched down the aisle, side by side, just like Wesley Lloyd and I used to present ourselves. This time, though, I turned my head neither to the left nor to the right, but I knew people were craning to see and I heard the buzz of whispers. I cut my eyes over to the side and saw LuAnne Conover's about to pop out of her head. And I saw Mamie Harrison pointing at us, whispering furiously to her husband, who was deaf as a post. I'd timed our entrance so there'd be no chance of anybody talking to us, and as soon as we were seated, we all had to get to our feet again as the choir entered the chancel singing the processional, and Pastor Ledbetter in his black robe stepped up to the podium.

I endured that service. That's the only way to put it. Little Lloyd began fidgeting after the first fifteen minutes, so I found a pen and whispered for him to draw something on the bulletin. Then I gave him a Life Saver and a Kleenex.

Pastor Ledbetter started off with how the Lord had burdened his heart all week long over the duties of women and mothers, and women who tried to be mothers but who weren't. Every word he said was aimed at me, and I knew it. I sat there staring up at him while he droned on about how Christian women were becoming tainted by the world and abandoning biblical precepts, taking on responsibilities that they were never designed to assume, making decisions, financial and otherwise, that they were not qualified to make. And all of this was leading to the worst crisis the church had ever experienced.

I didn't take my eyes off him, and after the first few minutes, he looked everywhere but at me. He had the podium, but I had the better of him. Several times he lost his place and had to repeat himself. Then he got a second wind when he came to the climax of his sermon.

"All my remarks to this point," he declaimed as he stacked his note cards preparatory to winding up, "have been laying the groundwork for us to consider with prayerful hearts the recent action by the General Assembly. An action that opens the door to the acceptance and *the approval* of homosexuality in our beloved church. This is just the latest step in the headlong rush to wipe out the biblical underpinnings of our faith. Beloved, this is indicative of the lengths liberals will go to if we give them an inch. And it all began twenty-five years ago when the General Assembly permitted women to be ordained and to become officers of the church."

He paused and looked out over the congregation, his eyes sweeping left to right and up to the balcony. You could've heard a pin drop.

"Now I know," he went on, lowering the tone of his voice to keep our attention, "what I've just said won't sit well with some of you, especially those women who have served as officers in this church. But hear me out, if you will. I'm giving you an example of what can and will happen when we ignore the clear teaching of Scripture. Whether we like it or not, the Scriptures teach that only men are to serve as deacons, elders, and pastors. Paul writes to Timothy that an officer should be the husband of one wife, a clear indication that he did not envision women as deacons or elders. Even more to the point, Paul writes further to Timothy that he does not permit a woman to teach nor to usurp authority over the man, but to be in silence. Now, that's a hard thing to accept, for it is a fact that women have served well and faithfully in all offices throughout our denomination. But that's not the point. The point is that we have been going against the teaching of God's Holy Word. And look what it's led us to: homosexuals in our schools, in our military, and in our pulpits. Beloved, we must be in complete submission to the Lord's will if our church and our nation are to survive."

I tried my best to tune him out, tired of church politics that pitted one group of men against another group of men over women's role in the church. I already knew

Pastor Ledbetter's position. He held that women's duties consisted of covering their heads, their mouths, and their casserole dishes, and I'd done all three about as long as I wanted to. But when he tied all the woes of the church to women officers, I could've wrung Paul's neck, and Timothy's, too, for giving men like Pastor Ledbetter justification for their prejudices. And don't tell me, as he'd done before, that a woman's submission elevates and ennobles her. I knew all about submission, and all it had gotten me was the humiliation in khaki pants sitting next to me.

When that interminable sermon was over, I grabbed Little Lloyd's hand and headed down the aisle. People were crowding out of the pews, but they gave us a wide berth and I knew they'd picked up on who'd been the pastor's target. Several smiled at me, their eyes drawn like magnets to the child with me. Others talked animatedly with their neighbors, keeping themselves too occupied to notice us. Yes, and when I got to the door, there was the pastor shaking hands with people as they left. I expect he thought I'd sneak out one of the side doors, but I marched up to him, ready to give him a piece of my mind. I managed to get Little Lloyd right up in front of him.

"Little Lloyd, this is Pastor Ledbetter, who's taken such an interest in your welfare," I said, and loudly, too. It stopped the conversation around us and held up the line as well. "Pastor, it was a privilege to hear your sermon this morning, but I'll have to tell you that I don't think the Lord's burdened your heart quite enough on the subject. You might want to consult Him on the duties of husbands and fathers, and men who try to be both in different households. And if permitting women to be officers in the church is what started us on the slippery slopes of sin, I'd like to know what mountaintop the church was sitting on for the two thousand years men had it to themselves."

I heard several women gasp at my outspokenness, but I didn't care. I took hold of Little Lloyd's hand and left, breathing hard but with my head held high.

I was so mad it took a few minutes of fierce walking before the car parked in front of my house registered in my mind. An old maroon-and-white vehicle with fins and a tilt in the back end. A rusted fender, too.

"My Lord, Little Lloyd," I said, clasping his hand harder and feeling my heart lift, the first time that'd happened in a number of days. "I believe that's your mama's car!"

"It is! It is! She's come back for me!" He turned loose of my hand and began running for the house.

CHAPTER THIRTEEN

—

"Wait! Watch for cars! Little Lloyd, don't you cross that street till I get there!" I hurried after him and we hastened across, up my front walk and onto the porch. My heart was racing with the anticipation of telling that woman what I thought of her. I intended to lay her low, but I didn't get the chance to do it.

A man was sitting in my rocker, hidden by the wisteria vine, with no sign of Hazel Marie Puckett.

The sight of him slowed Little Lloyd's steps and stopped mine. He was of a husky build, not tall, but solid as a wall. His hair, blacker than his eyebrows or the carefully shaved outline of a goatee and mustache, was slick with pomade or gel or some such.

One lock curled on his forehead. He wore a suit, grayish green, a white shirt, and a tie that was splotched with green and maroon colors. And white socks, for the Lord's sake. He wore a large gold watch turned to the inside of his right arm and a heavy gold ring on each middle finger. A soft leather Bible, with gilt-edged pages, was clasped to his chest. I pegged him for a preacher of some kind—well, the slick kind—before he opened his mouth. But far be it from me to be critical.

He stood up, a smile of welcome on his face, when we stepped up on the porch. Little Lloyd edged close to my side.

"Miz Springer," the man said with great solemnity as he bowed in what I can only describe as a deferential way. "I'm here to offer my humble apologies for the disgraceful way my niece, Hazel Marie Puckett, has conducted herself and to convey the deep gratitude of all the Puckett family for your kind acts of Christian charity, praise God. All of us, myself not the least, will be forever in your debt for taking Junior in and caring for him like you done. I'm here to relieve you of that burden and to take Junior back into the fold of his loved ones, who have sorely missed him."

Well, hallelujah, I thought, and couldn't help but smile at my most unlikely looking savior.

"Forgive me, ma'am," he went on before I could reply. "Let me introduce myself, though I would hope you'd already recognized me from the *Fanning the Flame* program, televised each and every Tuesday evening from nine till ten over WCHR, channel eight, coming with the power of God into thousands of Christian homes in Western North Carolina and the Upstate." I shook my head and mumbled that I didn't watch much television. He smiled like he recognized me as a potential viewer and contributor. "I'm the Reverend Vernon Puckett, known far and wide as Brother Vern, which I would be honored to have you call me." He held out his hand, which I shook, noticing how sweaty it was. Still, it was a hot day.

"Have a seat, Mr. Puckett," I said, "and tell us where this boy's mother is."

"Well, she's down in Raleigh," he said, sighing, lowering himself into the rocker, his thighs bulging like hams. I don't generally notice such intimate details of a man, but polyester makes for a snug fit. He pulled out a large handkerchief to mop his face. "I declare, that girl has been a trial to all us Pucketts, and I'm sure I don't have to tell you why, Miz Springer." He glanced up at me with a penetrating look, letting me know that he knew all about her connection to Wesley Lloyd. "Now, as you may not know, the Lord's work takes me all over this state and into others as well. I been in the great state of California, lo these many months, and I tell you, Miz Springer, that place needs the Word of God as bad as anyplace I ever been. Wherever I get a call, I go, praise God, He keeps me busy. As it happens, I been called to hold revival services all next week at Bethany Crossroads Baptist, and that's right outside Raleigh. It was the Lord's doings, Miz Springer, 'cause we got a call from Hazel Marie not two days ago, asking if any of us was down that way could we bring Junior to her." He turned his eyes, black as raisins, on Little Lloyd and said, "You want to see your mama, boy?"

"Yessir," Little Lloyd answered. He stood beside me, his hand gripped to the arm of my chair. Excited and pleased, no doubt.

"Well, then," Brother Vern said, slapping the floppy Bible on his knee, "go get what you come with and we'll be on our way. I got to be down there by nightfall for an early morning telecast, praise God. Got to be up with the chickens!" He threw his head back and laughed, showing me large, artificial teeth. I didn't much care for the man. Something about him was a little too smooth and practiced for my taste. But then he was a television personality, so I guess he had a bit of the actor in him. Most preachers do.

Little Lloyd hesitated beside my chair. I couldn't understand the child. Here was an answer to both our prayers, a way to his mother for him and a way out of this mess for me.

"Go on, boy," I said. "Put everything in that suitcase I gave you, your new clothes, too. I want you to have them. Your mama's sent for you and I expect she can't wait to see you."

"Will you tell Deputy Bates 'bye for me?" he asked, cutting his eyes toward his uncle. Great-uncle, I guess.

"Of course," I assured him. "He'll probably want to come see you when you get back to town."

He gave a quick smile and dashed into the house. I heard his feet pounding up the stairs. I sat back, thankful that this child from the wrong side of the blanket was being taken back to it. I turned my attention back to the man beside me in time to see a broad smile wipe out the frown he'd directed at the boy.

"Mr. Puckett—"

"Uh, uh, uh," he admonished me, wagging his finger to and fro.

"Brother Vern, then," I said. "I hope you give your niece a piece of my mind for me. I never heard of anybody dropping off a child on perfect strangers before. Especially in these circumstances, as you've indicated you know about."

"Indeed I do," he said. He leaned forward in that confidential way that all preachers seem to learn in seminary. I got a whiff of a dark, musky cologne, and noticed the gleam of a jeweled cross in the center of his tie. Zircons? Diamonds? Surely not. I leaned back out of the aroma field as he went on. "I don't mind telling you that when I learned some years back of how my niece was living, I was shocked to my innermost soul. I prayed about that situation, I can't tell you how many times I laid it before the Lord, and I talked to her and I pled with her, and all to no avail. And I prayed for you, too, Miz Springer, and I didn't even know you."

"Well, I declare," I said, touched in spite of myself.

"Yes, that girl has caused us all untold heartache, but I know she loves that boy. And a mother's love overcomes the worst of sins, praise God."

"Maybe so, but what am I thinking? You and Little Lloyd can't go off on that long drive without a thing to eat. It'll take just a minute to put something on the table. And while I'm at it, I'll see what's keeping that child." I got up to go to the kitchen, but he was on his feet faster.

"No need, ma'am, no need at all. I plan on stopping at the Burger King out by the interstate. We'll eat as we go, praise God for the conveniences provided for His people. I'm really pushed for time, and Hazel Marie is anxious for us to get there. I thank you for the offer, though, praise God."

Little Lloyd came out on the porch then,

with his suitcase in one hand and his blazer in the other. His glasses had slid down on his nose and he looked out over them in a dazed and addled way. The child must've been blind without those thick lenses. I'd intended to get him some better-fitting ones if he'd stayed much longer. But at least he was leaving with a good haircut.

"Well, Little Lloyd, we'll miss you," I said, sure the Lord would forgive me for the lie. But what else are good manners but lies? "Lillian's going to be upset when she comes tomorrow. And Deputy Bates won't know what to do with that tire swing back there. I hope you'll come back to see us." Well, lightning didn't strike the first time.

"Yes'm," he mumbled, ducking his head and looking ready to cry. Taking in his look of misery, I felt a sudden twinge of pity. Not that I cared about the boy, you understand, but it was just that I didn't know how his mother could look after him. I did have a certain responsibility here, however little I'd wanted the care of him.

"You know, Mr. Puckett, I'm a good mind to keep the boy till I hear directly from his mother. Not that you wouldn't look after him," I added at the sharp glance he gave me. "But you have your hands full already, what with your television shows and revival services, and what if you miss connections with his mother? You can't be dragging a child all over the countryside, keeping him up late, feeding him fast-food hamburgers and I don't know what all. Yes, I think the boy should stay here."

I glanced from one to the other, saw Little Lloyd's indecision and Brother Vern's startled look.

"Oh, no, that won't do." Brother Vern raised his hand like he was stopping traffic. "Beg your pardon, Miz Springer. I didn't mean to speak so sharply. But, you see, I'm under commission to get that boy to his mother. I promised her and, well . . ." He stopped, shook his head, and narrowed his eyes. "I'll tell you the truth, Miz Springer, you don't want to cross that woman. There's no telling what she'd do and, believe me, you don't want to find out."

"Well, if you put it that way," I said, images of my ransacked house flitting through my mind. But it couldn't have been the Puckett woman. She was in Raleigh, wasn't she? "I declare, I don't know what to do. What do you think, Little Lloyd?"

"He wants to be with his mother," Brother Vern pronounced. "Don't you, boy?"

"Yessir, I—"

"Thank the nice lady, then, and let's get on the road." Brother Vern pushed himself up from the rocker, a gleam of sweat on his face, and buttoned his suit coat. Double-breasted, too, which was not the best choice for a man of his girth. He tucked his Bible under his arm and walked toward the steps. He was ready to go.

"You sure you have everything?" I asked the boy. "Coloring book and crayons? A book to read on the trip?"

"Yes'm, I've got everything." He lifted his head and stared at me hard, frowning as he looked me straight in the eye like Wesley Lloyd used to do. Not at all like the retiring child who'd been moping around my house for days.

"Well, what about—?"

"I got everything in my suitcase," he said, his eyebrows wiggling as he frowned and squinched his eyes and carried on until I thought something was wrong with him. Then he surprised and shamed me by saying, "Thank you for letting me stay. I'm sorry for all the trouble."

"Why," I stammered, "no trouble. It was nice having you around." And while I waited for lightning to surely strike that time, I realized I'd spoken with a smidgen of truth.

Brother Vernon Puckett picked up the suitcase and, with a firm hand on Little Lloyd's back, guided him down the steps and out to the car. I stood watching them, waiting for the relief of a burden being lifted and not feeling it. The car started with a roar and black smoke billowed out the tailpipe.

"My Lord!" I exclaimed, stunned at my density. *Somebody* had been driving this very same car when the Puckett woman had hopped into the passenger seat hardly a week before. Who'd been driving then? How had Brother Vern ended up with it?

"Wait!" I cried, running down the steps and waving at them. The car roared off, Little Lloyd's face looking back at me through the side window. They turned right on Lincoln and were lost to sight, black smoke drifting down around my boxwoods.

Before I could turn back to the house, a deep, growling rumble reverberated in my head and filled the empty street. I looked around, unable to tell where it was coming from. Then I saw a black pickup, hiked high on monster tires, edging around the far corner of the block and rolling toward me. My Lord, I thought, my heart pounding like sixty, that's the very truck, or its twin, that followed me the other night. The very same yellow lights across the top, the same tires, the same black windows. As it passed within ten feet of me, I saw an orange lightning flash painted on the door. I watched it pass, too unnerved to move, as it went slow enough and loud enough to deafen me. I watched it turn right on Lincoln, and heard the sound of that awful motor fade away like thunder in the distance.

I hurried back to the porch and hid myself in the wicker rocker behind the wisteria, shaken by the coincidence. If that's what it was. I sat there staring off at the empty street, worrying about Little Lloyd, wondering if the truck was after him and not me at all.

A wisp of black exhaust curled along the steps, and I felt more lost and lonesome than I had even during the time of my recent bereavement.

CHAPTER FOURTEEN

—

Later in the day I tried to read the newspaper, even the "Over 50" section that was supposed to appeal to people like me but didn't, trying to fill the long Sunday afternoon that stretched out before me. The air was still and hot, the house quiet and so lonely that I wondered what I'd do with myself from then on. My throat felt closed and tight, and it got worse whenever that child came to mind, which was more often than I wanted to admit. Where was he, what was he doing, and why did I care?

Well, I didn't, I reminded myself. He was no longer my problem, if he ever had been. I folded the papers and then my hands, and looked around the empty room. Maybe I'd replace the velvet draperies with something lighter, maybe re-cover the furniture. Maybe a decorating project would take my mind off my recent troubles. Maybe it wouldn't.

I was glad to hear a knock on the front door around four o'clock, and even gladder to see Sam standing there.

"Come in, Sam," I said, opening the screen door for him. "I know you'll rejoice with me that my problems have all been solved."

"How'd you manage that, Julia?" He settled himself in one of the Victorian chairs by the fireplace. His familiar bulk seemed to fill the room and the lonely afternoon. I noticed how his hair had lightened, and how blue his eyes seemed in contrast.

I took his hat and placed it on the marble-topped chest, then took a seat on the sofa. "His uncle, or rather his mother's uncle, was waiting for us after church. He'd heard from Hazel Marie and she wanted him to bring Little Lloyd to her down in Raleigh. I guess she found a place where she could have him with her. They left about twelve-thirty, quarter to one, something like that. They're well on their way by now."

I looked at my watch, wondering where on I-40 East that child would be. I hadn't been able to get his face, staring at me from the car window as they left, out of my mind. Nor that business with his eyebrows before they left.

"That does solve your problem, then," Sam said. He paused, studying my face then; in that mind-reading way of his, he went on. "So where's all that rejoicing you mentioned?"

"Well, the thing is," I said and stopped to finger a button on my dress, "I began to have second thoughts about letting him go, and Little Lloyd didn't seem all that thrilled about it, either. I didn't really notice it at the time, because *I* was so thrilled to have him go. I mean, he wanted to see his mother, I know that. But there was just something about the way he acted, now that I've had time to think about it, that makes me wonder about the whole thing.

"And, I might as well admit it, I didn't have my wits about me enough to question Brother Vern. That car, for one thing."

"Why don't you start over," Sam said, "and tell me from the beginning. Who's Brother Vern, and what's worrying you about the car?"

So I told him, and the more details I laid

out, the more I realized how wrong I'd been to let the child go off with somebody I didn't know from Adam.

"But the boy knew him, didn't he?" Sam asked.

"Yes, he did. He just didn't seem to like him very much, but I could be wrong. What I should've done, Sam," I said, standing up and pacing the floor, "was to've found out where the Puckett woman is. Then I could call her and make sure the boy gets there all right. That's what I *should've* done. Now there's no way to know where he is or where she is. Or where Brother Vern is, for that matter. I should've stuck to my guns. Instead, all I could think of was getting Wesley Lloyd's child out of my house and out of my life. Totally self-centered, that's what I've been."

"You're too hard on yourself, Julia. You were willing to look after the boy—"

"Yes, but I didn't *want* to. That's the difference between the letter of the law and the spirit of it. It's the attitude of the heart that counts, Sam, and you know it as well as I do. And," I said, taking a deep breath, "I better tell you about that deformed truck, too."

When I finished, Sam was so agitated, he stood up and put his hands on my shoulders, bringing me to a stop. "Julia, why in the world were you driving around the countryside by yourself after dark?"

"Because I wanted to," I snapped. "Sam Murdoch, Wesley Lloyd treated me like a ten-year-old all my life, and I'm not going to be treated that way by you or anybody else again."

He dropped his hands. "You're right and I apologize. I'm just worried about you, Julia. Will you allow me that?"

I pretended to think about it, then nodded and said, "Yes, you can worry, but give me credit for having some sense."

Wesley Lloyd would've told me to act like I had some, but Sam smiled and said, "I give you more credit than you know, Julia."

Not knowing how to respond to that, I changed the subject. "What should we do about that child?"

"First thing, now that you don't have to worry about social services taking him from you, let's ask Deputy Bates to contact the Raleigh police to locate the Puckett woman. They can confirm that the boy's there and being cared for. Nothing will

come back on you except a little reassur-
ance."

"Good, let's do that. Deputy Bates
worked late this morning, but he ought to
be up any time now. In fact, let's go out to
the kitchen and I'll put on a pot of coffee for
him. He'll need something to eat, too.
Would you like some eggs for your supper?"

"Don't mind if I do," he said, following me
down the hall. "But, Julia, I didn't know you
could cook."

"Anybody can scramble eggs, for the
Lord's sake," I said, though if the truth be
known, I wasn't much of a hand for any
kind of cooking. And didn't care to learn.

I had another restless night, in spite of
Sam's suggestion and Deputy Bates's will-
ingness to make an official inquiry into
Hazel Marie Puckett's whereabouts. The
sheriff would be interested, too, he'd told
us, since she was wanted for questioning
about the blood on her garage floor and
walls. Deputy Bates hadn't been too happy
to learn that Little Lloyd was gone. I'd seen
disappointment and concern written all

over his face, and his response had rankled me.

"I'm going to miss that boy," he said.

I took that as criticism and snapped back, "Well, I won't. How do you think I felt, having that illegitimate child underfoot every day, all day long?"

My eyes welled up, and Sam said, "Now, Julia."

That wasn't much help, because I had been remiss in letting that child go off. They knew it and I knew it, but what could I have done when his own kin showed up to claim him? A lot of things, as it turned out. I could've wakened Deputy Bates, for one. I could've questioned Brother Vern, for another. I could've asked, even demanded, that he give me her address. I could've gone upstairs with Little Lloyd and made sure, out of his great-uncle's hearing, that he wanted to go with him.

Oh, there were a lot of things I could've done and should've done, and now I had to live with it all. I got up sometime in the middle of the night and walked across the hall to Little Lloyd's room. The empty bed made me realize how empty my house was, and maybe my life, as well.

I was just a selfish old woman with nothing but a few million dollars to her name. No husband, no children, nothing to look forward to but more of the same. Even the thought of writing checks and buying things couldn't lift my spirits.

I cried. Sitting there in Little Lloyd's room, not a light on in the house, an old, slightly blue-haired woman who'd thought of nothing but herself all her life. Yes, I cried.

But not because I missed the boy, not at all. He'd been nothing but a reminder of Wesley Lloyd and, I hate to say this, I wasn't missing *him*. It was because I was worried about the child and because I'd been lax in looking after him. If I could be assured that he was safe with his mother, I could put the whole week behind me and get on with my life. I might even plan a tea and invite all the women of the church. Wesley Lloyd hadn't been gone a year yet, but there was no reason I couldn't entertain if I wanted to. It'd show everybody that I could still hold my head up. So I went back to bed and filled my mind with cucumber sandwiches and layered cream cheese sandwiches, and cheese straws and petit fours and flower arrangements and linen napkins, planning the most elaborate tea anybody'd had since Lula Mae Harding had her last one before she passed and the ladies' Sunday school class named itself after her.

Sam arrived that Monday morning about the same time Lillian did, one at the front door and the other at the back. We all ended up in the kitchen, drinking coffee and eating the toast Lillian had fixed. She wouldn't sit at the table with us because she'd once told me that it wasn't right for her to visit with my company. I didn't care, especially since Sam wasn't real company, but she busied herself around the stove, getting a big breakfast ready for Deputy Bates when he got off duty. She listened to us, though, and made her opinions known by the expressions on her face. She hadn't liked it one little bit that I'd let Little Lloyd go off with "somebody callin' hisself his uncle."

"What you do that for, Miss Julia?" she'd asked. "That baby need lookin' after, not let go off with ever' Tom Dick that come by."

I said, "It was his mother's uncle, not any

Tom, Dick, or Harry. So don't blame me for
his own mother's neglect and careless-
ness."

"That be a pitiful excuse," she'd told me.

Sam stirred his coffee, then reached over
and put his hand on mine. "I went by this
morning and talked to Sheriff Frady. Just
laid it all out for him. I don't have to tell you
he was mighty interested in the relationship
between you and the boy. Then he called in
this lieutenant and I had to tell it again. That
lieutenant is sharp. He put it right together
with the blood Coleman found at the boy's
house."

"I'd have thought Deputy Bates would've
already reported it all," I said, surprised at
where Deputy Bates's loyalty seemed to be
placed.

"No, apparently Coleman just explained
that the boy was staying with you and that
the three of you had driven out to check on
the house. He let them assume that the
Puckett woman knew you and that you had
agreed to look after the boy. He was trying
to keep social services out of it."

"I hope he won't get in trouble over it."

"I doubt it. He could only tell what he
knew for a fact, and that's what he did. Still,

he respected your wishes to keep the boy
out of a foster home. But, Julia, you're going to have to talk to them yourself. That
lieutenant, what's his name, Peavey, he
wants to know what you know and what
you suspect about the whole situation. He's
treating the Puckett woman as a missing
person and, after hearing what I had to say,
is about ready to treat the boy as one, too."

"But he's with his uncle!" I protested.
"Great-uncle, I mean. I know, I know. Lillian,
quit looking at me that way. I know I
shouldn't have let him go off, but what was
I supposed to do?" I wanted to cry again.
Instead, I refilled our cups. It was all so un-
fair. I hadn't asked to be betrayed by my
own husband, and I hadn't asked to have
his bastard dumped on my doorstep, and
the Lord knows, I hadn't asked to be
blamed for it all, either.

"Nobody's blaming you, Julia," Sam said,
reading my mind again. "Tell you what. Why
don't you go fishing with me tomorrow?"

Lillian started laughing, and I glared at
her. "Yes, and I can see me going fishing
with you, Sam Murdoch. First off, I've never
fished in my life and, second off, if this town

didn't already have enough to talk about, that would do it."

"It'd be good for you, Julia, and who cares if the town talks? The men would just wish they were in my shoes, and the women would be jealous of you for landing the handsomest man in town."

Lillian laughed out loud. "Don't sound like no fishing I ever heard of."

"You two," I said, feeling my face redden. "I've got enough worries without adding you to them, Sam Murdoch."

"Ah, Julia," Sam said, cocking his head to the side and lowering his voice. "I don't want to be a worry to you. I want to help you, if you'll let me. Getting away for a few hours out on a lake would make all the difference in the world. You'd like it, I promise."

"No, and that's that," I said, refusing to look at him. "You can fritter your time away if you want to, but I have things to do."

"You better listen to him, Miss Julia," Lillian said. "Not too many men knocking on yo' door that I been noticin'. 'Specially not one like Mr. Sam."

"You tell her, Lillian," Sam said, smiling

now. "Tell her she's letting the best man she'll ever know slip through her fingers."

"That's about right," Lillian agreed, with a long look of warning at me.

"The subject is closed," I said, tired of being teased. I was in no mood for it.

I heard Deputy Bates's car pull in and was glad to see him come in the back door. He looked tired, but maybe he'd turn the conversation to something more sensible. Lillian and Sam took on over him, Sam pulling out a chair for him and Lillian hurrying over with coffee.

"I'm fixin' you two eggs over light, sausage, and grits. That all right with you?" she asked him.

"Sounds great," he said, twisting around to turn off his walkie-talkie that was giving out bursts of static and a jumble of words from somebody with a real bad cold. "What a night," he went on. "I'm glad to have it over with."

"Lotta calls?" Sam asked.

"Man, yes. A robbery out at the Motor Inn. Three fights down on Mercer Avenue, and speeders all over the county. Then an Alzheimer's patient walked out of a nursing home. Had to get the trackers and dogs out, but we found him. It just never stopped."

"What you need," Lillian declaimed as she flipped eggs, "is a little honey in yo' life." Then she laughed so hard I was afraid she'd break the yolks.

Deputy Bates grinned and said, "What makes you think I don't already have some?"

She whooped then and told him she could tell when a man had a little or a lot or none at all, and he was in the last category. Sam sat there laughing with them, but to me the conversation was getting a little too racy. It was my kitchen, after all.

"Has there been any word on Little Lloyd or his mama?" I asked, and everybody got serious again.

"Not a thing," Deputy Bates said, going after his breakfast like he hadn't eaten all night, and he probably hadn't. "We put out a description of the car and notified the state troopers to watch for it, but there's been nothing. The Raleigh police're going to check all the beauty schools down there as soon as they open this morning to see where the Puckett woman's registered. Other than that, there's not much else we can do. Oh, yeah, Lieutenant Peavey's going down to Benson's Gap sometime today and question some of the Puckett clan. He knows a bunch of them, arrested most of 'em at one time or another, and if anybody knows anything, he'll get it out of them. Lillian, if it's not too much trouble, I believe I could eat another egg."

"No trouble a'tall," she said, beaming like she did when anybody appreciated her cooking. I didn't tell her that he'd eaten four of mine the night before.

When Deputy Bates finally pushed his plate away and praised Lillian to the skies, more than she needed, to be honest about it, he took a deep breath.

"Miss Julia," he said, "Sheriff Frady's coming over this morning to ask you about Little Lloyd and his mother. It'd be best to go ahead and tell him everything."

"Sam's already warned me," I told him. "And I don't plan to leave anything out. I want that boy found so I can quit worrying and get some sleep. I'll tell you this, though, I am certainly glad I didn't try to hide the fact that Little Lloyd is my husband's son. It'd be so much worse if I had, because I'd have to reveal it now anyway.

See, Lillian? Sometimes I do know what I'm doing."

"*Some*times," she admitted.

I heard car doors slam out front, and my heart gave a lurch inside my chest. I'd never been questioned by law officers before and I wasn't looking forward to it. It could be about as bad as being counseled by my preacher. Earl Frady wasn't much, but he represented a lot, even if I did know his wife went on a spree now and then, and only stayed out of jail because none of his deputies was willing to arrest her.

Sam stood up with me and said, "Come on, Julia, let's go let them in."

Then Deputy Bates got up and Lillian folded her dish towel as they came to join Sam and me. The four of us went to the living room to greet the sheriff.

CHAPTER FIFTEEN

—

I'd known Earl Frady for all the eighteen years he'd been sheriff of Abbot County, and he still looked like a none-too-prosperous shopkeeper in his brown polyester suit and black wing tips. He smiled his quick, nervous smile when I came to the door, and smoothed the thin hair over the bald spot on his head. He looked even more uncomfortable and unprofessional than usual, standing shoulder high to the big, sharply uniformed man behind him.

I opened the screen for them, and Deputy Bates introduced Lieutenant Wayne Peavey. He was far and away the largest man in the room, towering over us and unnerving me, what with those dark glasses that reflected my image without giving away anything of himself. He had a thin, firm mouth that looked as if it would split his face if he smiled.

None of us had to be introduced to Earl Frady; he'd been getting elected every four years like clockwork. Not because he knew so much about law enforcement, but because he knew county politics and county politicians inside and out. And because he knew enough to hire professionals, trained and experienced deputies, to keep the peace. And because he had enough sense to leave them alone and let them do it. That was enough reason to keep returning him to office.

He showed up only when he thought something might make the newspaper or when, like now, somebody important might be involved in a crime.

We all took seats except Lillian, who leaned against the double opening to the dining room. She'd placed herself behind Lieutenant Peavey, but where I could see her. Deputy Bates took the piano bench, and Sam pulled up a chair next to Sheriff Frady. We looked at the sheriff, waiting for him to start, but the big lieutenant cleared his throat and took out a little notebook.

Then he commenced questioning me about everything that'd happened since Hazel Marie Puckett showed up on my porch.

Lillian frowned every time he opened his mouth.

Right at the start, Sam interrupted to state in no uncertain terms that I was answering questions only in a spirit of cooperation, and that if the sheriff had anything else in mind, my attorney of record had to be present. Lillian crossed her arms and nodded in agreement.

"Nothing like that is on our mind," Sheriff Frady said, straightening out one leg and plucking at the stretchy material to get enough slack to go over his knee. "We just need to know the sequence of events leading up to the break-in here Saturday. In broad daylight. That's mainly what we're investigating, and to see if Mrs. Springer's discovered anything missing."

"Mind your questions, then," Sam said, giving the sheriff a squinty-eyed look.

Sam was a Democrat, born and bred, and so was Sheriff Frady, who knew which side his bread was buttered on. The sheriff nodded at his lieutenant to continue, while he leaned back in his chair and looked around like the proceedings had nothing to do with him. And they didn't.

The lieutenant took me step by step through the past week, making notes as he went. After I went over in detail how the boy had left my house the day before, described Brother Vern and his car, and declared that as far as I knew, Hazel Marie Puckett was filing nails down in Raleigh, he closed his notebook and stood up.

"All right, Mrs. Springer," he said as I craned my neck to look up at him. "We don't know what happened in that garage. Neighbors tell us that the woman and her son lived there, but they're both missing. Seems the place belongs to you, and the boy was here with you, so there's a connection to you whichever way you look at it. And not only was there blood in that garage, we also found a couple of teeth. We're waiting on the investigation report to confirm if we're dealing with human substances, but we still don't know who they belong to or how they got there."

"Well, I don't, either," I said.

"No'm, I guess not, but what we found hadn't been there much more than twenty-four hours, and from what you've told me, nobody knows where you were Friday afternoon."

"Why, Friday afternoon I didn't even know where that house was, much less that it belonged to me. And I told you I was driving around. All evening for some three hours. Ask Lillian. Ask Deputy Bates. They were both here when I came in." Deputy Bates had been leaning his arms on his knees, staring at the floor. He looked up and confirmed my statement with a nod. Lieutenant Peavey didn't notice.

"But according to you, nobody saw you during that three hours."

"Well, the black truck did."

Lieutenant Peavey aimed those black sunglasses at me and said, "What black truck?"

So I told him. He shrugged one shoulder, and didn't even open his notebook. "Black pickups all over the place. You need a better witness than that."

"Now, just a minute," Sam began, getting to his feet. "Are you accusing Mrs. Springer of having something to do with all this? I told you, Earl," he said, turning to the sheriff, "and I'll tell you again. If you want to use anything said in this room, you're in trouble.

Mrs. Springer has not been represented by counsel, and I warned you about it before you began."

"Now, Sam," the sheriff said, getting up and edging toward the door. "We're questioning everybody and, so far, nobody's been charged with anything."

"I should hope not," Sam said. "Since, so far, you don't have any charges to file. What crime has been committed except for a break-in right here? Is Mrs. Springer a suspect in that?"

"No, no, of course not," the sheriff said, aiming a hard look at his lieutenant, who ignored him. "We just have to, you know, cover all the bases."

The lieutenant turned to me. "You're not planning any trips out of town, are you? I may want to talk to you again."

When they left, Sam was fuming at the idea of me as a suspect in a crime without a habeas corpus, or delicti, or some such. I didn't pay much attention, because my head was in a swirl again. That child had turned my life upside down when he entered it, and was still doing it now that he was out of it.

———

It had just gotten dark good that Monday night, about nine o'clock, and I was hoping for a good night's sleep. Though now that my whereabouts last Friday had been called into question by the authorities, I didn't have much hope for it.

I went into the kitchen to heat some milk for a cup of Ovaltine, figuring that might help. Then, on second thought, I put the pan up and took down Lillian's cooking sherry. That ought to do it, I thought. Presbyterians aren't supposed to use alcohol, but a lot do. Not Wesley Lloyd, though, who was a teetotaler by conviction, which meant that I didn't either. However. It came to me as I tasted the vile stuff that the ABC store ought to have something better, since so many people seemed to like it. I resolved to take myself down there and buy something decent to drink. I didn't care who saw me, either. Just to get a little something to help me sleep, you know. And to aid the digestion. Nothing wrong with that, since Paul told Timothy to take a little wine for his stomach's sake. If you can find a verse of Scripture to back you up, even Presbyterians will leave you alone.

I was just putting the bottle back when I

heard a scratching at the back door. Then two little taps. I froze. Scared to death. Who could be at my back door that time of night? Anybody I knew would come to the front and yoo-hoo along with the tapping.

I hesitated, trying to think what to do. Get to the phone? Scream my head off? Run through the house and out the front? *In my bathrobe?* Stay real quiet and pretend I wasn't home?

Lord, it wasn't possible. I was directly in line with the window in the door, and whoever was out there could see me, plain as day.

I grabbed the sherry bottle by the neck and went to the door. I flipped on the porch light and nearly fainted.

I couldn't get the door open fast enough, and when she stumbled through it, I wished I had fainted.

Hazel Marie Puckett fell against me and clung so that I was looking right into her poor smashed and swollen face. "Miz Springer!" she gasped. I held her upright, feeling the frailness of her bones. "I'm sorry to bother you," I think she said. Her words were so slurred I had trouble understanding her. "I need to see Junior. Please, I have to see him."

"Sit down, sit down," I cried, putting my arm around her waist and guiding her to a chair. "What happened to you? You look terrible!"

Her eyes were almost swollen shut. Her mouth was split and swollen out of shape. Dried blood caked the corners of her nose and mouth, and her whole face was blue and yellowish-green with the worst bruising I'd ever seen. Her nails were dirty and broken, and right from that I figured she hadn't been in Raleigh at beauty school. Her dress was torn and streaked with dirt, and her bare feet were scratched and filthy. All in all, she was a mess.

"What happened to you?" I asked again, as tears poured out of those battered eyes. Fresh blood leaked from her split mouth, and she put a hand up to cover it. "Have you been drinking?" I demanded.

"Oh, no'm. I . . . an accident. I've been in an accident. Please, Miz Springer, I got to see Junior."

She wasn't in any shape to see anybody but a doctor, and I wasn't ready to admit that her Junior was in Raleigh looking for her. I took out some ice cubes and wrapped them in a dish towel.

"Here," I said, "put that on your face. It'll help the swelling. Have you been to the hospital? You may need some stitches around your mouth."

"No'm, it's all right. Just some teeth," she said, pressing the ice pack to her face.

"Teeth! You lost some teeth? You need to see a dentist, and right soon, too. You want to take care of your teeth. I go twice a year. Every year. Whether I need to or not." I was chattering, but I did that any time I got upset and this was one of those times.

"I need Junior," she said into the towel. "Please, is he in bed? I just need to be sure he's all right."

"Well," I said, taking a deep breath. "Of course he's all right. It's just that somebody's wires have got crossed. 'Cause he's in Raleigh, looking for you."

"Raleigh!" She looked up from the towel with the most stricken look I'd ever seen. "But . . . he's supposed to be here! With you, where he'd be safe. I left him here, he can't be gone! Tell me, Miz Springer, please tell me he's here with you."

"Hush, now," I comforted, "he's all right.

Your uncle picked him up yesterday to take
him down to you."

"You mean . . . Brother Vern? You mean
Brother Vern's got him?" The look on her
face made my heart sink.

"Well. Yes."

"Oh, God," she sobbed, and her whole
body seemed to shrink into itself. "How
could you let him go? I counted on you to
take care of him."

"Now just a minute, miss," I said, taking
immediate umbrage at being blamed for
one more thing on a long list. "You left him
here with not so much as a by-your-leave.
You didn't tell me word one about where
you'd be, and you called Brother Vern to
come get him and he did. Was I supposed
to keep him from his own uncle? Great-
uncle?"

She shook her head. "I didn't call nobody,
wasn't able to. And 'specially not him. I
thought Junior'd be safe here."

"He would've been, if you'd told me what
was going on," I said. I don't mind saying
that I was on the defensive. I hadn't felt
right about Brother Vern ever since they'd
been gone, and I hated being told that not
feeling right about him was the right feeling

to have. "I'm not a mind reader, you know. And if you'd had the courtesy to tell me not to let Little Lloyd go off with, *I remind you,* one of your own family, then I wouldn't have let him go. What else was I supposed to do?" Seemed I'd been asking that an awful lot lately.

"I'm sorry, Miz Springer," she whispered, burying her head in the towel again. That blond hair needed washing, and a new color job, too. "It's just, well, Brother Vern's been looking for something since Friday. He tried to get me to tell him about it, but, Miz Springer, I didn't know what he was talking about."

"He tried to get you . . . ?" Light dawned in my slow mind. "Are you telling me you weren't in an accident? Are you saying that Brother Vern did this to you?"

She shook her head, but kept it in the towel. "No, but he let somebody else do it."

"Thay Lord," I gasped, and sank into the chair beside her. "And him a preacher! I can't believe this."

"Being a preacher don't mean a thing, Miz Springer," she said. "Or calling yourself a Christian, neither."

"Well, child," I said, shrinking up a little

myself. "You're not telling me a thing I don't already know.

"Why did Brother Vern want Little Lloyd so bad?" I asked.

"Who?"

"Little Lloyd, the one you call Junior," I snapped. "I hope you don't expect *me* to call him Junior."

"Oh," she said. She lifted her head out of the towel and took a deep breath. Then doubled over with a gasp, holding her side. "My ribs. I think something's broke inside."

"I'm calling a doctor," I said, getting up to go to the phone.

"No, please." She touched my arm, stopping me. "We've got to find Junior. I've lasted this long, I can keep going till we find him."

I studied her a minute, looking at the various colors of the bruises and the blood that was dried and cracked on her face. That beating had not been recent. I didn't know how she'd managed to last without medical treatment, but she wasn't dead from it, so maybe she could keep going.

"All right, then," I conceded. "But we've got to get you in better shape."

"Maybe," she said, pointing at the sherry

bottle still gripped in my hand. "Maybe a little of that would help."

I gave it to her and watched her turn it up. She took several long swallows straight from the bottle. When she came up for air, she coughed and sputtered and had a hard time getting her breath back.

"Shit! What is that stuff?"

"Watch your language in my house, miss," I told her. "And keep in mind that beggars can't be choosers."

"Yes'm, sorry. I thank you for it." She turned away, trying not to gag.

"Come on over to the sink," I said, helping her get up. "I'll fix some warm saltwater so you can rinse out your mouth. That'll help that missing tooth."

"Teeth," she said, pulling back her lip to show me where two had once been.

I thought I'd start gagging, too, but I got her to the sink. When she finished rinsing her mouth, I gave her some aspirin and started her toward the stairs.

"A good, hot shower will make you feel better," I said.

"But I have to find Junior."

"Listen to me," I said, stopping on the landing and taking her by the shoulders.

"You're in no condition to find anybody. You can't even think straight, and straight thinking is what we need right now. So you just come on with me and get yourself cleaned up and feeling better. Then we'll decide what to do."

By the time I got her out of the shower, dried off, and into one of my gowns, it was all I could do to get her into Little Lloyd's bed. She was out on her feet. Pretty tired, I guessed. To say nothing of four aspirins and a fair slug of cooking sherry.

I closed her door, but left mine open. I lay in bed, thinking about this turn of events, wondering if I should call Deputy Bates or Sam or who. Nothing they could do that night, though, as dead to the world as she was.

I'd wait till morning, then try to get more out of her, like why did Brother Vern have her beaten half to death, and why did he want Little Lloyd, and what in heaven's name was it all about?

I finally went to sleep and dreamed about tires as tall as my head trying to run me down while I searched all over creation looking for that child.

Chapter Sixteen

—

It was not a restful night. I came awake fully about five o'clock and got on up, with that child still on my mind. He was all I could think of, for he'd been wandering in and out of my dreams most of the night. And, Lord, what was I going to do about the woman across the hall? I thought about calling the sheriff, or telling Deputy Bates, and just washing my hands of the whole mess. On the other hand, it would be worth keeping her around just to see Pastor Ledbetter's face when he heard of it. Maybe I'd remind him of David's harem, and see if he would excuse Wesley Lloyd then.

And at that thought, I began to feel down-right dejected again. My house had become a way station for Wesley Lloyd's second family, people popping in and out, and me not knowing who to trust and who not to.

One thing I did know. I'd been tricked again, and this time by that preacher in sheep's clothing. Wesley Lloyd Springer had tricked me, just pulled the wool over my eyes as slick as you please, and now Brother Vernon Puckett had done the same thing. They'd taken advantage of my trusting nature, and I was getting mad as thunder, not only at them, but at myself for being so easy to fool. It wasn't going to happen again, believe you me.

And in the bed right across the hall was the loose woman who'd slept with my husband for untold numbers of years, and here she was sleeping now in my house. If Wesley Lloyd hadn't been six feet under, all he'd have to do would be to walk from one bed to another.

The thought made me sick to my stomach. I needed my morning coffee.

I put on my robe and tiptoed down the stairs to the kitchen. Strange, I thought, to start the day with pictures in my mind of Wesley Lloyd with that woman, yet the night before when she'd stumbled into my house with the evidence of a beating all over her, I hadn't given one thought to Wesley Lloyd. And what they'd done together.

I made the coffee and sat at the table with a cup of it before me. Thinking. Trying to understand what was going on. Trying not to worry about Little Lloyd. A hard thing to do, now that I knew his mother was worried sick about him.

It's funny about women and children, isn't it? There was Hazel Marie Puckett, with no money, no home, and no husband. Yet she had a child. And here I was, a respectable married woman with everything to give to a child, and the Lord hadn't seen fit. This was just one more situation where I wondered what in the world He was thinking of.

I'd fully expected, within a decent time after being married, to welcome a blessed event. But it hadn't happened and I hadn't questioned it. But Wesley Lloyd had. He'd announced one morning a few years into our marriage that I had an appointment with Dr. Monroe to find out what was wrong with me. I didn't like it, but who was I to question Wesley Lloyd's decisions?

I won't go into too much detail about what that doctor did to me, but you wouldn't have liked it, either. They put me up on a table and stuck my feet in these metal contraptions; then the doctor pulled on the bottom sheet and said, "I'm going to scoot you down, now." And when he did, my knees splayed out on each side, and I thought I'd die when he threw up the sheet and sat down on a little stool to get a good look. And that nurse of his was right down there getting an eyeful, too. And in the midst of that, another nurse opened the door so that anybody in the hall could get in on the picture show. I'm not going to describe how Dr. Monroe poked, prodded, and mashed around down there. Nor where he put his fingers.

It was a mortifying experience, and I decided as soon as they let me off that table they'd never get me back on it. If that's what it took to have children, I'd just pass altogether.

And wouldn't you know it, the very next Sunday there was Dr. Monroe waiting in the narthex to usher us to our pew. I couldn't look him in the face, especially when he smiled and squeezed my arm, so pleasant and genteel with that pink rosebud in his lapel. Humiliating, was what it was, after what he'd looked at and fingered and handled on his examining table. And I didn't like the way he shook Wesley Lloyd's hand and asked how things were going.

That did it for me as far as seeking help from medical science. As a predestinated Presbyterian, I had reason not to go messing around with what wasn't meant to be. I told Wesley Lloyd that I'd just do what Sarah and Hannah and several other barren women had done, and depend on prayer alone. He couldn't very well argue with that, since that was what he was always recommending to me. I figured if the Lord wanted me to have a child He'd give me one.

Coffee slopped out of my cup as Little Lloyd's pale little face came to mind. I stiffened in the chair and said aloud, "But, Lord, I didn't mean give me one *this* way."

The night was slowly giving way to morning, with the gray shadows of shrubs and trees taking shape in the yard. I heard the chirping calls of birds break the stillness of the night. Early birds getting their worms. Which reminded me that an Oreo would taste good with a second cup of coffee. That was not the kind of breakfast that Wesley Lloyd would've approved of, but as

we've all noticed, he was no longer around
to pass judgment.

I went to the pantry and commenced
rummaging around to find the cookies. Lillian liked them, too, and we'd been known
to hide the last few from each other. I
moved cans of Luck's beans and Camp-
bell's soup, and jars of Jif peanut butter and
Hellmann's mayonnaise, and sacks of Lily
Maid flour, Dixie Crystals' sugar, and Yel-
ton's cornmeal, but I couldn't find the
Oreos. I was determined, so I went through
the folded grocery sacks that Lillian saved
and, bless Pat, I came across one with
something in it.

"Lillian, you sneaky thing," I said to myself, smiling at the thought of her searching
for the Oreos I was fixing to eat.

I reached in the Winn-Dixie sack and
pulled out a picture book. I stood looking at
it for a minute, coming to realize that I was
holding Little Lloyd's precious sack. The
one he always had with him, the one he
slept with, the one he never let out of his
sight, the one I'd never thought in a million
years he'd go off without. I'd thought it held
a little boy's treasures, that's what Lillian
had told me. And she'd also told me to

keep my hands out of it, and here I was holding a child's well-used picture book that'd been hidden away among the empty sacks. I should've put it back right then. The child had a reason for leaving it there, even though I couldn't think why in the world he would've.

But, as I'd already discovered its contents in all innocence, I opened the front of the book and read the inscription. In for a penny, in for a pound. I recognized my husband's heavy, confident penmanship. He'd written: "For your birthday," and signed it with his full name, "Wesley Lloyd Springer." I sighed, my heart heavy with the thought of my husband's rich private life and my barren one. I turned to the title page. *Aslan's Book of Pictures.* Wesley Lloyd had no more an idea of what a child wanted for his birthday than I did. But I think I would've picked out something better than a book about lions.

I heard Lillian on the porch and felt guilty for plundering through somebody else's belongings. Then I thought better of it. Lillian should know about this so she wouldn't gather up all the empty sacks and throw them out.

"What you doin' up and in the pantry?" she asked as soon as she came in the door.

"Come see what I found," I said, holding out the book. I told her how I'd come to find it, without mentioning Oreos. "I was looking for a pencil," I said.

"Well," she said, "you just put that book back where you found it."

"I intend to."

"You know what it mean, don't you?"

"What?"

"It mean," she said, "that he want to come back. When you leave something you loves somewhere, it draw you back to that place."

"Lillian, you know better," I said, putting the book in the sack and folding down the ends the way Little Lloyd had left them.

"I don't mean it act'ally draw you. I mean it what you want it to do. That chile left here intending to come back, 'cause he left what meant the most to him."

"Well, I declare," I said, touched in spite of myself. "I do believe you're right. I can't think of any other reason he'd leave it. He certainly put a lot of stock in this sack, or what was in it, or both. And, Lillian, he found a good hiding place for it. I would've never thought to look here, if I was looking for it. So," I said, thrusting the sack under the empty ones, "back it goes, and it can wait right there for him."

I closed the pantry door and sat down at the table. "Get some coffee and come sit down," I said. "I've got something else to tell you."

When she was settled, I told her about our new houseguest and her pitiful condition. She punctuated my recitation with a series of "No's!" and "You don't mean it's!," but I finally got it told and admitted I didn't know what to do next. Which was no surprise to her.

"That chile in trouble, an' his mama, too," she declared. "What we gon' do 'bout it, Miss Julia?"

"I wish I knew. I'll take something up for her to eat, it'll have to be something soft or liquid, Lillian, two of her teeth have been knocked out. Maybe when she eats a little, she'll be able to help us decide what to do."

"Soup," Lillian said, getting to her feet. "I'll heat some soup and crumble up some sody crackers in it. That be good for her. You pour some milk. She'll need building up.

"Now, what I want to know," she went on as she put a pan on the stove, "is what you gon' tell Deputy Bates? He be here pretty soon."

"I don't think I'll tell him anything," I said. Then, at her quick glare, hurried on, "At this time. He's in a bad position, Lillian. The sheriff, or rather that big lieutenant, wants to question Miss Puckett and that could take all day when we could be looking for Little Lloyd. If I tell Deputy Bates she's here, he'll have to report it and no telling what that would lead to. If he doesn't know it, he can't report it. So, I'm just thinking of what's best for him."

"Uh-huh," she said. She poured soup in a bowl and crumbled in saltines until it was a thick mush. She put the bowl, a spoon, a napkin, and a glass of milk on a tray. I added a bottle of aspirin.

"You take this on up to her," Lillian said, "and I'll fix his breakfast. Go on, now, I think I hear his car turning in. And put yo' clothes on, too. Sound like we got lots to do soon as Deputy Bates close his eyes."

I hurried upstairs with the tray, wanting Deputy Bates to think I was still in bed. Hazel Marie Puckett groaned when I touched her shoulder. Lord, she looked worse in the daylight.

"Shhh," I whispered. "Here's something to eat, but we have to be quiet. There's a deputy sheriff in the house."

Her eyes flew open, as much as the swelling would allow, and I could see the fear in them.

"Is he here for me?" Her mouth was so misshapen that she could hardly form the words.

"Should he be?" I asked sharply, realizing again how little I knew about her.

She shook her head. "You never know."

Well, that was the truth, especially after my run-in with Lieutenant Peavey. "Eat," I told her, "but be quiet about it. Deputy Bates lives here and pretty soon he'll be sleeping right down the hall."

When she'd finished the soup, I helped her across the hall to my bedroom and ran a hot bath for her. Deputy Bates would think it was my morning ablutions. I told her to soak out the soreness while I dressed. I gave her some of my underclothes and then went to the closet to pick out a dress for her. When she came out of the bathroom in my slip, hunched over against the pain in her ribs, I had three for her to choose from. None of them Sunday dresses, just my good, everyday shirtwaists. She looked at them for quite a while.

Then she said, "Do you have anything else?"

"What's wrong with those, I'd like to know?"

"I'm sorry. I just meant, maybe some jeans or shorts."

"There're some things," I informed her, "that ladies don't wear. And jeans and shorts are two of them."

"Sorry," she said, and picked up the first one and put it on. It was maybe a size too big for her, but she was skinny to start with, and it was somewhat longer than she was accustomed to wearing, which wasn't a bad thing. I started looking for some slippers that would fit.

We heard a tap on the door, and Lillian stuck her head in. "He gone to bed," she said, sidling in and closing the door behind her. "I come to fix you up," she said to Hazel Marie, holding up a roll of Ace bandage.

So we helped Hazel Marie undress again, and Lillian displayed another of her unsung talents as she wrapped the bandage around the chest of the woman who'd had my husband's arms around the same places.

CHAPTER SEVENTEEN

—

As soon as Lillian finished, Hazel Marie Puckett swallowed hard a few times, then clapped a hand over her mouth.

"Sick!" she gasped, clutching her ribs with one arm and scrambling for the bathroom. She made it to the sink before soup, saltines, milk, and aspirin came spewing out.

I went to the far corner of the room, as far from the sound of it as I could. I'm sensitive to things like that, don't you know, and I couldn't bring myself to go in and help her. I moved the curtains aside and looked down on the street. Cars passing, people going to work, two runners panting and sweating as they pounded by on the sidewalk. Normality everywhere except in my house. Help me, Lord.

I heard water running in the bathroom, and Lillian comforting Hazel Marie. I turned back as Lillian led her toward the bed. She wiped Hazel Marie's face with a wet cloth, then pulled down the covers on the bed.

"Lay back down, now," Lillian told her. "You too weak to be doin' anything. You need a doctor." She glared at me.

I sat down on the side of the bed, trying not to think about how this woman was now in my bed. Wesley Lloyd's bed. But I had to put first things first, and that little boy was the first thing.

"Miss Puckett," I said, "I know you don't feel good, but I need some answers and I need them now. We're both concerned about Little Lloyd, and if you're out of commission, as it seems you are, I need to know how to proceed in finding him."

"Please," she said, "please find him."

"We will. Now, listen to me and give me some straight answers. Who was driving that car when you left Little Lloyd here?"

"Brother Vern," she said, her voice weak but determined. "He was going to take me to Raleigh—I didn't lie to you about that. I had a place in beauty school, and Brother Vern had just come home from preaching somewhere out in California. He was all tore up about Wesley Lloyd's passing. He didn't know about it until he got home, and he offered to drive me down so I could get a new start."

I nodded. "So why'd you change your plans?"

"I didn't change them." She put a hand over her eyes, but I could see tears leaking down her face and into her hair. "I thought we were on our way, but as soon as we left Junior here with you, he told me he had to see some people on church business and it wouldn't take long." She dabbed at her eyes with the corner of my three-hundred-count Egyptian cotton sheet, took a deep breath, and continued on. "He drove way back in the hills, up near the edge of the national forest, I think. I'd never been up there before, but we ended up at a couple of trailers. Single-wides, and the sorriest bunch of people I'd ever seen. Just trailer trash, with outhouses and filth all over the place."

I thought to myself that they must have been a motley crew indeed, since her own people were considered pretty sorry. But I didn't say anything.

"So what happened then?"

"Well, he kept making one excuse after another for not leaving, kept having meetings with the people living there and telling me he was on the Lord's business and I'd have to be patient. And all the while, he was counseling me—that's what he called it— reading the Bible and praying over me."

"Uh-huh," I said when I heard the word "counseling."

"I didn't know what was going on," Hazel Marie said, looking first at me and then Lillian. " 'Cause he kept asking about Wesley Lloyd, how he died, was he saved, had he been right with the Lord, and had he straightened out his affairs before he faced judgment. I didn't know, Miz Springer, I swear Wesley Lloyd never talked about anything like that with me. You have to believe me!" She commenced crying again, burying her face in the sheet.

"Oh, I believe you," I said. "He never discussed things like that with me, either. But don't worry about him being saved. He was a Presbyterian and therefore one of the elect, which makes me wonder about the election process. But that's neither here nor there. What happened then?"

"Well, Brother Vern kept on at me, saying that Wesley Lloyd had promised to provide for me and Junior. He thought I was holding out on him, told me I was being selfish and ungrateful, and I had to respect the hierarchy of order that the Lord instituted because woman is the weaker vessel. It just got worse and worse, and he's got a temper, Miz Springer, a temper you wouldn't believe. I thought he was gonna hit me right there, but the Lord stayed his hand."

"I don't understand," I said, though I'd heard Pastor Ledbetter expound on that hierarchy more times than I cared to recall. In a family, according to him, children are under the wife, and the wife is under the husband, and the husband alone is answerable to God. But I couldn't figure where uncles came into it. "Did he think he had a right to whatever you had?"

"Yes, ma'am, but that's kinda the way it is in our family. The men take care of the money, if there is any, even if it belongs to the women. And since my daddy's dead, and I don't have a . . . Well, you can see how he figures it's his place to look after things for me. But I don't have any things for him to look after."

"Thay Lord," I said, about to roll my eyes until I realized that my situation hadn't been much different from hers. Except for the violence. But then, I'd never refused Wesley Lloyd anything. "So how'd you get away from him?"

"I kept asking to go, telling him I had to be in Raleigh, and he'd promised. Finally, after a day or two, I forget now how long it was, I just decided to walk outta there. I didn't know where we were, but I thought I'd just walk till I come to a road and follow that. Soon as I started out, though, some of those people took hold of me and wouldn't let me leave."

"Well, I never," Lillian said. "Don't tell no more till I get back. You need some liquids in yo' stomick. Jes' lay right still while I go get you something to drink."

She came right back with a glass of chipped ice, a spoon, and a can of ginger ale.

"Suck on this," she commanded, shoveling a spoonful of ice into Hazel Marie's mouth. "An' soon as yo' stomick feel settled, we'll start on this drink."

"Go on," I urged. "What happened then?"

"Well, Brother Vern was still trying to get me right with the Lord, he said, so things wasn't too bad. Except I couldn't leave. He preached at me till I thought I'd go cross-eyed. He just would not believe that Wesley Lloyd hadn't left me anything. All I had was three hundred dollars for beauty school. I offered him that and he took it, then he went on and on about Wesley Lloyd's papers. I didn't know what he was talking about, and still don't. I swear I don't.

"The next thing I knew, he told me to get in the car. That was Friday, I think, Friday evening. He drove me to my house, I mean the one I'd been living in, and, Miz Springer, I got such a shock when we pulled in. Two of my cousins, twice removed, was moving my furniture out, Jerome and Donnie. They just loaded it up in a U-Haul and a pickup. I tried to stop them, but they wouldn't listen to me. Said Brother Vern'd told them they could have whatever they could move. They come from the other side of the family, and that whole bunch is not worth a hill of beans."

I almost smiled as I thought of the pot and

the kettle, but I didn't. "So they took your furniture?"

"Yes'm, every stick," she went on, wiping her eyes and taking a quivering breath. "I tried to get Brother Vern to make them quit, but he told me that your lawyer was going to take possession if the family didn't get it first. He said he'd looked through everything I had and couldn't find Wesley Lloyd's papers, and he'd run out of patience."

She turned away and hid her face. Lillian reached over and patted her on the arm. "Now don't you worry, honey. You safe here with us."

I rolled my eyes at that, and asked Hazel Marie, "So what happened then?" I asked.

"He talked awhile to my cousins. Then he left."

"And?"

"They beat the shit outta me," she said.

My mouth tightened as the shock of the word resounded in Wesley Lloyd's bedroom. I was not accustomed to such language. However. What she said seemed to be pretty much the truth.

"Brother Vern come back sometime later," she went on, "but, Miz Springer, I couldn't give what I didn't have. And he said if I

wasn't gonna be obedient like I was supposed to be, he'd just have to keep Junior
away from me. Said I wasn't fit to raise a
child, being outside of God's will like I was.
Miz Springer, I was alayin' in that garage,
hardly able to get my breath and hurtin' so
bad I thought I was gonna die, and he said
he'd just keep Junior till I decided to submit
to the Lord's will. And he left me there,
bleedin' and hurtin', and I knew he was going after my little boy."

She was sobbing by this time.

To give her a chance to collect herself, I
told her how we'd gone to her house and
how Deputy Bates had found blood all over
the garage, and teeth, too, and how, when
we got back to town, we'd found that my
house had been broken into.

"It had to've been Jerome and Donnie,"
she said. "Maybe Brother Vern thought you
had Wesley Lloyd's papers."

"I do," I said. "Or rather my lawyer does.
But there's nothing concerning you or the
child in them. I'd know it if there was."

"I bet he tear up the house 'cause Little
Lloyd wadn't here for him to get ahold of,"
Lillian said. "That man's mean as a snake.

But, honey, how you get from that place to here in the shape you in?"

"Walked and crawled," she said. "I was afraid to try to get a ride, lookin' like I do. Afraid somebody'd call the law on me. And afraid Donnie and Jerome would be looking for me, too. So I went through fields and woods, hiding out in the daytime and come into town after dark, so afraid he'd get to Junior before me. And he did." More crying.

I felt bad about it all. There I'd been so anxious to be rid of the child, and blithely let him go off while his mama was walking miles to get to him. I felt real bad.

"Drink some of this," Lillian urged, holding out the glass of ginger ale. "I 'spect you keep it down now."

"I still feel sick," Hazel Marie said, "but I got to get up and look for Junior."

"The problem is," I said, "is where're you going to look? You think Brother Vern took him to Raleigh, like he told me?"

She thought for a minute. "No. He just told you that to get Junior away from you. No, he's still around, 'cause he thinks I've got something of Wesley Lloyd's. Oh, me," she said, as she began to untangle herself from the sheets. "I feel like I'm gonna throw up again."

Lillian helped her to the bathroom, saying, "This girl need some medicine or a doctor or something."

"Not a doctor," Hazel Marie said. "I'll be all right."

"Watch after her, Lillian. Get her into one of my gowns while I walk downtown to the drugstore. I ought to be able to find something that'll make her feel better."

I put on my hat, hung my pocketbook on my arm, and commenced walking. Perkins Drugs was only two blocks away on the corner of Polk and Main, so I could walk it quicker than I could find a parking place.

I marched down the sidewalk, intent on my errand, going over in my mind what purchases to make for the Puckett woman. Miss Myrtie Gossett came walking toward me, that ugly tote bag on her shoulder, and wanted to stop and talk. I waved and passed on by. I had no time for gossip. Besides, I was the hot topic, so she couldn't tell me anything I didn't already know.

Troy Beckworth was leaning on the door of his insurance office, hoping for a calamity that would scare up some business for him, and I do mean scare. He'd taken to advertising on the Asheville television, warning people about the dangers of flooding from the sea surge of hurricanes, and us two hundred miles from the coast and three thousand feet above sea level.

"How do, Miz Springer," he said.

"Sea surge," I replied. "For the Lord's sake." And passed on by.

And when I went into the drugstore, who should I run into but Norma Cantrell in her big hair and a turquoise pantsuit. She was getting a prescription filled instead of taking care of the pastor's office, which is what she should've been doing.

"Why, Miss Julia," she said, patting that hair to be sure it was still a foot high. "What you doing in the drugstore?"

"Minding my own business," I said, looking at my watch. "Particularly since I'm not supposed to be working in anybody's office."

She huffed a little at that, but her salary and the preacher's came out of my pledge and I had a right to demand a day's work for a day's pay.

I went about my business of picking out the things on the mental list I'd made. A box of straws, a bottle of Extra Strength Tylenol, another Ace bandage, and a hot-water bottle for the soreness. I carried it all to the counter by the cash register where Norma was standing. She pretended she wasn't interested, but she eyed everything I put down, and I saw her trying to get Buck Tatum's attention by making little sideways jerks of her head at my pile of merchandise. He kept on counting pills, and I went back down the aisle.

After considering all the places where Hazel Marie had been messed up, I picked up two more hot-water bottles. I don't like those heating pads with electric cords that plug in the wall. They're all right if you're holding them to a sore place while you're sitting up, but try turning over in bed.

I took the hot-water bottles to the counter and with a look at Norma dared her to say anything. I stood there tapping my fingers on the counter, trying to think of what else I needed.

"Uh-huh," I said, turning on my heel and catching a glimpse of Norma's avid stare. I paid no mind as I went looking for a tube of Ben-Gay. Good for muscle soreness and stiffness. I added some Q-Tips, Band-Aids, and Mercurochrome. Then, on the Puckett woman's request, a bottle of foundation to cover her bruises. Cover Girl, which seemed apt.

When I got back to the counter, I called Buck to come help me. I needed one more thing.

"I'll be through here in a minute, Miz Springer," he said from behind his drug counter. "Just getting a few things together for Miz Cantrell."

I didn't mind waiting a few minutes, but Norma said, "Oh, that's all right. Go ahead and wait on Miz Springer. I'm in no hurry." She turned and looked me straight in the eye. "Pastor Ledbetter sent me." Letting me know she was on the job.

"All right, then," Buck said, "what can I do you for, Miz Springer?"

"I need some paregoric."

Norma's eyebrows went up like they were on springs.

"Can't do it, Miz Springer. Have to have a prescription now."

I rolled my eyes at that. Somebody's always changing rules that've worked well enough for years. I said, "And just what are people supposed to do when they need re-lief? Call a doctor and pay his bill, too?"

Buck and Norma exchanged knowing glances, as if they thought I was blind or too crazy to notice.

"Well, now, Miz Springer," Buck said, pulling at the tail of his white jacket. He loved to dispense medical information along with his pills. He'd wanted to be a doctor or a veterinarian. I couldn't remember which, but they wouldn't let him in.

"It's a controlled substance now," he informed me. "Too many people self-medicating themselves with it. Want me to call your doctor and get a prescription for it?"

"No, if I need it bad enough I'll call him myself." I wasn't ready to explain to a doctor why I wanted a prescription for a painkiller. "Just give me a large bottle of Pepto-Bismol for now."

Norma couldn't stand it any longer. "What're you going to do with all that stuff, Miz Springer? If you don't mind me asking."

"I do mind, Norma," I said. "But since you have, I'll tell you. Instead of letting the church tear down my house, I'm going to turn it into a home for injured cats and dogs. And when they're better, I'm going to let them run around in the church parking lot. So be prepared to do some scooping."

I paid for my purchases and left the drugstore, aware of Norma's squinty-eyed appraisal following me down the sidewalk.

Chapter Eighteen

—

Lillian and I doctored on Hazel Marie for some time when I got home with the medical supplies. I kept hoping she'd drop off to sleep, but every time her eyes began to close she'd think of Little Lloyd and start crying again. And every time I turned around Lillian was handing her another drink. If it wasn't ginger ale, it was a milk shake or a glass of lemonade, saying she had to have something on her stomach. It's a wonder she didn't begin to float. After a while, she ate a slice of dry toast and kept it down, which relieved me considerably.

She kept wanting to get up and look for the boy, but we convinced her that the best thing she could do was stay in bed until we knew where to look.

I volunteered to call all her relatives down in Benson's Gap, and we decided that I'd pretend to be somebody wanting Brother Vern for a preaching service and not mention Little Lloyd at all.

"That's the best way to do it," I said. "We don't know how many others are in this with him, but I'll bet that wherever the Reverend Vernon Puckett is, the boy is, too."

"He may have him hid somewheres," Lillian said.

"Don't create problems," I told her. "Besides, if I find Brother Puckett, you better believe I'll find Little Lloyd. I'll have that man in jail so fast his head'll swim. The idea of lying to me to get that child. To say nothing of ransacking my house. I tell you, he'll think twice about messing with me again."

Hazel Marie slept most of the afternoon, except for the times Lillian woke her with another glass of something to drink. During that time, I spoke to more Pucketts than I'd ever known existed. At first it was hard to do, unaccustomed as I am to lying. But after a while, I about convinced myself that the little church I'd made up really needed Brother Vern's ministry. Most of the people

I spoke to had that local mountain twang, and I found myself following along.

"I'm alookin' for Brother Vernon Puckett," I'd say. "They's a need for his preachin' in our church, 'cause it's about to split in two, and we need a revival real bad."

That certainly got more cooperation than when I said something like, "I wonder if you could tell me, please, where I might find the Reverend Puckett."

But none of them knew where he was. Or if they did, they weren't telling.

After that disappointment, I had another idea. It was Tuesday, and Brother Vern's telecast was supposed to run at nine o'clock that night. Unless he canceled out and ran a substitute in, we'd know he was in Spartanburg for at least an hour.

When I told Hazel Marie what I'd come up with, she wanted to head down the mountain right then and wait for him to get to the studio.

"No," I said. "If he sees you before he starts his program, he'll just drive off. You ought to wait and see if he's on live and not just running a tape. Which he might be, if he thinks you're able to get to him."

When Lillian heard what we were going to

do, she announced that she was staying to watch, too. So we kept Hazel Marie in bed in my room until Deputy Bates was up and gone, and then we helped her downstairs. I'd offered her either my cotton chenille zip-up robe or my blue satin wraparound with lace inserts, the one I kept in case I ever had to go to the hospital. She chose the blue satin, and why wasn't I surprised?

"Come to the kitchen first," Lillian told her. "You need to rinch yo' mouth again with salty water. An' I fixed you another milk shake to put some meat on yo' bones."

Hazel Marie brought the milk shake into the living room, and Lillian made her comfortable on the sofa with pillows behind her back. I turned the television on and we all leaned forward to watch the *Feeding the Flame* program, coming to you live with Brother Vernon Puckett, the anointed of God, preaching with Holy Ghost power the good news of the Gospel.

And there he was, in a royal blue suit and matching tie with a white dove on it. His hair looked wet and slicked back, except for that little curly swirl on his forehead. He made a big thing of attaching what he called a lavaliere microphone to his lapel, laughing and pretending he didn't know how it worked. Just your average workingman, unfamiliar with technical devices. Uh-huh, and those one-eight-hundred numbers running across the screen in front of him.

"Pray with me now, all you brothers and sisters in the telecast-viewing audience," he started out, but not a one of us bowed our heads. *"Lord, we ask that You send the devil packin' tonight, and let your angels just camp around us so we'll be in a frame of mind to receive your blessin', praise God, amen.*

"Now then," he went on, hardly taking a breath. *"I want you-all to know that a special blessin' is comin' to you tonight. I don't want to say I'm happy about this, you know how it is, but Brother Winslow, who has the next hour after us, has taken sick, and we're prayin' for you, Brother Winslow, but the good people here at the station has asked if I can go on for two hours instead of my usual one."* He paused, looked around, and put this surprised look on his face. *"Can I go on for two hours? Brethren, I can go on for ten hours! It don't take no effort for me to preach just as long as somebody's out*

there to listen! But now, before I get revved up good, let's hear from Sister Rubynell. Come on out here, Rubynell, and backin' her up is the Glory Boys Band; take a bow, boys. They all down here from up in Shelby, North Carolina, and we thank you for it."

Hazel Marie sat up and said, "He's going to be there for two hours, and I can be there in that time. I'm going to Spartanburg and make him tell me where he's got Junior."

"Wait," I said, waving her back. "You don't have a way to get there, and we don't know yet if this is a rerun. Let's be sure this is live before you do anything."

By that time, Sister Rubynell had appeared in what looked like one of my housedresses, and she was a sight to see. Her hair was silvery white and teased so high that Norma Cantrell's couldn't hold a candle to it. She looked about my age, with a few more pounds on her and a whole lot more wrinkles. In spite of that curled mass of hair, she wasn't wearing a lick of makeup except for a thick layer of blue eye shadow. The contrast was jarring, to say the least.

"That woman look like she been rode hard and put up wet," Lillian said, frowning at the screen.

She sounded it, too, because when she opened her mouth, without so much as an introduction by the band, she came out with a loud, piercing rendition of "Will the Circle Be Unbroken?" Fingernails on a chalkboard, I thought, turning down the volume. But she evermore got into it, at one point snapping her fingers and saying, "Pick it up, boys," in spite of their flailing away to do just that, and she didn't miss a beat. She had a set of lungs on her, I gave her that.

I cut my eyes over at Lillian and Hazel Marie to see how they were taking this, not wanting to offend anybody by saying what I was thinking. Lillian's church likes hand-clapping, foot-tapping music sung on key by rich voices, so she was sitting there with a frown on her face. Hazel Marie, on the other hand, was watching intently and nodding her head in time to Sister Rubynell's screeching. We Presbyterians like semipro-fessional choirs to do our singing for us, with only a few congregational hymns to mumble our way through.

"Thank you, Sister, and all you Glory Boys," Brother Vern sang out on the last twang of the electric guitar. There was a

smattering of applause as the camera panned across an audience of a dozen or so people sitting on folding chairs.

"Now, I want all you folks in the telecast-viewing area to listen up, 'cause I got some good news and I got some bad news," Brother Vern said. *"The bad news is, there's a devil loose out there lookin' for whoever he can devour. Make no mistake about it, he don't want no New York strip with A.1. sauce and he don't want no strawberry shortcake neither. He craves the souls of men. And women's and children's. Don't matter to him, he'll take 'em all. But the good news is, JEE-sus was hungry, too, and you know what he ate? Help me now, He swallowed up death. Praise God, He took death and swallowed it whole and not a one of us has to be afraid of the devil's appetite no more. Listen to me, now, 'cause I'm agonna tell you all about it. Just as soon as I wipe my face here."*

He laughed in that folksy way of his, and took a large white handkerchief from his pocket. He mopped the sweat from his face, which was glistening in the television lights.

"All right, lissen to me now," he went on

as he paced back and forth. *"You got to have JEE-sus in your heart. Wait a minute, wait a minute. Lissen here, you don't have to mix up a cup of Kool-Aid or hitch a ride on Hale-Bopp to find Him. Nossir, that ain't the way to do it. All you have to do is say, 'Come on in, Jesus,' and that's it. Wait a minute, don't turn that dial, all you gonna see is somebody trying to sell you a car or a double-decker hamburger. You don't need that, so stay tuned 'cause I got lots more to tell you.*

"But first, I want you to meet a real special guest right here in the studio with us. He come all the way from Memphis, Tennessee, to tell us about a special ministry that God has called him to. Come on over here with that television camera." As Brother Vern moved to the side, he kept looking over his shoulder to be sure the camera had him in view. He pulled up a chair beside a sofa where a very wide woman was sitting. She held a toddler on a lap that looked full of an unborn child. Beside her was a wisp of a man, bald head shining, who was holding another toddler. Between them was a little older child.

"This here's Brother Stedman Jones and

his good wife, Sister Leesie. Welcome to the Fanning the Flame program, *good people. Now, folks,"* Brother Vern said, looking directly into the camera, *"Brother Stedman and Sister Leesie take to heart the Lord's commandment to be fruitful and multiply, 'cause they got, count 'em now, sixteen children, praise God!"*

The camera panned quickly across a row of children bunched up behind the sofa. Lillian shook her head and said, "Sixteen head of chil'ren. How they feed 'em?"

The camera came back to Brother Vern, who leaned toward his guests and said, *"What's the Lord got you doing now, Brother Stedman?"*

"Glad you asked," Brother Stedman said, unrolling a narrow two-foot long piece of paper. *"I want everybody to call in right now to get this special gift for only twenty-three dollars, plus postage and handlin'. See, it's a bumper sticker that tells everybody where you're goin'. And, believe you me, it ain't to no Wal-Mart's."*

"What that thing say?" Lillian asked.

"It says," I said, squinting against the glare of the television lights on the shiny paper, " 'Warning! Driver May Disappear at

Any Moment.' What in the world does that mean?"

"It's talking about the Rapture," Hazel Marie said, surprising me no end. "You know, when all the believers will be taken up in the air." I vaguely remembered hearing something about that from a visiting evangelist in First Church. But most of us mainline Presbyterians are post-dispensationalists, or so Wesley Lloyd told me.

"I declare," I said, turning my attention back to the set.

"Hear that, folks?" Brother Vern took one end of the banner and held it up high. *"Put one of these on your bumper, and you'll be doing your neighbors a favor, telling them to watch out for cars going every whichaway when that final trump sounds. In the twinklin' of an eye we'll be swept right up outta our sports-utility vehicles and our pickups and our living room recliners, ain't that right, Brother Stedman? Now, why don't you tell us what all you been doing over in Memphis. I know you been busy."*

"Yessir, I sure have," Brother Stedman said, and I thought of those sixteen children and figured out what he'd been busy doing. *"Besides running off these bumper stickers,*

*I been workin' on them abortion clinics. I've
closed down two of 'em and been put in jail
three times, praise God. I need your prayers
real bad, 'cause you got your liberals, and
your secular humanists, and your homasex-
als, and they're all dead set against me."*

"Well, you got my prayers, Brother,"
Brother Vern assured him. While Brother
Vern went on, it came to me how some
Christians seemed to always need to have
something or somebody to be against. If it
wasn't desegregation, it was women's lib. If
it wasn't sex education, it was secular hu-
manism. And if it wasn't one-worlders, it
was just plain Democrats. Now it was abor-
tionists and homosexuals who were ruining
the country and destroying Christianity.
Well, I had more faith in the Lord of Calvin
and Knox than to get carried away over that
unlikely possibility. He'd been running
things since the beginning, and I didn't figure He'd have much trouble keeping a lid
on things in this day and age. Besides, we
didn't have any abortion clinics in Abbotsville. Or homosexuals, either.

"Now," Brother Vern said, drawing my attention back to him. *"Brother Stedman, I
want to give our telecast viewers a good*

*look at your fine family. Smile, young'uns,
you're on Candid Camera! Come on, put
the camera on ever'one of 'em, praise God
for the stars in your crown, Sister Leesie."*

That poor woman had sat all through this
with a smile plastered on her face, without
a word to say for herself. Of course, nobody
had given her a chance to speak, and she
was probably too tired anyway. I kept wondering how she got all those children fed,
washed, and dressed to make their appearance on television.

"Look!" Lillian yelled, jumping up and
pointing at the screen. "Look right there!"

"What is it?" I strained to see what she
was pointing at.

"It's Junior!" Hazel Marie came off the
sofa, holding her ribs and spilling her milk
shake all over my Oriental. "It's him! Brother
Vern's got him in that family! He's right
there, don't you see him?"

"It is him," I said, seeing that little pinched
face with the thick glasses sliding down his
nose. All the children were smiling and pos-
ing for the camera like they'd done it a hundred times before, while Little Lloyd stood
in their midst looking lost and forlorn. I noticed that he had on his clip-on tie because,

I was sure, he didn't have anybody to make the knot in his good one.

"I got to get down there," Hazel Marie said. "Miz Springer, I hate to ask you, but could you loan me enough money for a taxi? I'll pay you back if it takes me twenty years."

"A taxi? To Spartanburg? That's forty miles from here, and I certainly will not." I stood up and clicked off the television. "We'll take my car. Get yourself together and let's get started."

Chapter Nineteen

—

"Wait for me," Lillian said. "I'm goin', too, but I got to get this milk shake up."

"Leave it," I said, "we don't have time to be cleaning rugs. It's forty miles down there, and he's going to be on the air for"—I looked at my watch—"another hour and a half. If we hurry, we can be down there about the time he's through."

"Oh, please, let's hurry," Hazel Marie said. She was so jittery that the blue satin robe was shaking and shimmering around her.

Lillian looked at her and then at me. "You want me to go get her clothes?"

"No," I said, "it takes too long to get her dressed. You two go on out to the car, and I'll lock up the house."

I got my pocketbook, checked the cash in

my change purse, turned out the lights, and hurried outside to the garage. Hazel Marie was already in the passenger seat, while Lillian stood waiting for me.

"You want me to drive?" she asked.

"I do not. I'm perfectly capable of driving this car."

"Well, I know you don't see too good at night."

"Neither do you," I said. "Besides, I do have headlights, so get on in and let's go."

She pulled back the driver's seat and started cramming herself into the narrow backseat, moaning and groaning as she did. "Whew," she said as she plopped in, "this ain't built for no normal person."

Hazel Marie had her hands clasped in her lap, staring straight ahead, willing us to get started.

I drove through town, seeing only a few cars at that time of night, but half blinded by the headlights of the ones we did meet. By the time we got to the interstate I'd learned not to look right into them. There were only a few headlights way off in the distance when I got ready to merge, so I was able to do it without having to fit in between a stream of cars.

"Miz Springer," Hazel Marie said softly and a little hesitantly, "you don't have to stop and look on a ramp. You can just go on out in the nearest lane. If you don't mind me saying so."

"I'm doing the driving," I reminded her, but I considered what she'd said. I thought you always had to stop and look both ways when entering a main road.

After a while Lillian said, "How fast you goin'?"

"I'm almost up to the speed limit."

"Well, get on up there and a little over," she said. "We got to get to that place 'fore he go off with that boy again."

"Oh, yes, please let's do," Hazel Marie said.

"Now look, you two, I want to get there as quick as you do. But I want us there in one piece, so spare me the comments."

"I probably could drive," Hazel Marie said, "if you need me to."

I glanced at her, hunched over with the pain in her ribs. "You can't hardly straighten up, much less take the wheel of a car. I'll get us there, don't worry. And in plenty of time, too."

In fact, night driving wasn't as hard as I'd

thought it'd be. There wasn't a lot of traffic, and what there was came in bunches that whizzed on past us.

"Uh-oh," Lillian said as a flash of lightning lit the southwestern sky. "Look like a cloud comin' up."

"Heat lightning, most likely," I said. Still, it worried me. I could do without one of our fierce mountain storms that usually followed a heat spell like we'd been having.

For long stretches, we were the only car on the road. The four-lane highway dipped and climbed, ran past the Continental Divide, and curved between high cliffs before streaming down the mountain to the flat country below. Our headlights cut a tunnel through the night as lightning occasionally flashed behind a cloud ahead of us. I thought I could hear the tires humming on the pavement, then realized it was Hazel Marie moaning. Or praying.

"I jus' thought of something," Lillian said, leaning forward between the front seats. "What that chile doin' in that fam'ly? Reckon Brother Vern give him away?"

"Oh, don't say that," Hazel Marie cried. "Surely he wouldn't do that."

"He might," I said. "He might want him

where he'd be out of your reach, and mine. But don't you worry about it. We know Brother Stedman lives in Memphis, and from what he said about his activities there, I don't expect we'd have any trouble tracking him down."

"I want to get Junior tonight. I just don't think I could stand it if we miss him."

"We'll get him," I said, with as much assurance as I could muster. I wasn't ready to drive to Memphis that night, but I'd do it if I had to.

"I jus' thought of something else," Lillian said. "Do anybody know where we goin' when we get to Spartanburg?"

Trust Lillian to say what had just occurred to me. That studio on television had seemed so real that I guess I just thought we could drive down the mountain and straight to it.

"I think I know where it is," Hazel Marie said. "I was down there one time when Brother Vern had the idea of a family band. The Puckett Pickers or the Pickin' Pucketts, he couldn't decide which, but it didn't work out. He said music was supposed to be to the glory of God, but we couldn't stay in tune long enough to glorify anybody."

"I declare," I said, wondering what other talents Hazel Marie had. Besides those Wesley Lloyd had appreciated.

"I jus' thought of somethin' else," Lillian said.

"For goodness' sakes, Lillian," I said, "what now?"

"We might ought to have a plan of some kind. I mean, do we go inside an' grab him? Or do we wait till he come out an' scoop him up then? Better think about what we gonna do."

So we all thought for a mile or so, considering the best way to snatch a child who'd been snatched from us. I wished I could think of some way to trick Brother Vern the way he'd tricked me, but I couldn't. I looked over at Hazel Marie, but all I could see in the glow of the dashboard lights was an intense frown on her face. She was either hurting bad or thinking hard. Maybe both.

"Uh, Miz Springer," she said, scrunching up her shoulders so that I thought her pain had gotten worse. "I hate to ask this, but you reckon we could stop for a minute?"

"You want to stop?" I took my foot off the gas and got a blaring horn from a lumber truck that passed us so fast it shook the car. I speeded up a little to keep from getting run over, and asked, "You going to be sick?"

"No'm, it's just that I got to, well, pee-pee, and I don't think I can hold it any longer."

"Pee-pee?" I almost laughed, then remembered what she could've called it. "Lillian, help me look for a filling station. I haven't seen one for miles, but we ought to come up on a sign pretty soon." But the roadsides were dark, and there were no exit signs ahead that I could see.

"I can't wait, Miz Springer. I got to go real bad."

"Well, I don't know what I can do. I can't make a filling station with a bathroom just appear out here on the side of the road."

She moaned.

Lillian said, "Be quicker to jus' pull over an' let her go beside the car."

"Why, that's plain trashy," I said. "Lillian, this is your fault, making her drink all day long."

"Ain't nobody gonna see her, so jus' pull on over. When you got to go, you got to go, an' don't matter if it do be trashy."

I didn't like it, but I pulled over onto the edge of the road. After fiddling around on the dashboard, I found my blinker lights. Hazel Marie had the door open before we stopped rolling good, and Lillian shoved out after her.

"Squat down right here," she told her, "an' I'll stand so cars comin' up can't see you."

"I don't even care," Hazel Marie said tightly, hiking up my satin robe and hunkering down beside the car.

"Reckon they's any snakes out here?" Lillian said, almost stopping Hazel Marie in her tracks, so to speak.

Suddenly a blast of light hit us. We were lit up like the sun had come up at ten o'clock at night. My heart nearly stopped when I heard the whooshing sound of air brakes behind us. A big truck, with running lights over the cab and a pair of headlights that put us on display for miles around, pulled up behind us.

"Thay Lord," Lillian said. She spread her skirt out to screen Hazel Marie from view.

"Hurry up. Hurry up," I urged. "My Lord, he's getting out!" I saw the shadowy figure of a man climb down from the cab and walk over to my window.

"You ladies need any help?" he asked, leaning down to look across me at Hazel

Marie's head, which she was covering with one hand. I gave her credit. I couldn't see much of him, but he wore a baseball cap and had a powerful masculine odor to him. Probably been cooped up in that truck for miles on end.

"No, but thank you for stopping," I said. "We're all right, just a, you know, a necessity stop."

"Well," he said, grinning and spitting on the road, "I know how that is, but you ladies need to be careful along here. They's been somebody 'long this stretch with a blue light that ain't no police."

"Hurry up, Hazel Marie," I said.

"I'm tryin'," she said.

"Where you ladies goin'?" the trucker asked.

"We goin' to Spartanburg," Lillian said. I glared at her, trying to stop her from telling a stranger our business. "You know where they's a television station down there?"

"You mean that Christian broadcastin' one? I know where that is. If y'all're headin' there, you can follow me. I'm goin' to the interchange and on up to the Milliken plant on I-85, an' we'll pass right by it."

Hazel Marie popped up right then,

straightening out her satin negligee. She said, "Oh, thank you, thank you. That's wonderful. We'll follow right behind you."

The trucker stood up to look at her over the top of the car. Then he leaned down to look at her through my window. He couldn't decide which view he liked best, but I doubted he'd seen many beat-up blondes in satin negligees on the side of the road before this. But I could've been wrong.

"Lemme see can I get back in this car," Lillian said, crawling over Hazel Marie's seat. "We needs to be there real soon, Mr. Truckin' Man, so don't spare the gas."

"Now, just one minute," I said. "We don't need to go too fast. Are you in, Miss Puckett? Reach over and get the door, Lillian."

"This ain't gonna be no problem," the trucker said, squatting now so he could get a good look at Hazel Marie through the window. "Just get behind me, stay a coupla car lengths away, and the slipstream'll do the rest. Y'all got a CB in there?"

"I don't think so," I said.

"Well, I won't lose you, and when we get to your exit, I'll blink my lights and blow the air horn in plenty of time for you to make your turn. Just stay in the same lane I'm in all the way down." He straightened up and began walking back to his truck. Then he turned around and came back. "I hope you don't mind me askin', but are y'all some kinda gospel-singin' group?"

I nearly choked, picturing Lillian in her white nurse's uniform, Hazel Marie in my blue satin robe, and me in my Leslie Fay shirtwaist singing gospel songs on television.

"Nossir," I said and, figuring we needed to provide some explanation for ourselves, went on, "we're going down for a healing service." Forgive me, Lord, but it was the only thing that seemed to fit us all. I don't hold with lying as a usual thing, but the ox was just about in the ditch.

"Aw, I'm real sorry to hear that," he said. "Don't you worry none; I'll get you there." He gave Hazel Marie a tender look, a change from what he'd been giving her.

"We need to hurry," she said. "The program goes off at eleven, and I just got to get there before then."

"You'll make it if I have anything to do with it." He ran to his truck, put it in gear and pulled out around us, tapping his horn as he went.

I followed, and it was as easy as he said because I didn't have to watch all the other traffic. He did it for me. All I had to do was click on my turn signal when he did, change lanes when he did, and stay right behind him.

"Uh-oh," Lillian said.

"What now?"

"They's another big ole truck comin' up behind us. He might want us to get outta the way."

"I don't think so," Hazel Marie said, gingerly turning to look back. "No, they've put us in the rocking chair."

"In the what?"

"We're between two eighteen-wheelers an' they won't let anybody else in. He must've called out over his CB an' told him we need to get there in a hurry."

Across the way on the interstate, two big trucks going west on I-26 blew their horns and blinked every light they had, which was plenty. After a while, a car pulled up alongside of us and just stayed at our speed, every person in it gawking at us.

"What them folks want?" Lillian asked. They were worrying me, too.

"See that antenna?" Hazel Marie pointed

at the car. "They got a CB, so they've heard about us."

"Good Lord!" I gasped as bright lights lit up the car beside us, and a horn blew a blast that sounded like Brother Stedman's last trump. Another big truck came rushing up behind the car, getting right on his bumper. This new truck kept blinking his lights and blowing that horn. The driver of the car spurted on past us like a bat out of you-know-where. Scared to death, and I didn't blame him.

The third truck then eased up until the trailer was even with us, and we moved on down the interstate with one truck in front, one behind, and one to the side of us.

"They got us in the pen," Hazel Marie said. "Thank you, Lord." She leaned back against the headrest, and seemed to relax for the first time since we'd started.

That was the easiest driving I'd ever done, and I resolved to get myself one of those CB radios and from then on call for an escort every time I went anywhere.

We rolled on down I-26 eastbound, the third truck occasionally pulling ahead to let a fast car pass, then easing back beside us. When we got to the I-85 interchange, I didn't even have to worry about getting on the right exit ramp or merging with the heavier traffic. I just leaned that little car in the curve right along with our trucking friends and let them clear a path for us.

"I think I see it," Hazel Marie said, pointing ahead of us. "See those red lights high up over there? I bet that's the tower."

"I can't look," I said, "but you must be right. He's moving us over to the outside lane. Yes, and there go his lights. Y'all watch for the exit."

The lights on the truck in front of us were blinking like a nervous Christmas tree, and the horn started blowing. I flipped on my turn signal to let him know he could let up, I'd gotten his message.

"There it is!" Lillian yelled. "Slow down! Turn off! Turn off 'fore you miss it!"

"Blow your horn back at him, Miz Springer," Hazel Marie said.

"I can't do everything at once," I cried, slowing down, straining to see the exit, blowing my horn, and hoping the truck behind wouldn't climb over us. When we were safely on the exit road, every truck on both sides of the interstate blew their air horns and flashed their lights. Truckers' prayers for poor Hazel Marie, I guess. Lord, forgive me for lying by indirection, but she could use whatever prayers she could get.

The broadcasting studio was a squatty cement block building with that steel-strutted edifice, blinking with red lights, towering above it. A weed-choked wire fence enclosed the parking lot, with a security light on a pole at the open gate. A half-dozen or so cars were parked in the uneven asphalt lot, but we didn't see any people. One yellow bulb burned over the entrance to the building, and there was a weak light coming from a small window high up beside the door.

"It sure looks closed up. Wonder if anybody's in there," I said, trying to decide the best place to park.

"Somebody's there," Hazel Marie said. "The studios don't have windows, that's why it's so dark."

I knew that.

"I'll park by the side of the building while we decide how to go about this," I said.

"If you don't mind, Miz Springer," Hazel Marie said, "park over in that far corner. I got to pee-pee again if we got time."

I rolled my eyes even though nobody

could see me, and drove over to the darkest corner in the lot. Hazel Marie slid out of the car and I was treated to the slithering of satin and the top of her head again as she crouched down beside the open door.

"She losin' a lot of fluids," Lillian said. "We ought to stop on the way home an' get her a drink."

I said, "Don't even think about it."

"Woo-oo," Hazel Marie sighed as she eased back in her seat. "That's a relief. I was 'bout to pop."

"All right, now," I said. "We're here, and Brother Vern's program'll be over in about ten minutes. What're we going to do?"

"I'm gonna sneak in and get Junior," Hazel Marie said.

"You ain't gonna do no sneakin' in what you got on," Lillian reminded her.

"I'll go in," I said. "Little Lloyd'll come when he sees me. He knows me."

"Uh-huh," Lillian said. "An' that Brother Vern know you, too. You think he jus' gonna let you come take that chile by the hand an' walk outta there? Ever'body in there workin' for Brother Vern, an' all he got to do is yell, 'Stop that woman!' an' they stop you."

"Well, what do you suggest we do?" I asked, edgy now that we were there without knowing what to do next.

"I bet those truckers would've helped us," Hazel Marie said. "Wish I'd thought to ask 'em. We coulda told them my little boy was kidnapped by a crazy snake handler or something." Once lying starts, it just keeps growing, which is why I'm against it as a general rule.

"Huh," I said, "too late now." But I shivered at the thought of a bunch of wild truck drivers crashing in on a live television program. Sister Rubynell'd really have something to screech about, to say nothing of all those children in there. "We better think of something quick."

"Brother Vern don't know me," Lillian said. "Lemme outta this car. I'm goin' in an' get our little boy."

CHAPTER TWENTY

—

"Okay," I agreed, because I couldn't think of a better way. "Miss Puckett, let Lillian out on your side. Then if you can manage it, see if you can get in the backseat. When she comes out with Little Lloyd, we won't have time to get you in and out of the car."

She nodded and opened the door again. When she was out, hunched over and holding her rib cage, Lillian crawled out beside her. Then, whimpering with pain, Hazel Marie managed to get over the seat and into the back. She groaned as she settled into the seat. A flash of lightning lit up the weeds along the fence, as well as her drawn face, frowning with pain.

"Lordamercy!" Lillian yelped as a roll of

thunder followed the flash. "I got to get outta this 'fore I get struck down."

She started toward the station, but I stuck my head out the window and called to her in a loud whisper.

"Lillian, Lillian! Come back here a minute."

She came to my window and leaned against the door. "What you want?"

"Take this," I said, rummaging in my pocketbook. I held out two new hundred-dollar bills from among several that I kept on me in case I needed anything. And also because Wesley Lloyd had never given me more than fifty dollars at a time. "I didn't see any of your people on that television show, so you may have trouble getting in. Tell whoever you see that you work for somebody who's too feeble to get out of the car, but who wants to contribute one of those bills to Brother Vern's ministry, and to buy a bumper sticker from Brother Stedman with the other one. Don't give them to just anybody. Make them let you inside where Little Lloyd can see you."

"That's a good idea," she said. "Money do talk. And open doors, too."

She hurried toward the building, shoes flapping on her heels. I admired her courage, knowing how frightened she was of lightning. To say nothing of knocking on a door belonging to white people in the middle of the night.

"As soon as she's in, I'll pull up right in front," I told Hazel Marie. "We'll keep the car door open, so all they'll have to do is jump in."

"Keep the motor running, too," Hazel Marie said through clenched teeth. Those she had left, that is.

We watched as Lillian tried the door at the front of the building. Then she began pushing a buzzer, and for a long while I thought no one was going to answer. When the door finally opened, we could see her talking to someone for what seemed like several minutes. Finally, she held up the two bills and the door opened wider. She went in and it closed behind her.

"She's in!" I eased the car up beside the front of the building, keeping the headlights off. I reached over and opened the passenger door wide.

My hands trembled on the wheel as I wondered what was going on inside. I slid my left foot onto the brake pedal so the other one could rest on the accelerator, ready for takeoff. Other than the rumble of thunder, Hazel Marie's painful breathing, and the muted roar of traffic on the interstate, everything around us was quiet.

"I hope nothing goes wrong," Hazel Marie said. "She's been in there an awful long time. What if he wants to put her on TV? He does that sometimes, just picks somebody out to interview as the Lord leads him."

Lightning flashed again, closer this time, and heavy raindrops began to spatter on the windshield. I looked out to my left, seeing the rows of cars on the interstate and dreading the moment of merging again.

"Lillian won't go on TV in her work dress," I said. Then to keep my mind off what was happening inside, I asked, "Where did Brother Vern go to seminary?"

"He didn't. He was working for the World of Boots and Shoes when the Lord called him to preach. He got the call right between the Bass Weejuns and the Converse hightops. He says fitting shoes on people's feet gave him more training in misery than any seminary could."

I left that alone, since Hazel Marie's soft voice told it so matter-of-factly. Far be it from me to disturb anybody's faith.

"Well," I said, "I guess it takes all— Oh! here they come!"

The door of the building flew open and Little Lloyd ran out with Lillian right behind him. Several men and a pack of children, pushing, shoving, and yelling, ran after them.

"Get in! Get in!" I threw back the passenger seat and Little Lloyd practically flew over it to land in the back.

"Mama! Mama!" he cried, lunging for her. She reached for him and pulled him close.

"Sweetheart," she said. "Oh, baby, are you all right?"

"Careful, Little Lloyd, your mother's hurt. Hurry, Lillian!"

She was in and trying to get the door closed. Men, teenagers, and little children swarmed around the side of the car. One of the men held on to the door while Lillian tugged and strained to get it closed. She screamed as somebody reached in to pull her out of the car. I stomped the gas pedal so hard the tires spun on the asphalt. When I took my other foot off the brake, the little car practically leapt in the air. The momentum swung the door wider, then slammed it shut, flinging the man holding it to the ground.

The chain-link fence loomed before us, coming at us fast. I jerked at the wheel, spinning it around, feeling the car swerve and rock on its frame. Before I knew it we'd turned completely around. Practically in our tracks. I heard screams, but they were all coming from inside the car. People, some of them children, ran from one side of the lot to the other, arms waving, trying to get me to stop. They scattered as I came back at them.

"Miz Springer!" Hazel Marie yelled. "Watch out!"

"What you doin'?" Lillian cried. "Don't run over them people!"

"I can't find the gate!"

"Turn on the headlights!" Lillian yelled.

That helped. I found them and the gate and sped out onto the access road.

"Oh, my Lord," I said, "how do I get over there on the interstate?" Bumper-to-bumper traffic moved along beside us, separated by a ditch of weeds and a metal railing.

Hazel Marie had her arms around Little Lloyd, but she sat up straighter to look out the windshield. "There's a ramp right up there past the rise. You can get on there."

My stomach dropped as we sailed over the rise and down the ramp to the interstate. One car after another, a continuous line of headlights and taillights, filled both lanes of southbound traffic. I didn't let it bother me, though, since Hazel Marie had told me how to manage an entry. I zoomed toward the nearest lane, looking neither to the right nor the left.

Little Lloyd screamed. Lillian called on Jesus, but I just sped up and slid the car into the traffic. I'd never heard such blowing of horns and screeching of brakes. I paid no mind.

I breathed a sigh of relief as we moved along with the traffic. Lillian's hand was practically white where she was gripping the armrest.

"Anybody following us?" I asked.

Lillian turned around and said, "Only 'bout two million cars, but I can't see who's in 'em."

"Well, let's hope for the best. Little Lloyd, are you all right? We're glad to have you back." The amenities done, I said to Lillian, "Help me look for the windshield wipers;

that rain is peppering down now. I wish this car wasn't so new so I'd know where things are."

"You know where you goin'?" she asked as I finally turned the right knob and got the wipers going.

"No, Lillian, I don't. I just know we're going away from Brother Vern. Other than that, I'm just driving and doing the best I can."

"We'll go to Atlanta if you keep on this way," Hazel Marie said. "Watch for a Greenville exit and come off on that. We can get back to Abbotsville that way."

"My Lord!" I said as the roar of a heavy motor surrounded us and bright headlights behind us nearly blinded me. I reached up to adjust the rearview mirror. "What's that truck doing so close to us?"

"I can't see nothin'," Lillian said, as she twisted in her seat and shielded her eyes with her hand. "He mighty close, but he don't look like one of them trucks we had before."

"Lemme look," Hazel Marie said, and I heard the intake of her breath as she tried to turn around. "Pull out in the other lane,

Miz Springer, if you can, and I'll try to get a look at him from the side."

I twitched the car over into the fast lane and got a horn blast from another car for my trouble. I had the turn indicator on, so it shouldn't've been a surprise. I speeded up, though, and lost the glare of headlights through our rear window.

"I see him!" Hazel Marie yelled. "Oh, my goodness, that's Jerome's pickup. I know it is, see how high it's jacked up."

A jacked-up truck rang a bell that I didn't want to hear.

"Look at them wheels," Lillian said. She'd turned completely around to kneel in the seat. "What he doin' with them big wheels on a pickup?"

"Truck pulls," Hazel Marie said, as if that explained anything. "I didn't see his truck back at the TV station. I don't know what I'd of done if I had."

"Maybe it was parked in the back," I said. "But if it's the same truck I've seen before, it has a habit of appearing out of nowhere. The question now is, how do we get away from him?"

"We got to think of something," Hazel

Marie said. "Miz Springer, we can't let him catch up with us. He's pulled into our lane now! Oh, God, don't let him catch us."

"Mama?" Little Lloyd said.

"Don't worry, Little Lloyd," I said, "he hasn't caught us yet, and if this car lives up to the claims they make for it, he won't."

"What you gonna do?" Lillian asked. "Outrun him all the way to Atlanta, Gee-A?"

I said, "Think of something, somebody."

"One good thing," Hazel Marie said, "we can't miss that pickup. It stands out even in the dark. Miz Springer, try and get back in the outside lane, but stay with some other cars so he can't tailgate us again."

"I hope you have a plan," I said.

"Don't turn on your blinkers," she said. "We don't want to give him any warning. Just scoot on over whenever you can, and let's hope he loses track of which car we're in."

I did, but nobody liked me doing it. People can be so rude about blowing their horns. I just blew mine back.

"All right," I said, "I'm over here. Did he follow us?"

"You look, Miss Lillian," Hazel Marie said. "Me and Junior're gonna scrooch down so he'll only see two heads in the car, and maybe he'll think it's not us."

"He still in that other lane," Lillian said, "and they's a whole lot of cars around him an' us."

"Good," Hazel Marie mumbled from the floorboard. "Miz Springer, take the first busy exit into Greenville, then turn into the first street you come to on the right. Park on that street and cut your lights. If he follows us off the exit, maybe he'll keep on going."

I couldn't argue with the plan. It sounded like something that'd worked for her before, and it did again. We came off the interstate with several other cars, and as we left the ramp, Lillian said the pickup was still trying to get in the exit lane.

I parked the car on a dimly lit side street, turned off the lights, and kept the motor running. We sat there in the dark, listening to each other breathe and Little Lloyd sniffing.

"There it is!" Lillian pointed as the monster truck, black as the devil, passed at the end of the street. Jerome didn't slow down, apparently trying to catch up to where he thought we'd be. The roar of the truck's motor reverberated down the side street. I shuddered at the sight and sound of it, for it had to be the same truck I'd seen twice before. Now, thanks to Hazel Marie, I knew who was in it and, as she would've said, it scared the . . . well, pee-pee out of me.

"Lord," I said under my breath, "that thing could run us off the mountain and nobody'd ever know."

"What we gonna do if it come back at us?" Lillian asked. Her hands twisted in her lap, and I felt a twinge of guilt for putting her in this dangerous situation.

"We're gonna be gone," Hazel Marie said. "Miz Springer, ease on out now and get back on the interstate. We'll go back the way we came, now that he thinks we've gone this way."

I pulled out slowly, easing out of the side street and heading across the overpass to enter the interstate on the opposite side. More heavy traffic, but there was safety in numbers so I didn't mind it so much.

"This is not going to fool him long," I said.

"Yes'm," Hazel Marie said, "but by the time he figures it out, we ought to be far enough ahead to make it home all right."

"Well, an' that's another thing," Lillian said. "What we gonna do when we get home? If he really after us, ain't no being home gonna stop him."

"We can get help there," I said, trying to reassure her. And me. "If we have to, we'll sic Deputy Bates and Lieutenant Peavey and Binkie Enloe on him. We'll be all right once we get there. I just don't want to be driving alone on that mountain with him right behind us."

"Look, there's that TV station 'cross yonder." Lillian pointed past my face, but I was too busy to look. "They's still some people out in the parking lot. Talkin' 'bout us, I 'spect."

I heard some whispering between Little Lloyd and his mother, then he stuck his head up between the front seats. "Miss Lillian, I want to thank you for coming to get me. And you, too, Miz Springer. Me and my mama really 'preciate it."

"You so welcome, honey," Lillian said, patting his hand.

"Some things are just right to do," I said, then fearing that I'd sounded ungracious, changed the subject. "Lillian, tell us what happened when you went in there."

"Well, first thing, I didn't think I was gonna get in. They didn't like somebody knockin'

on they door that time a night. But them big
bills you give me changed they minds, like
it would anybody's. That first man what
come to the door, he wanted me to give
'em to him, but I say, 'No, I got my 'struc-
tions an' they got to go dreckly to Brother
Vern and Brother Stedman.' He keep tellin'
me they on the air an' can't be 'sturbed an'
I keep tellin' him I wait for 'em. Finally, he let
me go in the studio, but he tell me to stay
over in the corner outta the way till Miss
Rubynell sing again an' then I can hand
over the donations. That suited me, 'cause
everybody so busy they forget about me,
an' I stood there lookin' 'round for our little
boy an' wonderin' how can I get him to see
me."

"I saw you, Miss Lillian!" Little Lloyd said,
so excited that his glasses almost fell off. "I
couldn't believe it was you over in that corner. I didn't even see you come in."

"Well, the next thing I had to worry 'bout
was you sayin' somethin'. You know, out
loud, that'd let everybody know what was
up."

"But I knew better, didn't I? I didn't say a
thing, did I?" He was bouncing on the seat
and I almost said something to him, but

thought better of it with his mother there. I declare, I didn't know the child had that much life in him, which is just as well. I can't stand a nervous, talkative child, can you?

"You sho' didn't, honey. You did it just right. I jus' put my finger on my lips to shush you an' then motion you to come on to me."

"And you know what else I did, Mama? Miz Springer, guess what I did then? I whispered to one of the big kids that was on the show that I had to go to the bathroom and he said okay. And I just got up and left and Miss Lillian followed me. And then we ran, didn't we, Miss Lillian!"

"We made us some tracks, all right!" Lillian said, laughing.

I have to confess that I admired Little Lloyd's quick thinking, in spite of having to hear about it at full volume. Not many nine-year-olds would have their heads on so straight.

"I'm real proud of you, baby," Hazel Marie said, "and so glad to have you back."

We were all quiet as I maneuvered the car through the loop to put us back on I-26. The traffic thinned out as we began the climb toward Abbotsville. Nobody spoke, thinking either about our close calls or about Jerome, one.

There were no bright-beamed headlights behind us, so I leaned back and began to relax, keeping my hands lightly on the steering wheel. In spite of everything that'd happened and in spite of the fact that we were safely on the way home, not a one complimented me on my driving. Even though I really had the hang of it by then.

"Uh, speaking of going to the bathroom," Hazel Marie said.

"Just hold your water," I said. "I'm not about to stop on the side of the road with that Jerome after us. I'll come off on the next exit and we'll look for a cornfield."

I don't know why they thought that was so funny, but they laughed about it all the way home.

—

CHAPTER TWENTY-ONE

We all had a slow start the next morning, except for Lillian, who was up before seven getting breakfast for Deputy Bates. We didn't want him guessing we'd been tooling around two states in the middle of the night. I'd cautioned her before we'd gone to bed, saying we all needed to get our stories straight before telling anybody about our nighttime activities.

"Lieutenant Peavey told me not to leave town," I reminded her. "But what he don't know won't hurt him."

I got up about eight and checked on Hazel Marie and Little Lloyd in his room.

"I think I pulled something loose, Miz Springer," Hazel Marie said as she tried to sit up. "I'm awful sorry to be so much trouble. But I got my baby back, thanks to you and Miss Lillian, and I'll be all right."

"You stay right there in bed," I told her. "Here's some Tylenol, and if that doesn't help I'm taking you to the doctor today. Little Lloyd, run down and let Lillian give you some breakfast, but don't wake up Deputy Bates."

"Yes'm," he said, a brighter, happier child than I'd seen before. Not much improved in looks, though, I'll have to say, since he inherited so much from Wesley Lloyd.

"Did Brother Vern treat you all right?" I sat at the kitchen table with Little Lloyd while Lillian puttered around the sink. I noticed that so far he'd not retrieved his Winn-Dixie sack; at least it wasn't in his lap or by his chair.

"Yes'm, it was all right," he said, giving me quick glances like he was still afraid to look me in the eye. "I thought he was taking me to my mama."

"I thought so, too, or I'd've never let you leave with him. I want you to know that. But he didn't hurt you, did he?"

"No'm."

"What did he want with you? Did he ever say?"

"He said my mama wouldn't let him have something my daddy gave her. He thought I knew where it was, but I don't even know what it is."

Lillian said, "That man up to no good, if you ast me."

"Amen to that," I said. "Little Lloyd, I want you to stay inside today, either with me or Lillian. Your mother's not feeling well, so she needs to stay in bed.

"Lillian, I don't want to scare this child, but Brother Vern and Jerome Puckett may not be through with us. If you see that truck, or hear it, let me know. I want us all to stay close until we see what they're up to."

"This baby's not gonna be outta my sight," Lillian said. "Come on over here, honey, le's us make some biscuits for when Deputy Bates have his supper."

He got out of the chair, smiling, and went to her. For the first time since I'd known the child, and for just the briefest time, he didn't resemble Wesley Lloyd in the least.

———

The front doorbell rang as I started to leave them to it. Lillian and I looked at each other, then at Little Lloyd, whose face had gone white.

"It's nobody; don't worry," I said. "Jerome's not going to come to this house and announce himself. Lillian, you and Little Lloyd stay in here. I'll see who it is, and get rid of them as soon as I can." Unless it's Sam, I amended to myself.

It wasn't. It was Pastor Ledbetter, smiling confidently and not at all abashed over the outcome of our last meeting. Standing beside him was a short, thin man in a blue-and-white seersucker suit, the kind Wesley Lloyd wouldn't've been caught dead in. The man had a few strands of reddish hair combed carefully across the bald area where his hair had receded to a remarkable extent. He smiled without showing any teeth, stretching the thin mustache into a straight, dark line between his mouth and his nose. Milky blue eyes stared at me through gold-rimmed glasses, and it took me a minute to remember my manners.

"Why, good morning," I said, tearing my eyes away from the nondescript little man who had such a mesmerizing stare, and focusing on Pastor Ledbetter. He was looking too friendly for me to expect another lecture on a woman's responsibilities. That took a serious mind and a long face, but if he brought up Wesley Lloyd's estate again, I decided I'd transfer my membership. Maybe to the Episcopal church, where grown men get down on their knees. Which a lot of men, including the Presbyterian kind, ought to try. "I wasn't expecting you, Pastor, but do come in."

"Miss Julia," Pastor Ledbetter said, smiling broadly as he ushered in the stranger and followed him. "Sorry not to call first, but I wanted our newest member to meet you, so we just stepped across the street to introduce you. Dr. Fowler, this is Miss Julia Springer, who is one of our most active members. I don't know what First Church would do without her."

"How do you do, Mrs. Springer," the man said, shaking my hand. "Pleased to meet you. I'm Dr. Fred Fowler."

I don't trust people who have to make sure you know their titles, do you? And I've noticed that people with honorary titles are the worst offenders, so my guard went up another foot or so.

I got them seated and asked if they cared for anything to eat or drink. No, they both said, this was just an introductory meeting, which struck me as strange since Pastor Ledbetter had never made such a to-do over a new member before. At least to me, he hadn't. They sat side by side on my sofa, the little man smiling what seemed to me a secret smile, like he knew something that gave him pleasure, and Pastor Ledbetter giving me his broad, outgoing one.

"How've you been feeling, Miss Julia?" Pastor Ledbetter asked. "A little run-down lately?"

"No," I said cautiously, wondering at his concern. "Can't say that I have. I've been too busy to worry about how I'm feeling. How about you, Pastor, you feeling all right?"

"Oh," he said, laughing and glancing sideways at Dr. Fred Fowler, who sat with his eyes glued on me. I hadn't seen the man blink yet. "Nothing wrong with me an afternoon of golf wouldn't cure."

"Well, an afternoon of golf would cripple me," I said. Both seemed to think that was an exceptionally amusing thing to say. "Do you have a family, Dr. Fowler? I'd like to meet them and welcome them to town."

"No, I'm sorry to say. The Lord hasn't led me in that direction, but maybe I'll meet someone here."

"Maybe so, but I'm afraid there's not much to choose from in Abbotsville," I said, thinking of the dearth of available women in their fifties. "Are you planning to practice in Abbotsville, or have you come here to retire?"

"Oh, I don't have any plans to retire. I like my work," he said, crossing one leg over the other like he was perfectly at ease. I wasn't, because those eyes of his had a strange, penetrating look to them. If he thought he was going to get me up on another table in those metal contraptions again, he had another think coming. He studied me for a minute and said, "What would you think if I opened my practice in Abbotsville?"

"I wouldn't think much one way or the other," I said. "I'm not the one to ask. The Chamber of Commerce, maybe, or some of the other doctors could help you. But you're not a young man, if you don't mind my pointing it out. Aren't you starting out a little late in life?"

His smile stretched out broader, still with no teeth showing. I wondered if he'd needed braces as a child and hadn't gotten them. Dr. Fowler and Pastor Ledbetter glanced at each other, and Pastor Ledbetter raised his eyebrows.

"No," Dr. Fowler said, "I've been in practice for a number of years over in Chattanooga, but I'm feeling the need for a change. Have you ever felt that way, Mrs. Springer?"

I twisted my mouth, glancing from one to the other of them, wondering at the strangeness of the conversation. I tried to make allowances, though, because even some educated people have poor social skills. "No, I can't say I have. My feeling is that if you move around too much, people think you're flighty. It's especially bad where doctors are concerned, as I expect you know. People always wonder about a doctor who picks up and moves somewhere else; they wonder if something's wrong with him. I hope I haven't offended you, but the way people are couldn't be news to you."

"No, indeed," he said, putting his hands together and resting his fingers against his chin. "Mrs. Springer, I can see that you're a discerning judge of people, and I'd like to speak with you again, if I may. Could you spare some time to, well, just sit and talk every now and then?"

"I'm not sure. I'm pretty busy these days, but I'd like to help you if I can."

"I'm sure you'll manage it," Pastor Ledbetter said, rising to his feet. Dr. Fowler followed, holding his hand out to me as my preacher kept trying to get a commitment. "You could meet over at the church," he said, resting a heavy hand on my shoulder. "You can show Dr. Fowler around and tell him about the church and the town and yourself, as well." Pastor Ledbetter turned to the doctor. "She knows all the local history."

"It would be a pleasure," Dr. Fowler said. "Can we say ten o'clock this Friday?"

"I'm not sure I can do it then," I said, feeling uneasy over their combined efforts. "In fact, I'm sure I can't this Friday. Maybe sometime next week, or maybe Pastor Ledbetter can find somebody else to talk with you."

"I'd really rather it be you, Mrs. Springer," Dr. Fowler said, holding my hand and giving it a little squeeze. He wasn't that young, but he was too young to be flirting with me. I'd heard of men who preyed on wealthy widows regardless of age differences. I drew my hand away and stepped back.

"It's got to be you or nobody, Miss Julia," Pastor Ledbetter said in his heartiest manner.

I smiled and walked them to the door. "Maybe you should prepare yourself for nobody," I said. They both thought that was a clever thing to say, and they left smiling and shaking their heads.

I watched them walk across the street, Pastor Ledbetter leaning over the shorter man, talking nonstop and gesturing with his hands. I crossed my arms and shook my head. This beat all I'd ever seen. I couldn't wait to tell Lillian that my preacher was now playing Cupid. I leaned against the door and laughed to myself. I might even tell Sam, too.

I turned back into the living room, still smiling. I don't care how old you get, the least hint of a man's interest is enough to lift up your heart. I hate to admit it, but it's the truth even when it's from a man so unlikely as to slightly turn your stomach. Wonder what makes a woman so dependent on a man's good graces? There was little about Dr. Fowler that appealed to me, except that I seemed to appeal to him. And that was enough to brighten my outlook considerably. I'm just as foolish as the next woman, I guess.

I sat down in the chair by the front window and looked across the street at the church. It stood there, benign and holy, with its spire reaching toward heaven. A place of sanctuary and worship, yet there'd been so many upsets and hurt feelings and cliques and intrigues and downright battles in it, you wouldn't believe. And something was going on over there now. If I could only figure out what.

Leaning my elbow on the arm of the chair, I studied the problem. Pastor Ledbetter, unlike our previous preachers, had never been one to be guided or instructed or counseled by anybody. Except by Wesley Lloyd, who was no longer around to make his will known. So, what Pastor Ledbetter wanted, he got. And now, I realized with a start, what he wanted was a money-eating monument to family values, whatever they were, that he called an "activities center." An activities center built with the assets of Wesley Lloyd Springer, that widely known paragon of traditional family values.

I jumped from the chair so fast I got a catch in my back. That's what was on the preacher's mind. *That's* why he was over here making me feel I was in the inner circle. Drawing me in, that's what he was doing.

But how did Dr. Fred Fowler, newcomer and special friend of the pastor, fit in?

I walked the floor, rubbing out the crick in my lower back, trying to figure how Pastor Ledbetter's mind worked. Not an easy job, unless you understood that he never gave up on anything. He had the patience of Job, because I'd seen him work his will in spite of opposition from the session. But only since Wesley Lloyd had passed, of course. So it stood to reason that he still had building on his mind.

Maybe Dr. Fowler had money to burn. Doctors make it hand over fist, don't you know. Maybe Pastor Ledbetter was thinking that, with contributions from Dr. Fowler and, if he couldn't break Wesley Lloyd's will, from me, he could break ground any day.

That was it, I was sure of it. Get Dr. Fowler and me together, make us feel *chosen* to donate to the church, and he'd get what he wanted. The man would stop at nothing to do the Lord's work as he saw it. It made no difference if somebody else saw the Lord's work in a different light. Pastor Ledbetter had a hot line to heaven and nobody could tell him it might be a party line.

Well, he was just going to have to dial in again, because I wasn't about to be manipulated by the likes of him. The thing to do was to find out if Dr. Fowler was in on the plan or if he was being played for a fool like I was. Some way or another I needed to get close to the good doctor and see if his interest was in me as a woman or in me as the means to a pile of bricks with a commemorative plaque on it.

And they'd given me the perfect way to go about it.

CHAPTER TWENTY-TWO

—

"Lillian," I called toward the kitchen, "I'm going over to the church."

"What for?" she yelled back, but I was already out the door.

I hurried across the street and the parking lot, hoping to catch Dr. Fowler before he left. If I could get him off in the bowels of the church by himself, I ought to be able to find out whether his interest was in me or my pocketbook.

When I swung open the door to the fellowship hall, I saw the two of them, still talking, at the far end near Pastor Ledbetter's office suite. Their eyes lit up when they saw me.

"Miss Julia," the pastor called, coming toward me with his hand out. "I hoped you'd change your mind. I was just telling Dr. Fowler how much we need your input and he's so anxious to get to know you better."

"Well," I said, "I find I have a little time this morning, so, Dr. Fowler," I said, turning to him, "if you still want a tour of the church, we can do it now."

"Indeed I do," Dr. Fowler said. "I'd be delighted to have a lovely lady show me around. Here, take my arm and let us proceed."

Now that's a gentleman for you. I put my hand in the crook of his seersucker-clad arm, smiling at him and wishing I could smile up at him, instead of across and maybe a little down. But beggars and widows can't be choosers, and I confess to a little glow at the thought of any kind of interested party, even if the party was on the short side.

"Splendid," Pastor Ledbetter said, showing his teeth in a wide smile. "I couldn't ask for a better arrangement. Now y'all take your time. Nothing's going on in the church right now, no meetings or anything, so just wander around as long as you want. I'll do some work on my sermon, then come track you down about twelve and we'll see about lunch."

"That's fine," Dr. Fowler said, staring at me as he spoke. "Miss Julia and I are going to explore this magnificent building. Aren't we, Miss Julia?" And he patted my hand as it still rested on his arm.

"Yes, and I'll begin by pointing out that we're now in the fellowship hall, where we have prayer meeting on Wednesday nights with covered-dish suppers. A Boy Scout troop used to meet here, until a former pastor put a stop to it on the grounds that they weren't Christian enough." I waved my free hand around the large basement room, linoleum-floored and stacked with folding tables and chairs along the walls.

Dr. Fowler and I climbed the stairs to the sanctuary on the main floor, with him holding doors for me and watching each step I took. Those strange eyes didn't miss a trick.

As we stood at the back of the empty sanctuary, I was struck again by how spacious and elegant it was. White walls with cream-painted moldings, deep red carpeting down the center aisle that attracted any number of brides because of its proces-

sional value, red velvet pew cushions donated by a group with bony backsides,
eight large Williamsburg brass chandeliers,
double pulpits, choir loft with rows of organ
pipes on either side. A beautiful and worthy
place to worship the Lord, and considering
what it cost to build and furnish, it ought've
been.

We strolled up the aisle, arm in arm, and I
pointed out the pew where I always sat. I
showed the doctor one of the hymn books
with Wesley Lloyd's name on a sticker inside the front cover.

"You must miss him very much," Dr.
Fowler said tenderly.

"Not especially," I said, feeling I should be
truthful in the Lord's sanctuary, and assuming that Dr. Fowler had been apprised of
some of Wesley Lloyd's inclinations.

"Well, the heart closes over pain and begins to heal itself," Dr. Fowler said, "and I
expect that's happening to you." He
seemed so sympathetic to my plight that I
gave him credit for being a better physician
than his looks suggested.

We walked behind the choir loft, glancing,
as we passed, into the practice rooms
where dark red choir robes hung in rows.

Then we strolled down the hall and into the new Sunday school building. By that time, Dr. Fowler had taken my hand from his arm to hold with his own. He had our hands clasped up close to his side. I pretended I didn't notice the change, chattering on about how this building had been attached to the original one, and how many Sunday school rooms it had, and how many members used it, and so on and so on. You know how I get when I'm nervous.

"Miss Julia," he said, slowing his steps and leaning slightly toward me. "Julia, you just seem so much at home here. I can tell that you are in your element, right here in this sacred place."

My heart, or something, fluttered. What a nice compliment, since I'd always considered myself a deeply spiritual person. And this doctor was the only one who'd recognized it. He was exceptionally perceptive, and I predicted he'd do well in his new practice. But this wasn't getting the information I needed, so I stopped that train of thought.

"I want to show you the chapel," I said, moving with him down the hall. "It's a very small sanctuary that was donated by the

Belcher family, and it got away with Wesley Lloyd something awful because he didn't think of it first. See, here it is." I opened a door with my free hand, and we looked into the beautiful room, shimmering now with the morning sun streaming through the stained-glass windows.

"Lovely," he breathed.

I nodded in agreement, then realized he was staring at me. I declare, I'd not had so much attention directed my way since Wesley Lloyd's funeral. I felt an unfamiliar tremble work its way down deep inside of me, and I had to work to pull myself together.

Still and all, it'd been such a long time since I'd been in proximity to a man that I believed I'd be forgiven for enjoying a tingle or two. Who would know? Wesley Lloyd hadn't been interred all that long but, let's face it, his mind hadn't been entirely centered on home life for some little while.

"The church provides for a lot of the needs of its members," I said, subduing a tremble in my voice. "But Pastor Ledbetter seems to think we need a new building for family activities."

"Family activities are very important," Dr. Fowler said, his voice lowered to match the holiness of the place, his eyes searching mine, "especially in this day and age. Now, dear lady, what else do you have to show me? I'm entirely in your sweet hands."

I swear, which I hardly ever do, my knees started to buckle. My mind was telling me that Dr. Fowler wasn't all that attractive—short, skinny as a rail, red hair, pale skin, and wispy hair, what there was of it, had never been to my taste—but my senses were being powerfully moved and not by the thought of building plans. And here was a man looking deep into my eyes, breathing in little gasps and saying the sweetest things. He could be appealing, in the right light, to any neglected woman.

"Why don't we walk over here," I said with a little quiver, as he covered my hand with both of his. "I want to show you the bridal parlor. We have a lot of weddings in the chapel, small weddings, you know, and especially second weddings." I believe I actually tittered as we walked into the parlor. "I mean, people who are marrying for the second time. Widows, and the like."

"Lovely," he said again, and glanced at me.

It was a lovely room, done all in shades of

green—carpet, walls, draperies, uphol-stered chairs and love seat. Very soothing and inviting. Wesley Lloyd had contributed toward the furnishings, especially the gilt-framed portraits of former pastors and leading lights of the church, which included his father and grandfather.

"I can see," Dr. Fowler said, rubbing his hand over mine, "how this room would mean a lot to someone just beginning a new marriage. Second marriages can be very fulfilling."

I took a deep breath and breathed out through my mouth. "It's a little warm in here," I said, fanning the bodice of my dress as discreetly as I could. "They don't keep this building very cool during the week."

I indicated the portraits on the wall, which was all I could manage at the time, and we walked slowly around the room. Dr. Fowler read the brass plate on each one, all the while keeping me close to his side.

To tell the truth, I thought the feelings that were coursing up and down inside of me had been banked years ago along with the ashes of my marriage, but skinny little Dr. Fowler was proving virile enough to stoke

my fire. And don't talk to me about age. If
you haven't lived sixty-some-odd years
maintaining a ladylike deportment in all areas of life, you don't know what'll suddenly
turn on when you least expect it. Age and
deprivation are powerful stimulants, and, if
you don't believe me, wait till it happens to
you.

Dr. Fowler turned away from the portrait
he'd been studying and caught his breath
as he brushed against me. He backed
against the wall, still holding my hand, and
I stepped closer before I could help myself.
Drawn by animal magnetism and Old
Spice. I leaned in for a bigger whiff. I'd always been a fool for Old Spice.

"Oh," I whispered.

"Julia," he said, his voice strident with ur-
gency.

I pulled his hand up to the middle of my
bosom, without letting it touch anything important, and leaned into him. Excitement
thundered like a drum in my head.

"Miss Julia!" His eyes darted around the
room.

"Don't worry. We're alone," I whispered,
wishing he had enough hair for me to run
my fingers through. In fact, there were a lot

of things I wished were different about him but, if I kept my eyes closed, I could concentrate on my feelings and not on his looks. It'd been a long time since I'd felt anything close to such heady emotion, and I wanted to make the most of it as long as he was willing. Which he certainly seemed to be.

"I . . . I know we are." His voice squeaked, high and shrill. But passion can do that to a man.

He twisted his hand in mine, but I held on tight and put my face against his neck, wet now with perspiration. A man in heat. I'd about forgotten what one was like.

"Miss Julia . . . please," he gasped, turning his head so I could snuggle closer.

Lord, when a man is so carried away that he begs for your favors, a woman can be forgiven for having her spirits lifted.

"Shhh," I whispered, not realizing I was so close to his ear.

He squawked. I have to be honest, that's what he did, and it almost closed me down. But I'd read that in the throes of passion some men make strange noises, some cry out, and others hold their peace. Wesley Lloyd had been in the last category, and I found it interesting to be tangling with a different sort this go-round. It takes all kinds, don't you know.

"Miss Julia," he whispered, frantically wiggling his body between me and the wall. "I *must*—"

"No, wait," I said, understanding now what the word *fast* meant.

"You don't understand," he said, putting his free hand on my waist and turning me toward the love seat.

"I believe I do," I gasped. Lord, I wished the man looked a little better, but I was running a fever by that time. Finding out about Pastor Ledbetter's plans had gone completely out of my head.

I closed my eyes tighter, letting the darkness bring Wesley Lloyd's preferences to mind. He preferred to conduct our business in the dark and by feel.

As Dr. Fowler clasped my waist tighter and pushed himself away from the wall and against me, I felt his rising interest.

"I have to . . ." he croaked, pushing me backward. "I *really* have to get—"

The door slammed open, and we both jumped about a foot. Away from each other.

"What in *the* world?" Pastor Ledbetter stood there, bug-eyed and open-mouthed.

". . . *out of here!*" Dr. Fowler bellowed. He ran to the pastor and edged behind him. "The woman's crazy, Larry, just like you said. My God, she practically ravished me!"

Dr. Fowler's flushed face glared at me. He patted his straggly hair and pulled his suit coat together. With trembling fingers, he buttoned it closed.

"This . . . this woman," he went on, his voice quaking with outrage. "Larry, you wouldn't believe."

"Yes," Pastor Ledbetter said, sorrow pulling at his long face and slumping shoulders. "Yes, I would. I saw it for myself. Miss Julia, what are we going to do with you? You know we can't have this sort of thing. And in the church, too. I am so disappointed in you, and so very sorry for you."

"I couldn't control her, Larry," Dr. Fowler said, finally getting his breathing under control. "I tried to get away, but I've never seen such a deluded patient walking around free before."

Mortification swept over and through me, as I reinterpreted Dr. Fowler's words and actions of a few moments before. My Lord, what a fool I'd made of myself.

I did the only thing I could. I fainted.

When my eyes popped open, I was lying on the green velvet love seat in the bridal parlor, my head flat and my legs dangling over the arm of the sofa. Pastor Ledbetter sat on a straight chair next to me, fanning my face with a legal-size envelope.

"I think I'll just lie here and die, Pastor," I said as the humiliating memory flooded my mind.

"No, no," he said soothingly. "You mustn't say that. You've allowed Satan to have the upper hand, Miss Julia, and now you have to fight back. He's left you with a sickness of the soul."

"You think so?" I covered my eyes with my hand, so tired and unnerved I couldn't bear the light.

"Oh, yes. Dr. Fowler says so."

I shuddered. "Where is he?"

"He's gone, don't worry. He thought he ought to leave in case his presence caused a, ah, recurrence."

"Little danger of that," I mumbled, and

turned my face into the sofa. "I just don't know what got into me. I thought . . . well, it doesn't matter now what I thought."

"Miss Julia, I know you were acting out of character, and that you weren't in control of yourself. Dr. Fowler thinks you need therapy before it happens again."

"Therapy?" I turned to face him, keeping my hand over my eyes but looking at him through my fingers. "He thinks I'm that bad off? What's wrong with me?"

"Have you ever heard of"—he lowered his voice to a whisper as he leaned over me— "nym-pho-*man*-ia?"

"Nympho . . . *oh!*" My heart skipped and thudded, and I clutched at my chest as he pronounced the name of my affliction in broad daylight. The word I'd only heard whispered about and guessed at, the word that was tinged with dark, voracious appetites. I could hardly get my breath.

"Do you understand me, Miss Julia?" he demanded. I just lay there, staring at the ceiling, trying to take it in. "We are talking mortal danger here, and something has to be done. You are not only risking your own soul, but also the soul of any man you come in contact with. You can't play around with something like nympho-*man*-ia. I've studied up on it, along with other sins of the flesh, and I know what I'm talking about."

"What does it mean?" I whispered.

"Opinions differ, Miss Julia." Pastor Ledbetter sat back in his chair and shifted into a teaching mode. "Some so-called experts say you're born with a natural inclination for unnatural acts and can't be changed. Others say it's a learned response to childhood trauma, an arrested state of emotional development, and that it's a normal, alternate lifestyle. Of course, Christians know better, don't we? We know it's sin, which can be overcome by exercising the will and being forgiven through grace. Afflicted people can choose to live normal, decent lives. And that's what you want to do, isn't it?"

"Oh, yes, I do. And, Pastor, I've always lived a normal, decent life. I really have. I couldn't've had this condition all my life and not known it, could I? This just had to've been an error in judgment, an aberration, or something."

"No," he said, so forcefully that I cringed against the cushion. "You have to call it what it is. It is *sin,* and nothing less. You have to admit it and face it head-on. You may've been able to hide these impulses even from yourself, but now, with the grief of Mr. Springer's passing and the upset of that errant child, you've allowed this, this *debauchery* to rear its ugly head. Dr. Fowler is practically a stranger to you and look what happened with him. Who can tell what you'll do with somebody you know?"

He was right. If I could go after somebody as unappetizing as Dr. Fowler, there wasn't a man in town safe from me. The thought of flinging myself on Brother Vern or Leonard Conover or Lieutenant Peavey caused an ominous rumble from my stomach. Then I thought of Sam, and covered my face again.

"Pastor, don't tell anybody about this," I begged as tears streamed down my face onto the velvet love seat. "Please promise you won't tell. I'll get some help. I'll do anything, just don't tell anybody." I clutched at his hand, pleading with him and trying to stop his infernal fanning. "Especially Norma Cantrell. She'll blab it everywhere."

"Listen to me now," Pastor Ledbetter said as he pulled a large handkerchief from his hip pocket and gave it to me. "I'm not going to tell a soul. But you must promise me to get some help, and I firmly believe you can be helped. With prayer and obedience to the Word of God and Christian counseling, this problem can be overcome. But, Miss Julia, you must have someone trustworthy look after your affairs while you're so incapacitated."

"Binkie's doing that," I said, trying to blow my nose from a prone position.

"Miss Enloe's not a member of our church, and I think your guardian should be someone with the same values that you have."

"Guardian?" I said, struggling against the velvet to sit up. "You think I need a guardian?"

"It's the usual procedure in cases of this kind, all perfectly legal and aboveboard. A guardian would be appointed to protect your interests, and it would be for your own good, Miss Julia. I don't want to see you put away by court order, which could happen if you do this again and it becomes public."

"Public," I repeated. I swung my feet to the floor, testing my balance and the floor's stability. "Pastor, I'll do anything to keep this from becoming the talk of the town.

And don't worry about it happening again. I'm staying away from red-headed men, for one thing. So as far as therapy and a guardian are concerned, I've got to give that some thought."

"Don't take too long, I beg you," he said, sitting back in his chair and observing me. "It would be better for all concerned if you did this voluntarily. If it comes to a hearing, your condition will become public knowledge. As an ordained minister of the Word, I can't continue to ignore a sin committed before my very eyes. You need to know that the Lord has already burdened my heart about you and some of the decisions you've made long before today."

Mercy, I thought, as my eyes rolled back in my head. When you're threatened with the leading of the Lord, you're in real trouble.

"I'd appreciate it if you'd call Lillian to come get me," I finally managed to say.

"I'll walk you home, or maybe I'd better drive you across the street."

"No. Thank you, anyway." It was all too much for me. I started crying again, wanting only to curl up in a corner of my house with a sack over my head. "Call Lillian for me. Please, I just want Lillian."

Chapter Twenty-three

—

As soon as Lillian showed up, Pastor Ledbetter told her I'd had a weak spell and needed to be watched carefully. She took one look at me and got me out of the church. She walked me across the street and into the house and, before I knew it, I was in bed with a cold cloth on my forehead and a lunch tray on my lap. And she did it without any questions or fussing or mumbling under her breath, much less any eye rolling. She was a tower of strength, which I badly needed.

"You can take the tray, Lillian. I can't eat."

"You better eat something," she said. "What happened to you, anyway?"

"Oh, Lillian, it was awful." I reached up and pulled the cloth over my eyes. I didn't know how I could ever face anybody again after mortifying myself the way I'd done.

"A weak spell can't be that bad, 'less you fall and show more'n you want to," she said as she stood with her hands on her hips. "What you need is a doctor and you better see one fast."

"I know, and I will. Just as soon as I get my strength back."

"Well, then, you can start with this soup. Liquids is what you need." That was Lillian's remedy for everything. She held out a spoon, and when I didn't take it she said, "You want me to feed you?"

"I do not." I pressed the cloth tighter to sop up the overflow. "Just let me rest a little, then I'll eat."

When she left for the kitchen, pictures of what I'd done during the past hour tormented my mind until I thought I'd throw up with the shame of it all. Worst of all, Pastor Ledbetter and that awful Dr. Fowler knew how I'd acted up, and they were going to make me go tell somebody else about it. How could I go into some doctor's office and say, *"Sorry to bother you, but I'm a nymphomaniac"*?

I ran through my mind all the doctors in

town. As far as I knew, none of them spe-
cialized in sudden and uncontrollable fits of
physical appetite. And they were all men,
and what if I had an attack of it while I was
being examined?

I moaned aloud.

And if they wrote me a prescription for the
condition, would Buck Tatum fill it and
know what I was being treated for?

I writhed with mortification. And sloshed
soup all over the tray.

What I needed was an expert, a confidential expert who wouldn't blab all over the
place.

An expert, I thought, and snatched the
cloth off my eyes. Lord, there was an expert
right across the hall, if I could only ask her.
But I couldn't. I couldn't confide in anybody. Not Hazel Marie, not Lillian, not
Binkie nor Sam. No one could know, and I
determined to do whatever it took to keep
my affliction a secret.

My head swam as I tried to think through
this sudden change of life. Pastor Ledbetter'd said I needed a guardian, but what did
that mean? Just someone to manage my
money, or someone who'd follow me
around all day to keep me from attacking

every man I met? And he'd implied, or maybe he'd said, that if I didn't appoint one myself he was going to take steps. Public ones, too.

Lord, I'd thought that child showing up on my doorstep was as bad as things could get. I was wrong. What in the world was I going to do?

My head snapped up as the answer suddenly came to me. I'd heard Pastor Ledbetter say a million times that prayer could move mountains, and here was the perfect test. I'd pray like I'd never prayed before and depend on the Lord to cure me so I wouldn't need a guardian.

Then I remembered what the pastor had said about it being a matter of will, which, coming from a Calvinist, didn't make sense. How could you exercise free will and, at the same time, have your life planned, plotted, and predestinated?

If I wasn't careful, I'd give myself a headache with such theological problems. I had to keep it simple. I'd pray my heart out, and I'd steer clear of men, all shapes and sizes of them. Yes, I'd pray for a cure and, while I was at it, I'd pray that the Lord would keep the mouths of those two shut.

And if that didn't work, I'd deny it till my dying day.

"Now, what was that about, I wonder?" I hung up the phone with hands shaking so bad I had to hide them from Lillian. In an effort to appear normal, I'd made myself come down to the kitchen. I didn't want to alarm Lillian by hiding in bed all day.

Little Lloyd was standing on a stool at the sink while Lillian showed him how to shuck corn for supper. I'd just assured her that I was fully recovered from my weak spell when the phone interrupted us.

"What?" she asked. "That wadn't that Brother Vern, was it?"

"No, not him," I said, frowning with concern. "It was LuAnne Conover, wanting to know how I'm feeling."

"What you troubled 'bout that for?"

"Because she was calling to ask the state of my health, that's why. She usually has a dozen things to talk about, not how I'm feeling. You want a glass of tea, Lillian? Little Lloyd? I declare, before another summer gets here, I'm going to air-condition this house."

"The whole thing?"

"The whole thing."

"I been meaning to ast you 'bout one of them little units for the kitchen," she said. "But the whole house'd be better. Sometime it get so hot, I have to open the Frigidaire and stand in front of it."

My land, I thought, no wonder the electric bill's so high.

I put my tea on the table and sat down, listening to Lillian tell Little Lloyd how to get the silk off the ears. Then, still frowning, I propped my elbow on the table and rested my chin on my hand. Unbidden images of the fool I'd made of myself flooded my mind, so that I had to hold on to the table to keep from crawling under it. Gradually, my thoughts centered less on my shameful actions and more on Dr. Fowler's responses to them. Mercy, I thought as I suddenly sat up straight, I couldn't have mistaken that. It'd been a long time since I'd been in a face-to-face situation with a man, but you certainly don't mistake a thing like that.

Anger flashed through me like one of Troy Beckworth's sea surges. They'd blamed it all on me, said I was crazy, called me a . . . well, a you-know-what, and all the while that man had been as interested as I'd been. And then denied it, and said I needed a guardian. And therapy, of all things.

I squinched my eyes together, recalling Pastor Ledbetter's opportune arrival. My Lord, could they have planned it all?

I couldn't believe such a thing of my pastor, but then, a good many men had been doing things I couldn't believe. I wasn't a nymphomaniac, couldn't possibly be. Not and crawl into a lonely bed every night, even when Wesley Lloyd had been in it.

Those two had been playing with my mind, and they'd done a pretty good job of it. Well, I'd show them a thing or two. Sam still had control of Wesley Lloyd's estate and it would take months to get that settled. Until then, no one else could lay a hand on it. And as far as a guardian for me, I'd go them one better and appoint two. Between Binkie and Lillian, I ought to be well looked after, even if I didn't tell them why they needed to watch me. And, just to be on the safe side, I'd watch myself whenever a man came around.

———

The doorbell rang, putting me to the test then and there.

"I'll get it, Lillian," I said, halfway hoping it would be Pastor Ledbetter so I could let him know that Dr. Fowler's actions hadn't been so innocent, either. I'd tell him I suspected a conspiracy between the two of them, and that I just might sue their pants off. Well, not that, exactly.

On my way to the door, I stopped dead still in the dining room. I couldn't threaten them with a thing. All they had to do was tell one person, and the news of my so-called affliction would be all over town by nightfall. I'd never live it down.

The doorbell rang again, bringing me to myself, as well as to the unwelcome presence of Lieutenant Peavey.

I invited him in, gathering my strength to put on a good show of being pleased to see him. He'd intimidated me even before I had so much more to hide. I offered him a chair, and I took one across the room where I hoped he'd be safe if my condition suddenly flared up. No telling what I might do if Pastor Ledbetter's diagnosis had been anywhere close to accurate. I figured it was better to err on the side of caution until I could get a second opinion.

I tried not to look too closely at Lieutenant Peavey, but he seemed bigger than anything in the room, including the mahogany breakfront with my collection of mother-of-pearl oyster plates.

"Mrs. Springer," he started, taking out his little notebook and clicking his pen. "I'd like to ask you a few questions about a matter that's recently come up."

"My lawyer's not here."

"That's all right, but you can call him, if you feel you need him."

"Her."

"Ma'am?"

"My lawyer. It's a her, Binkie Enloe."

"Well," he said, twisting his neck like his collar was too tight. Binkie had that effect on people. "Well, she's a good'un. But, Mrs. Springer, I guess I misspoke myself. I'm here not so much to question you as to pass on some information and see if it has anything to do with what happened here last week."

I sat up at that. "What information?"

"Our department, along with several others in the area, has been notified by the

Spartanburg Sheriff's Department that a
child, a little boy, was kidnapped last
night."

My eyelids fluttered. "Kidnapped?"

"Yes, all the surrounding law-enforcement
units are working on it, and they'll probably
call the FBI in before long. Seems a black
female walked into a television studio down
there, and took the child before anybody
knew what was happening. When I saw the
name, Puckett, I figured it might be one of
our Abbot County Pucketts."

"Why, that's terrible," I said, wondering if
he could hear my heart pounding away.
"Lieutenant, excuse me for just a minute. I
left something on the stove and I need to
turn it off before it burns." I got up and hurried toward the kitchen. "I'll just be a
minute," I called back.

I slipped through the kitchen door and
closed it behind me. "Lillian," I hissed, motioning to her. "Don't say a word; don't say
anything. You and Little Lloyd get over here
quick."

"What you want?"

"Shhh, I told you, don't say anything. Get
in the pantry. You, too, Little Lloyd, get in

here." I pushed them both into the pantry and closed the door behind us.

"What is it? What is it?" Little Lloyd jittered around so much that his glasses went cockeyed on him. Then he clutched at Lillian.

I patted his shoulder. "Don't worry," I told him. "We're going to look after you, but you two need to stay in here and not make a sound. No matter what you hear, you've got to stay quiet."

"What's goin' on out there?" Lillian asked. Whispered, rather. "Who was that at the door? Was it that Brother Vern?"

"No. Worse than him. It's Lieutenant Peavey, and all the police in two states are looking for Little Lloyd."

I clamped my hand over her mouth. "Don't scream. Stay quiet. I'm going to get rid of him before he finds out we've got this child and takes him away from us. You're not going to scream, are you?"

She shook her head, her eyes rolling as much as mine ever had. She grabbed my hand and jerked it away. "I ain't about to do no screaming. What you think I am? Now, you ain't gonna turn this chile over to the law, are you?"

"Of course not. Why do you think we're in the pantry? Little Lloyd, you stay right here with Lillian and don't be afraid. We'll figure out what to do as soon as he leaves."

I went back into the living room, apologizing for having to interrupt the lieutenant's flow of information. "You know how it is," I said. "When you've got several pans on the stove, you have to watch them like a hawk. I declare, I do love to cook." If he believed that, he'd believe anything.

"Now, tell me more about that poor little kidnapped child," I said, smoothing my dress as I sat down.

"I'm trying to establish if the child who was taken in Spartanburg was the same one who left here Sunday. The one you told me about yesterday. What was his name?"

"Wesley Lloyd Junior Springer. Puckett, I mean Puckett."

"Which is it? Springer or Puckett?" He was making notes in his little book.

"It's complicated, Lieutenant. I think he's known as a Springer, but legally he's a Puckett."

"I don't understand."

"I don't either."

He shook his head, frowning as he studied his notes. "Could you describe the child you know? The fax we got didn't have much of a description. About nine years old, wearing glasses, sandy hair."

"Sounds close," I said, thinking that I could show him a picture of Wesley Lloyd and he could get a fairly accurate description of the child. But then, I could've produced the child himself. "Do they have a description of the person who took him?"

"African-American female in a nurse's uniform, heavyset but not fat. Quick on her feet, they said. Got into a car that tried to run over the people chasing them, so she had at least one accomplice."

"Accomplice," I repeated, hoping he didn't notice the tremor in my voice. "What kind of car?"

"New, dark-colored, possibly foreign make," he said. "That's the best they could do, 'cause the car didn't have any lights on and witnesses said the driver tried to run them all down. One scared bunch of people, from what I understand. The officer I talked to said there were a lot of children appearing on a program at the time. The parents were convinced that it was a liberal plot to kidnap one of theirs to stop their ministry. Pretty confusing, I gather. A dozen kids taken to the station, all crying and terrified. Parents demanding police protection, and it was a while before the officers determined who'd been taken. Turned out to be this Puckett kid, but the uncle who claimed to be his guardian couldn't or wouldn't give them much information." I could tell he was watching my reaction, at least those dark aviator glasses were trained on me like a double-barreled shotgun. "It's a strange situation."

"Very strange," I said, making every effort to look straight back at him. "I hate to hear it anytime a child's been kidnapped and I hope to goodness it wasn't the little boy who visited me. But I understand there're a lot of Pucketts."

"They are that," he said, closing his notebook and standing. "Well, Mrs. Springer, if you hear from the boy you know, call me so I can at least eliminate one of them."

"I'll surely do that, but as far as I knew on Sunday, he was going to Raleigh to be with his mother." That was certainly what I believed to be true on Sunday. "You were going to find out if he made it, weren't you?"

"Right. I'll double-check that today. Well, I 'preciate your time, Mrs. Springer."

"You're quite welcome," I said, walking him to the door. "I'd like to know how this turns out. I do hope you find the child. And whoever took him."

"We'll find 'em," he said, that mouth set in a hard line. I looked away, determined not to notice mouths anymore. "One thing I can't stand is somebody who'd hurt a child. I don't know how you feel, Mrs. Springer, but most of us in law enforcement are glad to have the death penalty in this state."

"Ah," I swallowed hard. "So am I." I hoped my face didn't look as bloodless as it felt. I closed and locked the door behind him, then ran to the kitchen.

Chapter Twenty-four

—

"Come on out," I whispered to Lillian and Little Lloyd. "But stay away from the windows. I don't want anybody to see you."

"How'm I gonna cook supper and stay away from the windows?" Lillian said, holding on to Little Lloyd and peeking around the pantry door.

"I just want to make sure he's gone and not coming back. I'll tell you, Lillian, I never knew that it's just as hard to keep quiet about the truth as it is to tell an outright lie."

"I ain't worrin' 'bout lyin', I'm worrin' 'bout goin' to jail," she said.

Little Lloyd said, "I don't want you to go to jail, Miss Lillian."

"Don't you worry," I said. "Nobody's go-

ing to jail, least of all Lillian. I mean, if anybody goes, we all will."

"My mama, too?" Panic washed over Little Lloyd's face as he clutched at Lillian.

"Miss Julia, you scarin' this chile, an' me
too."

"I'm sorry, I'm sorry. I was just thinking
out loud. Now, let's get ourselves together.
Lillian, do you think Miss Puckett would be
able to get along by herself?"

"She can't hardly get outta bed by herself.
You not aimin' to put her out, are you?"

"No, no," I said, waving my hand. "I
thought, if she could manage it, I'd take her
and Little Lloyd off somewhere till this all
blows over."

"This ain't gonna blow over," Lillian reminded me. " 'Specially since they got the
police in it. How you reckon they knowed to
be lookin' for him?"

I was afraid she'd ask that. "Well," I said,
"the fact of the matter is, somebody down
there reported it. Claimed the boy's been
kidnapped."

"Kidnapped!" I was surprised they didn't
hear her down on Main Street.

"Shhh, not so loud. Now, look, it's not so
bad—"

"Don't tell me it's not so bad. It can't get no worse!"

"Actually, it can. They have a description of you as the one who kidnapped him."

"Oh, Jesus!" She grabbed Little Lloyd and hugged him to her, almost suffocating him in the process. "What we gonna do, Miss Julia? You know I ain't no kidnapper. I jus' get this baby back to his mama where he belong. Oh, Jesus!"

"Lillian, Lillian. Listen to me now. This is certainly an unexpected turn, but we're going to handle it. They don't know it was you, just somebody like you, and they don't know that Little Lloyd is here, or his mother, either. They're not even thinking of looking here for either of them."

"They gonna be lookin' for me an' this chile ever'where an' they not gonna stop till they find us." She wiped her eyes with her apron, then clasped Little Lloyd again. "But don't you worry, honey, you worth all this worry an' then some."

He didn't look convinced. And I certainly wasn't.

"Here's what we're going to do," I said, with more assurance than I really felt.

"Much as I hate to do it, I'll have to get Sam over here, and Binkie."

"How Miss Binkie gonna get us outta this mess?" Lillian asked. "They say she smart, but I went in an' got this chile an' you drove the getaway car, an' this the evidence right here in front of us." She rubbed her hand across the head of the "evidence."

"You forget, Lillian, that his mother is right upstairs. How can he be kidnapped if he's with his mother?" I stopped, remembering Lieutenant Peavey'd said that Brother Vern had claimed to be Little Lloyd's guardian. If that was true, and who knew what legalities Wesley Lloyd had entered into, then Hazel Marie could be a party to kidnapping, too.

Surely not, I assured myself; Wesley Lloyd wouldn't've had anything to do with somebody like Vernon Puckett. I groaned, because I'd never thought he'd have anything to do with somebody like Hazel Marie Puckett, either.

"Little Lloyd, were Brother Vern and your daddy friends with each other?"

"I don't know," he said.

"Well, I mean did they visit together? Talk about things together? Anything?"

"No'm, 'cept one time right before

Brother Vern went off to California, he was talking to my daddy out in the backyard." He untangled himself from Lillian's arms and pushed his glasses up.

"Well," I said, "what did they talk about?"

He squinted his eyes and gazed off above my head, thinking hard. "I heard Brother Vern say my daddy ought to take everything into account. And my daddy told him it wasn't any of his business, and that he'd make arrangements when he got ready to. Or something like that."

"Sounds like Wesley Lloyd," I mused aloud. "So, as far as you know, they weren't what you'd call friends?"

"No'm, Brother Vern didn't come see us much 'cause he was always preaching somewhere. And my daddy worked real hard and couldn't be home much, either."

Lillian and I looked at each other over his head, and I shook mine at the way this child had been raised.

"Sooner or later," I said to Lillian, "the lies have got to stop. But not till we know what we're up against. If anybody finds out we have Little Lloyd, the police will send him right back to Brother Vern or to social services, one. And I'm not going to let that happen, even if it means lying my head off."

"He suspects us, I know he does." Hazel Marie lay in bed, her hair a mess of brassy tangles on the pillow. The bruises on her face had faded to near the same yellow tint. Still swollen, though, around her eyes and mouth.

"No, I don't think so," I said. "Lieutenant Peavey might be wondering a little, since he picked up on the Puckett name. However," I said as I tucked in the sheet at the foot of her bed, "if they're treating this as a kidnapping, we could be in big trouble. I just wanted you to know what we're up against now."

"I don't think I can stand anymore." She turned her face away as the tears started again. "I don't know how it could be kidnapping when he's my own little boy. I'm about at the end of my rope."

"Get hold of yourself," I told her as I snatched a Kleenex from the box and handed it to her. "If there's one thing I've learned in all this, it's that you have to stand up for yourself. Nobody else is going to do it for you, least of all the people you ought to be able to depend on." That was as close as I wanted to get to discussing Wesley Lloyd.

"You are so strong, Miz Springer," she said, dabbing at her sore face with the tissue. "I wish I could be like you."

I snorted at that and told her to get some rest. As I walked downstairs, it came to me that I was strong, if that's what I was, only because I had the money to back it up. If I'd been like Hazel Marie, without a penny to my name, I'd be overwhelmed and ready to give up, too. A pitiful commentary, but there it was.

I stopped on the stairs as my knees began to tremble. Money wasn't going to protect me from my sickness, or sin, or whatever it was as long as Pastor Ledbetter held it over my head. Regardless of Wesley Lloyd's estate, I wasn't any stronger or safer than that poor, pitiful woman in my guest bed. In fact, I might even've been worse off because of it.

In spite of the fluorescent lights overhead, the kitchen had begun to take on a greenish glow by late afternoon. An ominous growl of thunder swelled overhead as a swirl of limbs from the nandina bushes scraped against the window behind the table. I looked out to see the light green undersides of leaves on the poplars as the wind swept through the branches.

"It's coming up a cloud," Lillian said worriedly. "No tellin' what gonna happen next. Honey," she said to Little Lloyd, "don't you get close to the windows, lightnin' be coming with that wind." He moved a chair beside the pantry and sat very still, his hands clasped between his knees.

"It does look bad out there," I said, and cringed as lightning clicked close by. Thunder boomed around the house barely a second later. "Close," I said. "I better unplug the television."

From the front window of the living room, I could see a sudden downpour of rain falling like a sheet, streaking the panes. Lightning continued to pop around the house, while thunder crashed and rolled. I shuddered and pulled the drapes. As the room darkened, I reached to turn on a lamp, then drew back as another flash of lightning warned me away.

As I started back to the kitchen, I heard running steps on the front porch and the doorbell ringing. I peeked out the window before going to the door. Too many people had been showing up to hand us more problems.

"Binkie, what in the world!" I threw open the door and held the screen for her. Her hair and clothes were soaked, and she stood there trying to dry her face with a wet Kleenex. "Come in! What're you doing out in this storm? Get in here and dry off."

"Sorry to drip on your rug, Miss Julia. I'll just slip my shoes off, they're wet through." She was laughing and gasping for breath. In spite of looking like a drowned cat, Binkie had some color in her cheeks, and her eyes were sparkling. "I haven't been caught in the rain in I don't know how long! And I haven't run like that in a long time, either! Wow, I'm wet to the skin! Just look at me!"

Her skirt and blouse were plastered to her form, making her look even smaller than she was. In fact, she looked more like the young girl who used to ride her bicycle past my house on her way to the picture show. She'd always call out and wave if she saw me in the yard or on the porch. Big personality, that girl, even back then. Since coming back to Abbotsville to practice law, Binkie'd had to work hard to be taken seriously. Everybody wanted to pat her on the head. Patronizing, you know. Some of the locals actually tried it, and ended up with a nub instead of a hand. She called herself Elizabeth T. Enloe now, but she'd always be Binkie to me.

"Let's get you dried off," I said. "Why in the world are you out in this storm?"

"I was on my way back to the office from the courthouse." She smiled and pushed her hair out of her face. "And just decided to walk on over here. Thought I could make it before the rain started, but I missed it by a mile, didn't I?"

She looked up and past me, smiled again, and I turned to see Deputy Bates come into the living room from the hall.

"Sorry, Miss Julia," he said, turning toward the kitchen. "Didn't know you had company."

"No," I said, holding out my hand and backing away. I didn't want him in the kitchen because I hadn't had time to prepare him for Little Lloyd's return. Well, to be

honest, I hadn't had time to prepare whatever story I was going to tell as to how we'd
gotten the child back. And of course I didn't
want him too close to me, either, since I
didn't know at what age a man might stir up
my condition. If I had one to stir, that is. "I
want you to meet Binkie Enloe, one of
the best women lawyers in town. Binkie,
Deputy Bates."

Binkie gave me a quick glance, chilling
me for a minute, and I didn't know why.

Deputy Bates walked over and shook her
hand. "One of the best lawyers, period," he
said, and then I did know why. "She's raked
me over the coals in court a few times." But
he smiled when he said it. And so did she.

"Let me get some towels," I said. "Keep
her company for a minute, Deputy Bates, if
you will."

"Coleman," he said, his eyes still on
Binkie.

"What?"

"Coleman. Call me Coleman." He was still
looking at her, but he was speaking to me.
I think.

"Coleman," Binkie repeated.

I hurried into the kitchen and told Lillian to
send Little Lloyd upstairs to his mother.

"I thought you not tellin' no more lies," she said.

"I'm not. It's just too soon and I don't know what Binkie's doing here. I've got to feel her out before we spring Little Lloyd and Miss Puckett on everybody. Now just get the boy upstairs, and stay quiet about everything."

She grumbled about it, but she sent the boy up the back stairs, promising him chocolate cake for dessert.

Binkie was standing by the door, water dripping on the floor from the hem of her skirt. The room was dark, that sort of dusky dark of a late afternoon storm. Rain fell steadily outside, but not as hard as before. Deputy Bates had his hands in his pockets, looking down at Binkie, a smile on his face.

"Come on back to the kitchen," I said, not wanting to offer one of my velvet uphol-stered chairs to a sodden guest. "Binkie, we need to get you out of those wet clothes."

Deputy Coleman Bates watched as he followed Binkie to the kitchen, and she was a sight to see from the back, what with her wet skirt molded to her hips and thighs.

Deputy Bates, I mean Coleman, almost ran into the kitchen door.

Lillian walked back into the kitchen and started to make a fuss over Binkie, declaring she had to get out of her wet clothes before she caught her death.

"I'll run get one of Miss Julia's robes for you," she said, "then we'll put your clothes in the dryer."

I took Binkie to the downstairs bathroom, where she disrobed and rerobed in my blue satin robe that Lillian had cleaned since its trip to Spartanburg. I don't know where Lillian's mind was, the heavy chenille one would've been more appropriate and considerably less form-fitting. By this time, I felt like I was clothing half the women in town.

I declare, I never knew what that blue satin was capable of, but when she walked back into the kitchen, Deputy Bates, I mean Coleman, couldn't take his eyes off of it. It'd had the same effect on the truck driver when Hazel Marie was wearing it. Binkie was embarrassed and hurriedly sat down, wrapping it close around her. She clasped the neckline to keep it from gaping, which it was inclined to do.

"These'll be dry in a few minutes," Lillian

said, bundling up Binkie's wet clothes. "Who wants coffee? Or lemonade, or what? Got some chocolate cake, too."

Lillian passed around the dessert plates and poured coffee. It was the first time I'd seen Coleman ignore any food Lillian put in front of him. He was paying a lot of attention to Binkie, though.

"Thanks, Miss Lillian," Binkie said, then looked across the table at me. "Miss Julia, I know you wonder what I'm doing, calling on you this time of day. I could've asked you to come to the office, but I thought it'd be better to talk here."

That sounded serious. I glanced at Lillian as she stopped in the middle of the room and lifted her eyebrows. What did Binkie know, and who'd told her?

"What?" I asked, fearful of her answer.

"I wanted to see how you were doing," Binkie said. She glanced at Coleman, then looked back at me. "Would you rather we talked about this in private?"

"I don't think so, since I'm doing fine. Why'd you think I wasn't?" The only thing to do was brave it out and deny everything. I tried a laugh, but it was a weak one. "What is this? Everybody and his brother is suddenly concerned about my health. First Pastor Ledbetter, then LuAnne Conover, and now you." I looked around at all of them as they looked back at me. "Why, Binkie? What've you heard?"

"I've had a few phone calls," she said, clipping her words as she did in her office. "And, since you're my client, I wanted to be sure you were all right. I see you are, so that's all there is to it."

"No, that's not all there is to it," I said, about ready to break down with the strain. "Somebody's telling tales, and I want to know what it's about. Now, what's supposed to be wrong with me? Heart attack? Gallbladder trouble? Brain tumor?" *Nymphomania?*

"Nothing like that," Binkie said. "Don't be concerned about it. It'll die down."

"Binkie Enloe," I said, "that's not good enough. I want to know what's being said because whatever it is, it's not true."

"Well," she said with some reluctance. She scraped up some chocolate icing with the side of her fork, looked at it, then at me. "This is just street talk, but I've heard that you might be slowing down. You know, getting a little forgetful, a little confused. All perfectly normal after a certain age."

"Me?" My mouth dropped open, not knowing if this rumor was tied to my recent shameful display or if it was something new. "They're saying I'm getting senile? Is that it? That's it, isn't it?"

Lillian stood stock-still in the middle of the room, and Coleman listened with a be-mused smile on his face. But this time it was for me and not Binkie.

"Lillian," I said, "did you hear that? Am I senile? Do I look confused to you? Do I for-get things?"

"No more'n you ever did," she said.

"Who's saying these things, Binkie? Where'd you hear them?" I swallowed hard, wondering if Binkie would help them put me away. By this time, I didn't trust anyone.

"A couple of people from your church called me. They were concerned, wanted to know what they could do to help."

"Thay Lord," I said, slumping in my chair. "And they sent you to check up on me?" Pastor Ledbetter had promised not to tell, but it crossed my mind that he might've felt the Lord leading in a different direction.

"No, not me," she said, slicking a strand

of hair behind an ear. "I'm looking after your interests. Somebody else is trying to determine how competent you are."

"Who?"

"Your pastor, Mr. Ledbetter," she said. "And some psychologist from a Christian counseling service. A new member of your church, I believe."

"Dr. Fred Fowler? Is that who you're talking about?" I gasped and buried my face in my hands to hide the red flush that burned through my skin. My Lord, that peaked little man was a mind expert and he'd said I was crazy. And no wonder, after what I'd done to him.

And my pastor knew all about it, maybe suspected something lurking in my character even before I'd given them proof. I jerked my head up, recalling my earlier suspicions about the two of them. Maybe they'd planned that fiasco at the church. And how had Pastor Ledbetter even known to read up on nymphomania, and him a man of God, unless somebody had put it in his mind? It certainly wasn't covered in any theological library I'd ever seen.

I narrowed my eyes, thinking *entrapment.*

"Do you know what they're going to do if

they decide I'm failing before their eyes?" I
wanted to fall on my knees and beg Binkie
to save me, but I didn't want to tell her why
I needed saving.

"I'm not sure, Miss Julia," Binkie said.
"But there's nothing they can do without a
competency hearing, which, I warn you, is
not hard to get. I want you to watch what
you do and say around them. Don't give
them any ammunition, so to speak. You can
call me anytime you get concerned about
anything. Now, Lillian, if my clothes are dry,
I'd better head on home. The rain's slacked
off some."

CHAPTER TWENTY-FIVE

—

I sat there, too stunned to be hospitable, and let Lillian get her clothes. I had enough awareness to note that Binkie was a sight in her wrinkled linen, but she wouldn't let Lillian plug in the iron.

I was still sitting and staring into space while Coleman insisted on driving her home, still sitting and staring when they said good-bye and left, and still sitting and staring when Lillian came to the table and stared back at me.

"It ain't like you to take this sittin' down," she said. She put her hands on the table and leaned over toward me. "I thought you gettin' some gumption since Mr. Springer passed and left you more'n anybody can spend in a lifetime. Now you actin' like you used to when he was alive, all shriveled and shrunk up, takin' whatever anybody hand out and scrungin' down in yo'self. That preacher ain't got no hol' over you, so what you doin' actin' like you doin'?"

"Oh, Lillian," I whispered. Tears stung my eyes, and the pain in my chest spread out to burn in my throat. "Seems like everybody's got some kind of hold over me. And my pastor . . . It just hurts, that's all."

"It can't hurt if it ain't so. All you got to do is show 'em yo' mind as good as it ever was."

"I thought I was already doing that. But there's a lot you don't know, Lillian."

"I know all I need to know, an' then some. Ain't nothin' wrong with yo' mind and you know it. Law, Miss Julia," she said, straightening up and shaking her head, "ain't nobody get the best of you yet. Why you think anybody start now? Now, get outta that chair an' help me get some supper for Miss Hazel Marie and that little honey upstairs."

By the time we'd fixed trays to take to them, Coleman had called to say he was eating with Binkie and wouldn't be home till late. Which was pretty quick work on somebody's part. So Lillian and I fixed trays for ourselves and carried them all up to Miss Puckett's room.

"A picnic!" Little Lloyd cried. "I've never had a picnic before!"

"Well, you have one now," I said, and busied myself distributing trays, helping Hazel Marie sit up in bed, and fussing at Lillian for not wanting to eat with us. "Sit down and eat, for goodness' sake," I told her. "If, that is, you're not too good for us."

"I'll eat with you, Miss Lillian," Little Lloyd said, hopping off the bed where he'd been sitting with his mother.

"Well, come on over here, honey," she said, "an' put yo' tray on this desk next to mine."

"I declare, Miss Lillian," Hazel Marie said, "I believe you're gonna steal my little boy away from me."

"No'm, I'm not gonna steal him, I'm jus' gonna love him up for you." Lillian patted his shoulder and he smiled like he couldn't be happier.

"Speaking of stealing little boys," I said, "what're we going to do about Brother Vern and this kidnapping charge? We can't keep you two shut up in this room forever."

"I know, Miz Springer," Hazel Marie said,

leaning back against her pillow and staring up at the ceiling. "And I want to thank you for everything you've done for us. You, too, Miss Lillian. I ought to be able to get out of your hair by tomorrow, if you can put up with us one more night."

I put down my fork. "And just where're you going to go?"

"I don't know. Back to my mama's house, I guess. Her new husband won't like it, what with his three kids there already, but I don't know what else to do. Junior'll have to start to school pretty soon, so I'll have to settle somewhere and find me a job."

Silence settled over the room, and I felt Lillian glaring at me. "There's no need to make a hasty decision," I said. "Besides, just going off on your own won't solve the problem if Lillian's arrested for kidnapping."

"Lord, don't say sucha thing!" Lillian stopped eating and stared at me.

"I'm sorry," I went on. "I didn't mean it that way. What I meant was, we may all have a charge of kidnapping hanging over us and we need to take care of that before going our separate ways. Now, Miss Puckett, think hard. Could Mr. Springer've made your uncle Little Lloyd's guardian and you not know about it?"

"No, ma'am! He wouldn't've done that."

"Well, as long as the police think he did, we can't just announce the boy's where-abouts and go on about our business. I want you to think now. Did Mr. Springer in-dicate in any way that he might do that? Could he've told or just implied to Brother Vern that he was going to do it?"

"No way, Miz Springer," Hazel Marie said. She moved her tray off her lap and sat up as straight as she could manage. "Wesley Lloyd wouldn't've done any such a thing. He always said I took good care of Lloyd, and besides, he couldn't stand Brother Vern."

That was one thing I could still agree with Wesley Lloyd about.

"All right," I said. "If you're sure about it, then we can admit we've got the child and the police can't take him away from us. If Brother Vern raises a fuss, we'll demand to see a legal document. Then we'll turn around and accuse him of kidnapping."

"How you do that?" Lillian asked. "You the one let this chile go off with him. That ain't no kidnapping."

"You're splitting hairs, Lillian," I said. "The least he's guilty of is false pretenses. Anyway, what we need is something to hit him with to counteract his charges against us. Miss Puckett, you haven't had enough to eat. You're skinny as a rail, as it is."

"Brother Vern's looking for something," Hazel Marie said, picking at a cucumber slice. "I told you how he kept wanting to know what Wesley Lloyd left us, and how he was going to use Junior to make me give it to him. I still don't know what he thought I had, 'cause I don't have anything."

"He probably thought you had a bank account," I said. "Or maybe the deed to your house. There's no telling what he thought, and from my recent experience, there's no telling what Wesley Lloyd could've actually done.

"Now, if you're sure we're safe from Brother Vern, the thing to do is bring in Lieutenant Peavey and tell him to call off the Spartanburg police and the FBI. We'll tell him all about Brother Vern. After we accuse him of everything we can think of, not even social services would put a child in his hands. But before we do that, I think I better talk to Sam and Binkie, just to be on the safe side."

I went down to the kitchen the following morning, way before my usual time of rising. Switching on the coffee, I pulled my robe closer against the coolness left by the thunderstorm. Wesley Lloyd'd had firm ideas about living on schedule. There's a time, he'd often said, for sleeping and a time for waking. Of course, his Thursday night bedtime didn't stick to the schedule, but I guess he didn't count that, since he'd likely been in bed part of the time at Miss Puckett's house.

One of the nice things about being a widow, though, was that you could pretty much do what you wanted to without getting any cold looks or sharp words about it. I found I liked going to bed and getting up whenever the spirit moved me. And I liked not having somebody asking if I was sick or if my conscience was hurting me if I broke that somebody's routine.

So, I sat there in the quiet kitchen, drinking coffee and considering all the things that I needed to straighten out: what to do about Hazel Marie and Little Lloyd, what to do about Lieutenant Peavey and the kidnapping charge, what to do about Pastor Ledbetter and the threat he held over my head, and how to fix Brother Vern's little red wagon.

I stiffened and looked around the kitchen. I'd heard something, a scratching or scuttling sound. I thought of the night Hazel Marie'd shown up at the back door, and tiptoed over to peek outside. Nobody there, but as I turned toward the table I heard it again.

The pantry, I thought. My next thought was mice. And I shuddered at that thought. I stood still, listening. The refrigerator clicked on, but nothing else stirred. I wasn't eager to confront a mouse, but neither did I want to eat anything that'd been rodent-nibbled. I looked around for something to throw and grabbed a saucepan by the handle.

I crept to the pantry door, leaning against it and listening. Nothing. But I had heard something, so something was in there. I jerked open the door.

"Scat! Shoo! Get outta there, you nasty things!" I cried, holding the pan high.

Nothing moved. I lowered the pan, thinking maybe Pastor Ledbetter was right on the money in more ways than one. Maybe I was beginning to hear things now. I started to turn away, but then I heard a definite hiccup and a muffled sob.

"Who is that? Who's in there?"

Little Lloyd answered from behind a stack of Bounty paper towels. "It's me. Please don't shoot."

"Don't shoot!" I exclaimed, and started laughing. "Child, I'm not going to shoot you! What're you doing in there? Come on out here and talk to me."

He edged out, ducking as he emerged from under a shelf. He wore the cowboy pajamas I'd bought him, and he had his Winn-Dixie sack in his hand. His hair, mussed from sleep, stood up at various points on his head. His glasses were crooked on his nose.

"I'm sorry," he sniffled, wiping his teary face.

"What're you sorry about? I don't care if you want to sit in the pantry at five o'clock in the morning, but sitting at the table is more comfortable. You want some coffee? Or a glass of milk?"

"Maybe some coffee, if you don't mind." He stood there in his baggy pajamas with his paper sack clutched to his chest, and I noticed a fine tremor running across his shoulders.

"Are you cold?"

"No'm. I just didn't want to bother you."

I poured a cup of coffee and set it on the table.

"You couldn't bother me, Little Lloyd," I said, pulling out our chairs. "Come sit down. I'm glad to have your company."

"Yes'm." He sugared and creamed his coffee with a heavy hand and, as he stirred, I wondered how he could drink the concoction. But to each his own.

I said, "Don't tell Lillian I gave you coffee, okay?"

He glanced up at me, saw me smiling, and smiled back. "Okay."

"So," I said. "We've got to get you and your mother settled, don't we? School's going to start pretty soon."

"Yes'm."

"You looking forward to living with your grandmother?"

"No'm, I don't reckon I am."

"Oh? Why not?"

"I don't know." He shrugged and looked around the kitchen. "I like it here."

"Well," I said, surprised, "I'm glad you do. But I expect you'll get used to whatever your mother decides on, don't you think?"

"Yes'm, pro'bly so."

We sat in silence, drinking our coffee and waiting for daylight. I couldn't think of anything else to talk about except the things that were worrying me, which weren't fit to share with a child.

He set his cup down and straightened his shoulders from their habitual slump. His eyes darted around from me to the table and back again. He took a deep breath. "Miz Springer?"

"Yes?"

"If somebody gave you something to keep, what would you do?"

"Why, I guess I'd keep it. Wouldn't you?"

"Yes'm, I would." He lifted the cup with both hands to his mouth, and blew on the hot coffee. Then he set the cup down without drinking.

He said, " 'Cept, maybe you'd need to know how long to keep it. Wouldn't you?"

I made a show of considering the question, twisting my mouth in deep thought. "I suppose so. You mean, I take it, if this somebody hadn't told you when to give it back?"

"Yes'm, but more than that. I mean, what if you can't give it back?"

"Ah," I said. "Like, if somebody gave you something to keep and you happened to lose it?"

"Oh, no'm!" He looked at me, eyes wide at the very thought. "No'm, I wouldn't never lose it."

"Well, I was just speaking hypothetically, you know."

"What? I mean, ma'am?"

"Hypothetically. Just in general, so to speak. I didn't mean to suggest that you would." Though of course that's what I'd assumed the conversation was about.

I said, "Let's start over. You want to know what I'd do if somebody gave me something to keep for them. I haven't lost it, but I can't give it back. And you want to know how long I should keep it?"

He nodded, watching me intently. Talking to a child wasn't proving all that hard to do.

"Let me think," I said, patting my mouth with my fingers and studying the problem. "I need some more information. It's not broken, is it? That's not the reason you can't give it back?"

"No'm."

"And you still have it. You haven't given it to anybody else."

He shook his head solemnly, from side to side.

"In other words, you've taken good care of it. Oh, I know. You've grown attached to it and don't want to give it back. Is that it?"

"No, ma'am, I don't want it anymore. I just don't know what to do with it."

"Well, just tell whoever gave it to you that you can't keep it any longer. That's what I'd do."

He slunk down in his chair, his head tucked into the collar of his pajamas like a turtle. "I can't. My daddy gave it to me."

Oh, Lord, and here I'd thought I was doing so well playing a game with this strange child.

"Well," I said, "that puts a different light on it. I guess, if he didn't tell you how long to keep it or who to give it to, he meant for you to have it. Yes, I'm sure he meant for you to keep it for your own."

The gold watch that Wesley Lloyd wore in a special pocket came to mind, the one with a heavy gold chain with a Rotary pin on it. But no, they'd taken that off him and given it to me when they closed the casket after the final viewing. Maybe it was a check or a large bill.

"If it's money, Little Lloyd, I can assure you that your father would be proud of you if you put it in the bank. That way, it could earn even more, and I know that's what he'd do with it."

"No'm, it's not money." He slowly turned his spoon around on the table. His hands were small, frail-looking like his mother's. It occurred to me that the child was deeply worried about this problem. It wasn't a game to him.

"All right," I said, leaning down to catch his eye. "Here's my advice. Talk it over with your mama. I expect she'd know what to do."

"I thought about that." His voice was so low that I had to lean even closer. "But my daddy gave it to me the very same night he went to be with Jesus, and he told me not to tell anybody."

"Well, my goodness," I said. "Was . . . did your daddy, I mean, do you think he knew he was going to, well, go be with Jesus when he gave it to you?" Images of that fearful night when I found Wesley Lloyd slumped over his steering wheel flashed through my mind, the whirling red and blue lights of ambulances and patrol cars, the tubes and black kits with dials and toggles that technicians worked with to revive him, the rough kindness of young deputies trying to comfort an old woman trembling on the porch steps.

"I don't know." Little Lloyd sniffed and wiped tears from his face with the back of his hand. I gave him my napkin. "He didn't feel so good, but he had to leave anyway. My mama wanted to call the doctor, and I think he got mad about that. Me and her stayed in the kitchen while he went to the living room to do something. Then he called me to walk out to the car with him, and that's when he gave it to me. He said for me to keep it and not tell nobody and he'd see me next week." He sniffed wetly. "But he never did."

Wesley Lloyd's last minutes revealed, and they sounded just like him. Calling a doctor because he wasn't feeling well would be admitting to weakness. It didn't surprise me a bit that he'd been too stubborn to take advice. But I was pleased to hear that Hazel Marie had tried.

"So, I guess you figure that if he'd wanted your mother to know about it, he'd've given it to her and not to you?"

He nodded his head. Then he lifted his glasses and rubbed his eyes with his fists.

"You've had a pretty heavy load to carry around." I patted his shoulder. "But listen," I went on, "don't be worried about having a secret from your mother. That's just the way your daddy was. He was treating you like a man, and he didn't think men should get women, even mothers, involved in their business." Wives or girlfriends either, I could've added but didn't.

"Did you know my daddy?" he asked, his voice breaking as he tried not to cry.

I studied him a few minutes, thinking how remiss I'd been in not realizing that this child had lost a father he'd loved, and was still mourning him. Somehow it'd never occurred to me that anybody beside myself could be hurting.

I took a deep breath that caught in my throat and tightened my chest. "Yes, I knew him and I'm sorry that he's gone. I know you miss him, but these things happen, don't you know. We just have to be strong and go on with what we have to do." Platitudes, but that's all I had to offer. I patted his back again.

"Yes'm, I guess so." The paper sack crackled in his lap as he shifted in the chair.

"So," I said, "we still have the problem of what to do with what he gave you. And I think I have the answer. You just pick somebody you trust, tell them what it is, and let them decide what to do. I don't think your daddy meant for you to keep it hidden forever. I think he just meant for you to keep it safe, don't you?"

Worry knotted his forehead, making his glasses slip down on his nose. "You really think he'd want me to tell somebody about it?"

"Yes, now that he's gone, I think he'd want you relieved of the responsibility. But I also think he'd want you to be very careful who you choose to tell. But there're a lot of people you could trust with his secret—Deputy Bates, Lillian, Mr. Sam Murdoch. Your mother, of course. Any of them would be able to help you with it."

He continued to look at the table, avoiding my eyes, his hands resting now on the sack in his lap.

"Would you?" he whispered.

"Me?" I was taken aback. What had I done to deserve his trust? Or put it another way, what had I done to have another burden added to the ones I already carried? "Why, of course," I finally managed to say. "I'll help you if I can, but somebody else might do a better job for you."

"No'm, my mama said you're the best friend anybody could have."

"Well," I said, "I declare."

"It's in here," he said, unrolling the Winn-Dixie sack, and I prepared myself to treat a book about lions with suitable seriousness. To tell the truth, I was beginning to wonder if the boy had good sense, considering how he was agonizing over such a trivial thing.

He pulled the book out of the sack, pushed his coffee cup aside, and laid the book on the table. Very carefully, he leafed through the book and removed a thin, pink envelope.

As he handed it to me, our eyes met, and this time I saw, not Wesley Lloyd, but Little Lloyd himself.

I held the envelope, slowly turned it over,

and saw that it was sealed. I was reluctant to open and read what my husband had written to his child in his last hours on this earth. I wasn't sure I wanted to know anything so personal, nor did I feel prepared to comfort his grieving child. A letter from the grave, so to speak, could only open the wounds again. I wished Lillian were there to help me.

"Have you read it?" I asked.

"No'm. I just kept it like he told me to."

"Well," I said, taking a deep breath, "let's see what it says."

I reached behind me to the counter for a bread knife and slit the envelope. I pulled out a flimsy pink page, unfolded it, and silently read the sentence written there in my husband's heavy handwriting, studied his unmistakable signature, and felt my world fall away.

"Little Lloyd," I whispered, "you were right to show this to me. It has to do with your daddy's business. I'll have to study on it a while before deciding just how he'd want it handled. Now, why don't you tiptoe upstairs and get dressed. Or you might want to get a little more sleep, if you can. It's still early, so try not to wake your mother."

"Okay," he said, relief shining on his face. "Now I can get rid of this ole paper sack." He wadded it up and put it in the trash can on his way out of the room. "Thank you for the coffee, Miz Springer."

I watched him leave and listened to his bare feet slither on the polished wood between my Oriental rugs. Then, with an aching heart, I looked back at the sheet of pink stationery that represented my husband's last will and testament.

Chapter Twenty-six

—

The boy trusted me, so that gave me some time. He hadn't read it, probably wouldn't have understood it if he had, so no one on God's green earth knew about it. Except me.

I studied the pink page, taking note of the drawing of pastel flowers at the top, and understood that Wesley Lloyd had used a sheet of Hazel Marie's stationery to cut me off without a dime.

I thought about how it must've happened that night, because that's when the sentence had been written. I didn't doubt that, since the date of the night he died was right there on the page. He must've known something was bad wrong with him, a premonition of some kind, to've made such a sudden and drastic change. Maybe if he'd taken more time to consider his responsibilities, he'd have made some provision for me. Then again, maybe not. Maybe nothing was exactly what he'd thought of me, and exactly what he'd wanted me to have.

I buried my face in my hands, my shoulders shaking with the pain of realizing that in his last hours he'd taken no thought of me at all. I was not included in this, his final testimony to what was important to him. I read the sentence again: "I name my only son, Wesley Lloyd Junior Puckett (Springer), heir and beneficiary of all my worldly goods, and Sam Murdoch as executor of my estate and guardian until the age of majority." Dated at the top and signed at the bottom.

With one sentence, my husband of forty-four years had pauperized me and put me on welfare and food stamps. My home no longer belonged to me, much less any of the other properties that I'd taken such pride in owning. My furniture, my car—everything—it all belonged to a child who should've never been born.

My hands shook with the rage that flowed through me like an electric current. I wanted to crumple the page and tear it to pieces. I wanted to stomp it into the ground. I wanted to tear my hair out and scream my head off. I wanted to hurt Wesley Lloyd like he'd hurt me.

I trembled with the effort of controlling myself, stricken with the power of my anger. I drew a rasping breath and tried to come to terms with my new and impoverished state.

This would certainly relieve Hazel Marie of the concern about supporting herself or about where she and Little Lloyd would live. They could live right here in my house if she wanted it. Lillian could work for her, and probably would for Little Lloyd's sake. Hazel Marie could entertain my friends, go to my Sunday school class, sit in my pew, drive my car, take on my life. She could take my place in everything, just as she'd taken my place in my husband's heart and bed. And on top of losing everything, my pastor and half the town thought I was demented, incompetent, and a danger to every man I met.

I couldn't face it.

I needed time to think about what to do. I folded the page, put it back in its envelope, and slipped it into the pocket of my robe. I lifted my cup of coffee, tasted and swallowed the cold and bitter dregs. Take one thing at a time, I told myself, and this new will was the most pressing problem.

Little Lloyd would assume that I was taking care of his secret; he wouldn't question me. He didn't know it had anything to do with him. Hazel Marie didn't know, thanks to her son's integrity in following Wesley Lloyd's instructions. Sam, involved in executing the older and more appropriate will, didn't know. If I kept quiet, then things would take their course the way they were supposed to. I ground my teeth together as I remembered how important it'd been to Wesley Lloyd to do what was *supposed* to be done. I would only be following his lead, because a wife is *supposed* to benefit from her husband's estate. It was only right.

Besides, I told myself, a case could be made that Wesley Lloyd was not of sound mind that night. Couldn't it? He was sick, even dying, when he set pen to paper. And besides that, he'd not had that will witnessed and notarized. That meant it was invalid, didn't it? I wished I could talk it over with Sam.

Then I thought of something that would make it right, or at least justify me in rearranging Wesley Lloyd's last-minute intentions. I'd set up a fund for Little Lloyd's education. And maybe a monthly allowance for his and Hazel Marie's living expenses. She would be so grateful. She and everybody else would think highly of me for such an act of Christian charity and generosity.

She'd think I was the best friend a person could have.

I covered my face again, sobbing at the position Wesley Lloyd had put me in, and realizing that if Pastor Ledbetter had his way, I wouldn't be able to be generous to anybody.

Then, hearing Lillian walking down the drive, I hurriedly got up and left the kitchen. I couldn't face her this morning. I went upstairs and closed my bedroom door. I couldn't face anybody with the knowledge that my husband had discounted me as unworthy of his care, and I couldn't face anybody with the knowledge that I was considering living a lie for the rest of my natural life.

———

I sat by the window in the floral chintz-up-holstered chair that Wesley Lloyd had hated. He'd never liked anything with flowers on it or that was pastel in color, and the wine-dark living and dining rooms reflected his preferences. I'd felt that the bedrooms could be softer, a little more feminine, but he'd put a stop to that when I'd had the chair re-covered. As I sat there, I thought again that it was the only thing in the house that I'd selected. And he'd hated it.

That was a symbol of something.

I rubbed my hand over the arm of the chair, trying to take in what he'd done to me and what he was still doing from the grave. My throat hurt down into my chest as I tried to convince myself that I had every right to destroy his last will and testament. Who could blame me if I did?

No one, I told myself, because no one would ever know.

I sat up straight as Brother Vern came to mind. Did he know? But he couldn't know. Not for sure, anyway. He'd been looking for anything Wesley Lloyd might have left the two Pucketts. He couldn't know there was a new will. Could he? Even if he suspected something, what could he do if it never came to light?

He could accuse me if Little Lloyd ever told anybody that he'd given me a paper from his father. Everybody would suspect what it'd been. I'd be ruined in this town. Hazel Marie might sue me. Little Lloyd would grow up distrusting me, always wondering if I'd stolen what belonged to him.

You could move away, I told myself, just sell this house and move to Florida. Leave this town and its suspicious minds and enjoy your old age in comfort and security.

I declare, I didn't think I could do it. Enjoy it, that is. On the other hand, whatever I decided to do—reveal the new will or destroy it—my feelings about Wesley Lloyd were going to make the rest of my life miserable. Lord forgive me, I prayed, for the bitterness in my heart.

I dressed slowly and carefully, feeling disconnected to the familiar morning routine. Zippers snagged, buttons refused to equal out with buttonholes, hairbrushes fell to the floor, hairpins flew from my hands, yet I overcame each obstacle with deliberate care while my mind whirled on some distant plane.

Dressed at last, I pinned the envelope to the inside of the bodice of my dress. I wasn't about to leave it where someone might find it. As I smoothed my hand across it, the answer came to me. It would be my secret for a few days at least. I'd see if I could live with it staying a secret. Nothing would be lost or gained by delaying a final decision.

Yes, that's what I'd do.

Now, I thought, let's pretend that the page doesn't exist. Let's pretend that everything is just as it was before Little Lloyd turned to me as his trusted friend. And, while we're at it, let's pretend I never laid a hand on Dr. Fred Fowler.

I had too much to do, I told myself, to worry with last-minute, undoubtedly invalid last wills and testaments that probably wouldn't amount to a hill of beans.

I went downstairs, my head high, to confront them all.

"What's the matter with you?" Lillian asked as soon as I stepped into the kitchen. "You look downright peaked this morning."

Lord, does it show already?

"I'm fine," I said. "Just not sleeping too well. Too many things on my mind."

"You need to start straightenin' them things out," she told me. "You can't keep hidin' Miss Puckett and that little boy, and you can't keep tellin' stories to the police."

"I know it. And I guess today's the day to do it." I sat down and propped my arms on the table, uncommonly tired and dispirited. "I don't know why I feel like I have to take on the problems of the world. Hazel Marie is a grown woman and capable of caring for herself and her child. There's no reason I should take it on myself to hide them from the police or protect them from their own relatives."

"That don't sound like you." Lillian stood in the middle of the kitchen frowning at me. She wiped her hands with a dish towel and said, "You sure you feelin' all right?"

The pink paper burned against my skin.

"I'm fine," I said again, looking in her direction but over her head. "It's just that I've come to realize that I've taken too much on myself and meddled in business that's no concern of mine. I aim to stop it."

"Hmm," she said, folding the towel and

laying it on the counter. "How you figure on doin' that?"

"I don't know yet." I rubbed my forehead, and felt the paper crinkle under my arm. "I've a good mind to move my letter to the Episcopal church, and dare Pastor Ledbetter to slander a member of another church. Then I ought to call Lieutenant Peavey and tell him all about Hazel Marie and Little Lloyd, and let the chips fall."

"You can't do that!"

"Well, I may have to."

"What about that Brother Vern? What if he claims Little Lloyd and gets him away from his mama?"

"He won't. The only reason he wanted the child was because he thought they had some money from Wesley Lloyd. When he learns from Sam and Binkie that neither of them have a nickel, he'll be gone quick enough."

The pink paper seemed to throb with each beat of my heart. It was taking on a life of its own.

"Well, and what about me?" Lillian demanded. "You think the police gonna just forget about what they callin' kidnappin'?"

"They will when they learn the truth, and

that's what I'm going to tell them." Except not all of it, not yet.

Knowing the risk I was taking, if Pastor Ledbetter was right about my sinful flesh, or rather the danger I was putting him in, I went to see Sam. Walking up onto Sam's broad front porch, I noted the fresh gray paint on the floor at the end of the soft rose-colored old brick of the steps and wide walk. White rocking chairs lined each side of the open front door.

"Julia." Sam stood holding the screen for me. "Saw you coming up the walk. What's wrong?"

"Everything, Sam." I went into the cool hall, and he led me into the living room. Books, stacked neatly on tables and the floor, and newspapers folded on the sofa indicated that Sam truly lived in this room. Unlike mine, which was always cold and polished, ready for company.

"Have a seat, Julia. Want some coffee?"

"I don't want anything but an end to all the mess I've gotten into."

Sam smiled, his eyes crinkling at the corners. "Where do you want to start?"

That was the question. Which secret sin did I most want help with? On the way to his house, I'd thought about showing him Wesley Lloyd's pink paper will and just accepting the fate it decreed for me. Then I'd thought I wouldn't, and by the time I'd gotten there I'd decided to put it off a while longer. To see if I could live with my secret knowledge in the same room as Sam's honesty.

Funny, it never occurred to me that Sam might collude in keeping the new will secret. There was no question that he wouldn't. Some people are honest to the bone. And some aren't.

"Pastor Ledbetter," I said, and told him how Dr. Fowler'd been brought in to have me evaluated. I couldn't bring myself to tell him that they might have reason to conclude I was riddled with sin and out of my mind. "Can they do that?"

Sam leaned back and, if it wasn't completely unlike him, appeared to roll his eyes. "I tell you, Julia, preachers have the least common sense of any group of people I've ever known. Unless it's doctors." He hunched forward in his chair. "Listen now. In this state, it's not difficult to have someone declared incompetent. All they have to do is demonstrate that you lack sufficient capacity to understand the consequences of your actions."

"I understand them, all right. I live with them every minute of the day. But, Sam, there's no telling what they might say about me. You just don't know what they're accusing me of. I need to do something."

"Do like Sophocles and write a play." He was laughing at me now.

"What're you talking about?"

"His son petitioned the court to have him declared incompetent so he could get at his father's estate. The old man asked for a chance to prove himself, and the judges agreed. So he went home and wrote one of the Oedipus plays. When the judges heard a reading of it, they not only acquitted him, they escorted him home. Probably broke open a jug of wine, too. So nothing's new, Julia, that happened back in the fifth century B.C."

"I knew that much," I said, but I wasn't the reader that Sam was. "But if proving the condition of my mind depends on writing a play, I'm in worse trouble than I thought."

Sam laughed. "Ah, Julia, that was just an

example." Then he turned serious again. "Look, I don't want to scare you, but I'd better talk to Binkie about this. And, just so you know the process, anybody can make application to have someone declared incompetent. After that, a guardian *ad litem* would be appointed to represent that person's interests at the hearing. If the person's adjudicated incompetent, then a permanent guardian would be named, and that's the end of it."

I thought about it. It would turn me inside out to have to go through such a humiliating experience, but it sounded as if there would be enough safeguards to protect me.

"Well, Sam," I said, "I'd hate it if it comes down to it, but you could be named the guardian *ad litem* and Binkie the permanent guardian. Seems to me that things would go on just the way they are now, except for signing some legal papers and such. Now that you've explained it, it doesn't sound so bad."

Sam shook his head and looked down at the floor. "No, Julia, it's not that simple, but let Binkie and me worry about this. We're not going to let them railroad you, so what you have to do is stand up to them. And I know you can do that. You do it to me all the time."

I managed a smile in spite of the pink paper burning a hole in my skin inside my bodice.

CHAPTER TWENTY-SEVEN

—

When I got back to the house, I went through the gate in the back garden and on into the kitchen. I nearly turned back around when Lillian told me that Pastor Ledbetter and Dr. Fowler were waiting in the living room. I grabbed the edge of the counter and prayed for a fainting spell so I wouldn't have to face them. It didn't work.

"I tol' them I didn't know when you be back," Lillian said, as she arranged glasses of lemonade on a tray. "But they say they wait anyway. You better go on in there, 'cause Miss Puckett in the room right above an' she's up tryin' to get herself dressed."

"Little Lloyd with her?" I managed to ask.

"Yessum, I done warned 'em both to stay up there an' stay quiet."

I watched Lillian arrange cheese straws on a silver plate, girding myself for the ordeal to come. I tried to overcome my embarrassment by building up a head of steam to confront those two about their meddling, but it was hard to do. Somehow that pink paper inside my dress was sapping my spirit, and nothing seemed worth the effort anymore.

I took a deep breath and held the door for Lillian as she preceded me into the living room. Both men stood as I entered the room, Pastor Ledbetter's broad smile masking his nefarious intentions.

I nodded a greeting, unwilling to risk a handshake, and took a seat on one of the Victorian chairs by the fireplace. Lillian placed the tray on the coffee table in front of the sofa where both men were seated. She offered the plate of cheese straws and, after an encouraging glance at me, left the room.

I sat and waited for them to begin, ignoring my natural inclination to entertain them with conversation and make them feel welome. This visit was their idea, and since it was so hard on me, I determined not to make it easy for them. I saw them glance at each other over the tops of their glasses of lemonade, then cut their eyes at me while I burned with shame. I couldn't meet Dr. Fowler's eyes, but I held my head up. I couldn't even reach for my glass on the tray, so I just sat there with my hands in my lap, waiting them out.

Finally, Pastor Ledbetter cleared his throat. "Uh, Miss Julia," he began, setting down his glass and patting his mouth with a napkin. "Have you given any thought to what I talked with you about over at the church? We can't let matters drag on forever, you know." He cut his eyes over at Dr. Fowler. To see if he was doing all right, I guess.

"Pastor, all I've thought about is what you said to me in the bridal parlor, and I've come to the conclusion that you were wrong. I've also concluded that you and Dr. Fowler here conspired to put me in a compromising position. I'd like to know how you'd answer that in a court of law, especially when I describe what Dr. Fowler had in his pocket. Well, I don't mean his pocket, but you know what I mean."

"Now, just a minute here," Dr. Fowler said, briefly levitating from my sofa.

Pastor Ledbetter held up his hand, taking charge. "Let me handle this, Fred. Miss Julia, Dr. Fowler has already explained it all to me. What that was, *if* it was anything, was an autonomic nervous system response to unwelcome stimuli, which any man in the world would understand, given the circumstances. It's incumbent on me to advise you not to use that in any way. It would only make you appear even more childlike not to understand these matters.

"Now," he said, hitching himself forward to lean toward me, "here's what I want to talk to you about. None of us wants to take any legal steps against you, but something has to be done. We want to consider your wishes as we decide these matters. Have you thought about what you'd like to do?"

"No, I haven't."

"You should, Miss Julia." He clasped his hands together between his spread legs and looked earnestly at me. "I'll be honest with you, that episode of you taking in that child claiming to be Mr. Springer's son should've been a warning to us that you weren't thinking right. And now"—he spread his hands—"look where it's led us to."

"I don't have an idea in the world what you're talking about, Pastor," I said.

"It's like this," he said, resting his hands on his knees. He gave another look at Dr. Fowler, who was leaning back with his legs crossed, staring at me with those strange eyes of his. "We, that is, the church, the congregation of this church, are your family, the only one you have in this town. It's up to us to look after one another. Now, Miss Julia, I come to you not only as your pastor but as a member of that family, to say that we are deeply concerned about you. Besides what I saw with my own eyes, I've had reports that you've exhibited other strange behavior. All of which points to the fact that I've been remiss in not pursuing this matter more vigorously. Now, I know—"

He raised his hand, palm out, to stop any argument to the contrary, but I overrode him. "Tell me about those reports."

"Oh now," he said, smiling and shaking his head, "we don't need to discuss the details. Suffice it to say that several people, people who care about you and want to help you, have noticed a few worrisome things."

"Who?" I demanded.

"Now, don't get upset. We need to talk about this reasonably and come to some decision that'll be best for you."

"Who?"

"Miss Julia," he said, sighing, "this is just the kind of thing I'm talking about. You're not thinking straight. You need to be thinking about what you'll do in the future, not what's happened in the past. That's behind us, and I'm concerned about you right now, and I want you to know that Dr. Fowler here has opened a retirement center, a fine, Christian place, offering the best of care for our senior citizens. It has what's known as lifetime care where you can have a room with your own furniture and personal things, but also have nursing care when you need it. I'll tell you, it's a wonderful place with chapel every morning and evening prayers at night. There're nurses on duty day and night, and a trained dietitian, and therapists of all kinds. Why, they even have a social director who plans outings and all kinds of activities for the residents, things like aerobics and sing-alongs and birthday parties. Why, the days are just filled with wholesome activities, and all your meals are prepared and served in a lovely dining room with white tablecloths and candles at the evening meal."

Some of the old fire flamed up inside of me and I forgot about the pink paper pinned to my bodice. I straightened my back, thankful for all the calcium I'd taken over the years, and looked him in the eye.

"Are you going to tell me *who* has brought reports of my strange behavior to you, or did you break your promise and start the rumors yourself?"

"Now, Miss Julia, you don't want to get upset."

"Upset?" My voice went up alarmingly on the last syllable, and I made an effort to contain myself. "I simply want to know," I went on in a calmer tone, "on whose reports you've made the decision that I need to be in an old-folks home."

"Well," he said, giving another quick glance at the silent Dr. Fowler. Pastor Ledbetter pushed his hair off his forehead and sighed. "Several people have come to me with their concerns. It seems, for one thing, that you're planning to open a kennel right here in your house. And going so far as to buy a number of unlikely medical items for which you have no need at all. Now, you have to admit that that is a little strange and not at all like you. And, for another, people speak to you on the street and they get unusual responses from you, or no response at all, as if you're off in another world. Those are just examples, Miss Julia, and of course, I have not and will not speak of another example if, that is, you get some help. And let's not forget the way you took in that strange child with no idea in the world who he was or what he was after. You're just not yourself, Miss Julia, and we want to see you taken care of. Because we care about you and we're all worried about you."

"Oh, I'm sure Norma Cantrell's just made herself sick with worry over me," I said. "As well as Buck Tatum and Troy Beckworth. Both of them ought to be minding their own business instead of poking their noses in mine. I wouldn't trust either of them as far as I could throw them, since they're the biggest gossips in town. Except for Norma, who you ought to know by now doesn't have a lick of sense."

I swung around in my chair and faced Dr. Fowler. "And what is your interest in this, Doctor, other than befriending lonely old women so you can fill up the rooms in your rest home?"

"I . . ." he began, uncrossing his legs and looking away from me for the first time, "I was asked by Pastor Ledbetter and the session to give my evaluation of your state of mind. For your own good, I might add."

My soul sank inside of me. If my competency rating depended on Dr. Fowler's evaluation, the rest of me was sunk, too. They were giving me the choice of voluntarily committing myself or having a judge do it for me. And either way, it was for my own good.

As I opened and closed my mouth, trying to speak, footsteps sounded on the porch and the doorbell rang.

CHAPTER TWENTY-EIGHT

—

"Why, Brother Vern," I said, staring at him through the screen door, my mind going a hundred miles a minute, wondering how much he knew or how much he'd guessed, and what he intended to do. I was so shocked I couldn't move, trying to figure out how to get rid of him. And Pastor Ledbetter and Dr. Fowler, too, while I was at it. My mind fluttered here and there, trying to think how to warn Lillian and Hazel Marie.

He took hold of the screen and said, "Miz Springer. May I come in?"

"Why yes," I managed to say. "Yes, come in."

He walked in, nodding to the two men who'd stood as he entered. I saw Pastor Ledbetter take in Brother Vern's brown polyester suit, yellow tie, and white shoes. Short-sleeved shirt, too, since no cuffs showed below his coat sleeves. Brother Vern looked hot, his face red and shiny, his black hair glistening.

I made the introductions and the two ministers of the Gospel looked each other over like two dogs circling. Dr. Fowler might as well not have been there for all the attention they paid him. I could see that Pastor Ledbetter's back was up, since he'd pretty well gotten Brother Vern's number right from the start.

"Reverend Puckett has a television program every week. *Feeding the Flame,* isn't that it?" I said, considerably relieved to steer the conversation in another direction.

"That's it," he said. "I preach to a congregation of some forty to fifty thousand people every week, praise God."

Top that, I thought, as I found myself taking a peculiar satisfaction in setting one against the other. Not that I especially enjoyed it, you understand, but at least they weren't going after me.

"A televangelist," Pastor Ledbetter said, cutting his eyes at Dr. Fowler. "I didn't know you were interested in that kind of ministry,

Miss Julia." More fuel for the flame he wanted to set under me.

"I don't expect the Lord is limited to eleven o'clock on Sundays," I said.

"No, indeed," Brother Vern agreed. "In fact, Brother, the Lord is changing a lotta things these days. Have you switched your Sunday night services to Friday nights yet?"

"What?" Pastor Ledbetter looked bewildered, unsure he'd heard right.

"It's the coming thing," Brother Vern went on, coming into his own now that he'd discovered a way to teach a mainline preacher a thing or two. "The Lord has spoken to any number of preachers, evangelicals mostly, and pointed out to them that Sunday afternoons are family times and shouldn't be interrupted for church services. Friday nights do just fine for a substitute, and start the weekends off right. The Lord figures it's a good way to keep people out of bars and dance halls on Friday nights. And," he added with a knowing grin, "country clubs, too."

That was a nice jab.

Pastor Ledbetter drew himself up and

said, "There's a clear mandate to honor the Sabbath and keep it holy."

"You certainly know your Bible, Brother," Brother Vern said with a sly gleam in his eye. "And our Jewish friends honor the Sabbath every Saturday that rolls around. But us evangelical Christians honor the Lord every day of the week, don't matter to us what the calendar says."

"Well, but I—"

"Mr. Puckett," I interrupted, "was there something you wanted to see me about? Pastor Ledbetter and Dr. Fowler were just leaving."

Pastor Ledbetter found his voice. "Miss Julia, if you don't mind, we haven't finished with our concerns. Why don't you let Mr. Puckett here state his business, and then we can pick up where we left off."

Pastor Ledbetter wasn't anxious to leave me alone with a preacher who used television to raise money to stay on television. He probably thought I was one of those poor souls who believed a preacher with a Cadillac needed their Social Security checks worse than they did. I noticed Dr. Fowler pulling a little notepad from his jacket pocket.

"Then let's all have a seat," I said. I didn't know how Brother Vern could help my current situation, but he was doing a good job of distracting the other two. And I was happy to note that I wasn't having even a twinge of interest toward him. "Now, Mr. Puckett, what can I help you with?"

He sat across from me in the matching Victorian chair and ignored the other two on the sofa. "You heard about how my precious little great-nephew's been kidnapped?"

Pastor Ledbetter and Dr. Fowler exchanged surprised glances, and Dr. Fowler began jotting notes on his pad.

"I heard," I said. "That is, I heard that a child was missing in Spartanburg. Don't tell me it was the same child! Why, Mr. Puckett, it couldn't be! I mean, you took him to Raleigh! Didn't you? That's what you told me you were going to do." I might've been overplaying it, but he didn't seem to notice.

"Well, now," he said, pulling out a large white handkerchief and wiping the palms of his hands. "We was on our way, but when the Lord leads you to preach, you just have to stop and preach."

"But you took the child on Sunday," I reminded him. "And according to the lieutenant who notified me, the child went missing on Tuesday night. Late Tuesday night, too late for a child of that age to be up. Sounds to me like somebody wasn't taking care of him."

"That boy was gettin' three a day and plenty of sleep," Brother Vern said. "And I was going to take him to his mama, just as soon as I finished my telecast. We was going to drive on down to Raleigh right afterwards." He wiped his face with the handkerchief.

Pastor Ledbetter's eyes bounced from one to the other of us, mentally taking note of what else I was mixed up in. Dr. Fowler was just taking notes.

"Mrs. Springer," Brother Vern went on, a pleading tone in his voice now. "I mightta done wrong by not taking that boy right on down to Raleigh, but my conscience is clear. I did my best by him, and can't nobody help it when some strange black woman comes outta nowhere and snatches him away. Now I've come here to ask your help in gettin' him back. The police're doin' all they can, and it looks like to me that what we need is to offer some reward money." He wiped his forehead and glanced at me with those black eyes. "I've come to appeal to your spirit of Christian charity."

Pastor Ledbetter sat straight up, opening his mouth to protest. I cut him off.

"How much?"

"Why, whatever you find it in your heart to give. Whatever you think best, but it ought to be enough to get people's attention. You know, so if anybody has any information, they'll come forward. Or so that black woman will be tempted. I'll put it out over my *Feeding the Flame* program, and everybody'll be looking for that precious child."

"How much?"

"Miss Julia." Pastor Ledbetter couldn't stand it any longer. "Think about this before you do anything. You need to pray about this. Who knows where that child is? Or who has him? Don't get involved with this until you have more information."

Dr. Fowler's eyes gleamed as his notes began to cover a second page.

I waved off my pastor and kept my attention on Brother Vern.

"How much?"

"Well, I was thinking, maybe, ten thousand?" Brother Vern said.

"Ten thousand," I repeated.

"Five, if that's all you can do."

"I was thinking more along the lines of twenty-five," I said. "For a start."

Brother Vern's face brightened and Pastor Ledbetter buried his in his hands.

"The Lord bless you, Mrs. Springer!" Brother Vern cried. "I'll get that boy back, the Lord be praised!"

"Miss Julia," Pastor Ledbetter said, "you oughtn't do this. You're not yourself, we know it and you know it. Don't make any rash decisions before a guardian can be appointed. I beg you, don't squander Mr. Springer's estate that he worked so hard for. This is just the sort of thing Dr. Fowler and I are trying to forestall by taking care of you."

"Pastor, I don't need taking care of, and Mr. Springer's estate is as safe as it was the day he left this vale of tears." I smiled at him, then at Dr. Fowler and Brother Vern. "If you need more, Brother Vern, just let me know."

"Lord bless you, Mrs. Springer!" Brother

Vern leaned back in his chair and gave Pastor Ledbetter a complacent smile.

The door from the kitchen swung open, and Lillian's run-over heels slapped on the floor as she came toward the living room. I started from my chair, my heart pounding.

"I brought y'all some more lemonade," she sang out, balancing a full pitcher on a tray.

Brother Vern sprang from his chair like he'd been shot. "That's her!" He pointed at her, index finger quivering, as he bellowed, "She's the one! Call the sheriff!"

"Jesus Lord, help me!" Lillian shrieked, throwing her hands up as tray, pitcher, and three quarts of lemonade sprayed the room. She turned and ran for the kitchen.

"Citizen's arrest!" Brother Vern cried, running after her. "Stop, woman, you're under arrest!"

"What in the world?" Pastor Ledbetter asked, standing and shaking out his trousers, soaked with Lillian's lemonade. "Has everybody lost their minds?"

Dr. Fowler nodded as he wet a finger and turned a page, then began scribbling even faster.

CHAPTER TWENTY-NINE

—

I ran from the room, heading for the stairs, as Pastor Ledbetter yelled, "The man's crazy! Call the police!"

"That's what I'm doing," I yelled back, hitting the stairs as fast as I could. No time for the telephone; I had a live-in deputy upstairs.

Brother Vern's voice, loud with outrage and righteous indignation, echoed from the kitchen under Lillian's screams for me to save her.

I got to the top of the stairs, out of breath and terrified, fearing what Brother Vern could do to us all.

"Deputy Bates! Wake up, get up, we need you!" I pounded on his door.

"What is it?" he called, but the door stayed closed.

I pounded harder. "Hurry, hurry! Open up, we need you right now!"

I heard rustling sounds behind the door, almost drowned out by the commotion downstairs. Pastor Ledbetter came to the foot of the stairs, adding his bass rumble to the din.

"Miss Julia!" he called. "If you won't call the police, I will. This is intolerable! We can't have this, we just can't have it!"

I leaned over the banister and said, "Pastor, I'm calling the police as fast as I can. Now, get in the kitchen and keep that fool away from Lillian." A pan banged off the kitchen wall and clattered on the floor.

I pounded at Deputy Bates's door again, screaming, "Get up! We got to save Lillian. Deputy Coleman Bates, get outta that bed, you hear me!"

Behind me, another door banged open and Little Lloyd ran out, eyes big and frightened, his mother right behind him.

"What is it?" she asked. "Is there a fire? Run, Junior, we got to get everybody out!"

"Fire! Fire!" Little Lloyd screamed, jumping around with his skinny arms flying every which way.

"No, no!" I grabbed him and held him close, trying to calm him down. "It's not a fire, it's Lillian. I've got to get Deputy Bates up to help us."

Hazel Marie banged on the door along with me as the racket from the kitchen grew louder. She had on one of my dresses, looking for the first time like she might rejoin the living.

"Deputy Bates!" we both screamed.

The door opened a crack, revealing one of Deputy Bates's eyes, glinting fiercely, and a shock of hair.

"What is it?" He didn't sound pleased at being summoned to duty.

"It's Lillian! And Brother Vern!" I felt Hazel Marie's shock at hearing the name, and thought for a minute that she was going to turn and run. "Get out here and arrest him! I want him in jail before he hurts Lillian!"

Deputy Bates reached down and zipped up his dark blue uniform pants. Then he grabbed a white undershirt and pulled it over his head. "Is he attacking her?"

"That's what I'm trying to tell you! He's attacking her and right here in my own house!"

"Deputy Bates," Little Lloyd cried, "don't let him hurt Miss Lillian!"

"Where'd you come from, Bud?" Deputy Bates stopped, clearly surprised to see Little Lloyd, then he got a good look at Hazel Marie. Her face had healed considerably, but it could still pretty much stop a truck if you weren't prepared for it. Which he wasn't.

"See there," I said, pointing at her. "There's an example of what that man is capable of. He did that, or let it be done. And had my house ransacked, too. Now he's trying to take Little Lloyd away from his mother!" Then I remembered that he didn't know her. "And this is his mother."

"Ma'am," he said, nodding at her. He may have been having trouble absorbing the situation.

A piercing scream from Lillian and men's voices yelling at her or at each other shook the rafters.

"He's killing Miss Lillian!" Little Lloyd screamed, his skinny little legs dancing up and down, his arms flailing like a windmill. "We got to help her!"

"Well, goddamn, I believe it!" Deputy Bates left the door open and ran barefooted to the closet. He reached up and brought down from a shelf his black-holstered police weapon. "Y'all stay up here outta the way."

He swung the door wide as he brushed past us, pulling the gun out and tossing the holster aside as he ran. I had no intention of staying upstairs, but the spectacle in his room stopped me cold.

"Binkie?" I asked, staring at her. I couldn't figure out what she was doing in my upstairs back guest room, rented now to a paying boarder. "Oh," I said, the light dawning as she hurriedly buttoned her blouse.

"Hi, Miss Julia," she said, two spots of red in her cheeks. "Nice to see you again."

She stepped into her shoes and ran her fingers through her hair. It needed a comb and a brush.

Hazel Marie and Little Lloyd stood beside me, unsure of what to do or where to go. I got myself together and made the introductions.

"Pleased, I'm sure," Hazel Marie said with a quick, knowing smile.

There was a sudden break in the action

downstairs, and in the quiet of the cease-fire, we heard Deputy Bates say, "Everybody just calm down now, and let's get this straightened out."

It's amazing what the appearance of a man in uniform, even half a uniform, can accomplish, to say nothing of a man with a gun in his hand.

"Well, Binkie," I said, pulling myself together. "It's a good thing you're here. I expect several of us're going to need a lawyer in the next few minutes. We better get on downstairs."

Not too long before, I would've been outraged at the thought of something illegal, illicit, and immoral taking place in one of my bedrooms. However. I had too many other worries to get bent out of shape over Binkie and Deputy Bates jumping the gun, so to speak. Wesley Lloyd would've had a different view, but so would every other hypocrite.

It crossed my mind that Binkie might have a touch of the problem that Pastor Ledbetter accused me of having. But if she did, Deputy Bates didn't seem to mind it very much.

CHAPTER THIRTY

—

Deputy Bates had Pastor Ledbetter, Dr. Fowler, Brother Vern, and Lillian all in the living room, seated and separated, by the time the four of us joined them. Deputy Bates stood in front of the fireplace, holding his gun down by his side, looking fully in control of the situation in spite of his state of dress, his bare feet, and what he'd been doing when I interrupted him.

"Oh, Miss Julia," Lillian cried, lifting her face out of her apron. "Don't let 'em put me in jail! You know I didn't go to kidnap that baby!"

Little Lloyd ran to her and put his arms around her. Hazel Marie stood beside her, patting her shoulder. I said, "You're not going to jail, Lillian. Binkie, do something."

"What's the charge, Deputy?" Binkie asked, all business in spite of her blouse being misbuttoned.

"No charges yet on anybody," he said, giving her a quick smile. "Still trying to find out who's done what."

"I can tell you that," I said. But everybody else started talking at the same time.

"That woman," Brother Vern said, pointing at Lillian and drowning out the rest of us, "kidnapped that child." He pointed at Little Lloyd. "And that one," he bellowed, aiming a finger at Hazel Marie, "is a woman totally without morals and unfit for motherhood."

"Miss Julia." Pastor Ledbetter started to rise, the better to pontificate, but Deputy Bates held up his hand. The pastor took his seat again. "Miss Julia, I have to protest. Just what is going on here? Who is that woman? Who is this man, and why are Dr. Fowler and I being held against our will?" He looked from Hazel Marie to Brother Vern, then raised his eyes to the ceiling. Dr. Fowler had filled his notebook and was now searching his pockets for scrap paper so he could keep writing.

"You're not being held—" Deputy Bates

started, but Brother Vern popped up out of his chair.

"I demand you arrest that woman for kidnapping! And if you won't do it, I'll make a citizen's arrest right here and now!"

"Just try it, buster," Binkie said, getting right in his face.

"Now, folks," Deputy Bates said. "Let's all calm down."

"I can't calm down," Lillian sobbed. "They gonna put me in jail!"

"No they're not, Miss Lillian!" Little Lloyd cried, throwing his arms around her. "I won't let them put you in jail."

"Stay out of this, boy," Brother Vern said, giving him a cold look. "You'll be in a foster home or juvenile hall. I've had all the trouble outta you I'm gonna take."

"You just shut your trap, Vernon Puckett," Hazel Marie said, pulling Little Lloyd to her and standing closer to Lillian. "We've all had all we're gonna take from you. I've been beat to within an inch of my life on your say-so, and you took my boy from me, and I'm gonna swear out a warrant on you!"

"Listen, listen," Pastor Ledbetter said, unaccustomed to having to struggle to be heard, "this has got to stop. I don't know what's been going on here, but it's evident that somebody's taken leave of their senses." He looked at me. "And no telling what's been allowed to take place upstairs in this very house, what with both these young women up there with this law officer. Looks to me like you've been keeping a disorderly house, Miss Julia, among the other things I know about. Somebody's got to step in and do something."

That was a clear threat if I'd ever heard one, and I shriveled up inside at the thought of him being led to tell everything he knew, or thought he knew. Even if his diagnosis was wrong, even if Dr. Fowler hadn't made a point of his own, so to speak, I didn't want to stand there and be shamed in front of them all.

"It's not what it seems, Pastor. Please, it's just a mix-up." I folded my arms protectively across my chest, bringing to mind the pink paper pinned to the inside of my dress.

"Knock, knock, anybody home?" Sam stuck his head in the door. He looked around the room and said, "Looks like you're busy, Julia. I'll come back later."

He turned to leave, but I called him back. "Don't go, Sam, I need you here." If I had to be relieved of responsibility for myself, I wanted Sam to see that it was done right.

"That'd be a change," he said with a wry smile, but his eyes were traveling around the room taking in the unlikely group gathered there. Hazel Marie he didn't know, and he hadn't met Brother Vern or Dr. Fowler, but I saw him make some quick associations. I wanted to go stand beside him, but I was afraid of what I might do and what Pastor Ledbetter would think of it.

Sam raised his eyebrows as he noticed the gun in Deputy Bates's hand. "Trouble?"

"More noise than anything," Deputy Bates said, laying the gun on the mantel. But he didn't move away from it. "Now, folks. Let's get some things straightened out, and I don't want everybody talking at once. Miss Lillian, you first. Did you kidnap that boy?"

"Nossir, I did not." She sat up straight and smoothed out her apron. She trusted Deputy Bates, knowing he'd hear her out and not jump to conclusions. "That Brother Vern got this baby away from Miss Julia under false pretensions, claiming he'd take him to his mama, but 'stead of that, he taken him off an' put him on teevee, an' then we find out he let Jerome beat up on this pore little thing here." She looked up at Hazel Marie. Then dabbing at her eyes, she went on, "An' knocked out her teef too. That man a menace to decent folk."

"Menace!" Brother Vern shouted, jumping out of his chair again. Deputy Bates tapped his shoulder, and Brother Vern sat back down. But he didn't stop talking. "I'll tell you who's a menace. It's all these women running wild, interfering with the Lord's work! Hazel Marie's been living in sin for lo these many years and borne its fruit, which all I'm trying to do is look after. His daddy would've wanted somebody responsible in charge, an' that ain't her!" The words poured from his mouth like the sweat from his forehead. Brother Vern was mortally exercised.

"And now," he shouted, "here's this woman, a black woman and kitchen help at that, who walked right into my studio while I was *on the air* and put that child right back into this den of iniquity! And that's what this place looks like to me!"

"I couldn't agree more," Pastor Ledbetter said, looking at Brother Vern with something close to approval. "And, Brother, you don't know the half of it."

I grasped the back of a chair to keep from falling. Lord, I prayed, don't let him tell. Please don't let him tell.

"Just a minute, here," Binkie said. "Let's take one thing at a time. It seems to me that the kidnapping charge is moot. Here's the child; there's his mother. Where's the kidnapping?"

"But," Brother Vern said, "she took him from me."

"But you took him from me," I managed to say.

"But he's my child," Hazel Marie chimed in. "And I left him in Miz Springer's care, not his, and he has no right to claim him or raise a fuss when I got him back."

"Kidnapping's not going to stick," Binkie said with all the authority of Wake Forest Law School behind her. "What do you think, Sam?"

"I think you're right. The boy's where he belongs."

"Well. Well," Brother Vern blustered, "well, what about the reward? Miz Springer, you offered a sizable reward and I think I have a claim to it. If it wasn't for me, this child'd still be hid away somewhere."

"I think you have a point, Reverend Puckett," Pastor Ledbetter said, astounding us all. Even Brother Vern was stunned to have such an unlikely defender. "Miss Julia made a rash promise against good advice, and it seems to me she ought to make it good. She's been doing too many rash things lately, and has to accept the consequences of her actions. If, that is, she is able to understand them."

"Just a minute, here," Sam broke in. "Before you go off half-cocked, what reward are you talking about?"

"Yeah," Binkie said.

Pastor Ledbetter silenced Brother Vern with a take-charge look. "Miss Julia offered a twenty-five-thousand-dollar reward for the recovery of this kidnapped child. I was witness to it, and so was Dr. Fowler, just as we were also witnesses to something even more astonishing. I think you have to honor it, Miss Julia."

"But—"

"There was no kidnapping," Binkie said, cutting me off. "No kidnapping, no reward."

"There's something we're all overlooking here," Dr. Fowler said, proving that he could speak as well as write. I braced myself for his contribution. "Now, I realize that I'm an outsider and not familiar with all that's gone on, but it seems to me we need the answer to one important question."

"What's that?" Binkie demanded, squinting her eyes at him.

"Well, my understanding is that the child was taken from somewhere in another town, but now he's found right here. This woman"—he pointed at Lillian—"admits to having him. But the question is, how did she get him? Did she walk? Did she drive? Did she have help?"

Hazel Marie and Little Lloyd looked at me. Lord, where was Dr. Fowler going with this?

"Miss Julia," Lillian wailed.

"That's right," Brother Vern cried. "Somebody was driving that car! Everybody agreed that somebody else drove the car." He turned to me and narrowed his eyes. "Was that somebody you, Miz Springer? Were you a party to kidnapping?"

Binkie said, "Don't answer that."

Sam said, "There was no kidnapping, so it doesn't matter who drove what."

"But there was a *conspiracy* to kidnap," Pastor Ledbetter said. "Then add to that all the aimless driving around the county, plans to turn this fine house into a dog kennel, bizarre answers to common questions, apparent lying to the police, attempting to buy narcotics, getting involved with people she doesn't know and taking them in like members of the family, promising to give away twenty-five thousand dollars to a virtual stranger, and certain intractable behavior that would repulse you all if I told you of it. Well, you can see how it begins to stack up. None of you is doing Miss Julia a favor by ignoring these clear changes in her personality. She needs help, and if it takes a court case to get it for her, then so be it. At least I and her church family care enough to prevent any harm coming to her. We mean to take care of her, since it's abundantly clear she can't take care of herself."

"Clear as a bell," Dr. Fowler said. "As I will so testify."

Chapter Thirty-one

—

My head swiveled from Sam to Binkie, waiting for one of them to say the accusations were ridiculous. Sam frowned, deep in thought, and Binkie chewed her thumbnail.

"Can they do that?" I asked.

"They'd have to prove it," Sam said hesitantly, as if wondering what I'd done that he didn't know about.

"Which they'd have a hard time doing," Binkie added.

"That depends," Dr. Fowler said. "It depends on what they're trying to prove. If it's a criminal charge, yes, it would be hard to prove. But Brother Vern's testimony, added to that of so many others, including mine and her pastor's, could well make a case for diminished capacity."

Binkie turned on him, her hair swinging in her face. "Who *are* you?"

"I'm Dr. Fred Fowler, certified clinical psychologist." He stood a little straighter as he said it. "And I've been retained by the session of the First Presbyterian Church to look into this matter."

"Good grief!" Binkie said, throwing up her hands.

Sam's eyes rolled back in his head worse than I'd ever seen. Hazel Marie tightened her arm around Lillian's shoulders, and Pastor Ledbetter sat back with his hands clasped over his abdomen, composed and content. Brother Vern's black eyes ranged avidly over us all, watching for any other unexpected advantage.

"Now, Mrs. Springer," Dr. Fowler went on, his voice as soft as if he were gentling a wild woman. "We don't want you to be concerned. No one's going to hurt you, I promise. And no one is going to reveal any embarrassing details as long as you allow us to help you. Everything's going to be just fine. All we're concerned about is your welfare. I suggest you let me admit you to my infirmary for a few tests. And you can have a well-deserved rest at the same time."

"Sam?" I said, beginning to realize that they really could have me committed to some linoleum-floored, Lysol-smelling dormitory for the demented, doomed to the droning of game shows and Jenny Jones for the rest of my life.

"You know we'll take care of you, Miss Julia," Pastor Ledbetter said. "I've already begun the process, because I know Mr. Springer would want us to look after you."

"What they talkin' about?" Lillian asked, her eyes big with the fear that was beginning to well up in me.

"Binkie?" I said, turning to her.

"I'm thinking, I'm thinking," she said, pacing back and forth. "The problem is, the *big* problem is . . . Sam, you see what I mean?"

"Yeah, the clerk of court."

"The clerk of court?" I gasped as my soul dropped down to my feet. "You mean *Leonard*? Leonard *Conover*?"

"That's right," Sam said. "Leonard Conover's the one who'd handle this, the one who'd have the final disposition of their application. And the one who'd appoint a guardian. But hang on, Julia, we're not without a few resources of our own."

"Don't be too sure," Pastor Ledbetter said. "You may not be aware of the details of Miss Julia's recent erratic behavior."

I looked at his confident expression and at the gleam in the peculiar eyes of Dr. Fowler, and I knew they were prepared to ruin my life forever. I pictured a line of my friends and neighbors testifying in open court about the changes they'd seen in me. I pictured Dr. Fowler describing that episode in the bridal parlor, and I pictured Leonard Conover, who thought the sun rose and set on Pastor Ledbetter, deciding my fate. I felt a tremor run through my body. Men, religious men, had been making decisions for me all my life, telling me not to worry, do what I tell you, I know what's best for you, what you want is not important. And I'd let them, always assuming that they were right, that they knew more than I did, that it was my place to agree and go along, even as the icy knife of resentment cut wider and deeper into my heart. While I smiled and kept on smiling. Only since Wesley Lloyd's passing had I felt like a real person. So, yes, Pastor Ledbetter was right; I had changed. I was different from what I'd always been. Now I said what I was thinking instead of packing it down inside. Now I did what I wanted to do instead of what I was told to do. Now I followed my own inclinations instead of waiting for instructions. I'd discovered that I was neither a child nor a half-wit, and I'd refused to be treated as either. I was a grown woman.

No wonder they thought I was crazy.

Yet I also knew that without Wesley Lloyd's money, there wouldn't be this concern for my welfare, even if I threw myself at every man in town. If I'd been as broke as Hazel Marie, they might bring me a few casseroles and a box of dusting powder at Christmas, but they wouldn't be trying to put me in a two-hundred-dollar-a-day nursing home. That money had given me a freedom I'd never known, and now it was about to bind me up worse than Wesley Lloyd ever had.

My hands shook as I reached up and began to unbutton the bodice of my dress.

Brother Vern drew in a sibilant breath, while Dr. Fowler and Pastor Ledbetter began to back away. Pastor Ledbetter's face paled, his mouth dropping open, as if he feared I'd choose him as my next victim.

"Don't," he gasped. "Fred, do something."

But Fred ducked his head and sidled toward the door. He wasn't about to tangle with me again.

I unbuttoned the second button. Sam and Binkie looked shocked, but no more than Lillian and Deputy Bates.

Hazel Marie was the only one who moved. She walked over and stood in front of me, shielding me from them. She placed both her hands on mine.

"Oh, honey," she said, so softly I could barely hear her. "Don't do this. Let's me and you go upstairs."

My bones went weak on me as her poor, battered face swam out of focus through the tears that flooded my eyes. I'd never before in my life been called a sweet name by somebody who really meant it.

"It's all right," I whispered to her. "It's really all right."

We looked at each other a long second, then she nodded and took her hands from mine. But she stayed in front of me while I continued to unbutton my bodice. I reached inside and unpinned the pink paper. When I had it out, Hazel Marie rebuttoned my dress for me and stepped to my side.

"Here, Sam," I said, holding the paper out to him. "This should go to you. I expect it'll change a few things."

CHAPTER THIRTY-TWO

—

Sam walked over and took the paper from me. He unfolded it, read it, and looked at me with what might've been a gleam of admiration in his eyes. It might've been pity, though, I couldn't tell which. Everybody watched as Sam looked down and read it again, shaking his head and pursing his mouth in thought. Hazel Marie slid her arm around my waist, and I was grateful for the support since I was feeling a bit wobbly. Everybody in the room was aware that the flimsy piece of pink paper was of great import. Only Sam and I knew how great.

Binkie said, "What is it?"

"It's a holographic will," Sam said.

"A holy what?" Hazel Marie asked.

"A handwritten will." He held it out to

Binkie to read. "Wesley Lloyd Springer wrote it the night he died, according to the date. And it does change things. A good many things."

"What do it say?" Lillian asked, picking up on the charged atmosphere and misinterpreting it. "What time Mr. Springer write that thing, befo' he passed or after?"

"Before, Miss Lillian," Binkie assured her, "before. Probably sometime that day."

"Read it out loud, Binkie," I said, "so everybody'll know."

"Here, Sam," she said, handing the paper to him. "It's your place to read it." She went over and stood by Deputy Bates.

"What it says," Sam began, "is that Mr. Springer left his entire estate to his son, Little Lloyd here."

Dead silence as everyone looked at the boy. Except me, who was still trying to control the trembling as I waited to feel their pity directed my way.

"What!" Pastor Ledbetter was the first to find his voice. "Why, that can't be! Can he do that? Is that thing legal?"

"As legal as it can get," Sam said. "I can attest to the signature."

"I don't believe it! Miss Julia, I . . . you, we

have to do something, fight it, take it to court, something!"

"Forget it, Pastor," Binkie said, standing under Deputy Bates's arm, which was stretched out across the mantel. "That will's as solid as a rock, much to Miss Julia's sorrow, I'm sure."

As Pastor Ledbetter looked for help from Dr. Fowler, who had none to offer, Brother Vern approached Sam. "Spell that out for me if you will, Brother."

"It simply means that the boy inherits his father's estate when he reaches maturity."

"Everything?"

"That's what it says."

"The Lord be praised! Child," he said, turning a benevolent face toward Little Lloyd, "you have been blessed beyond belief and, undoubtedly, your family with you. Hazel Marie, you gonna need help raisin' this boy. It's a great responsibility, but I'm here to help every step of the way."

Hazel Marie had not moved from my side. She looked from Sam to Brother Vern, and back to Sam again.

"You mean," she said, "Wesley Lloyd left everything to Junior when he gets grown?"

"Yes," Sam said, "but it also means that

he, and you, will be taken care of financially from now on."

Hazel Marie was trembling worse than I was by this time. She put her hand up to cover her mouth. "I don't understand," she said.

"It means, Hazel Marie," I said, "that you won't have to crack a lick at a snake ever again."

She crumpled against me, both hands covering her face as she sobbed. "Oh, Miz Springer, that's just not right."

"Of course it's right," I told her, patting her back. "Sam wouldn't make such a mistake."

"No, I mean it's not fair. You were his legal wife, can he do this?"

"Mama?" Little Lloyd came to us, his face wrinkled with worry to see his mother crying. "What's the matter, Mama? What's going to happen to us?"

"Not a thing, Little Lloyd," I said. "All your troubles are over, and your mama is crying from happiness. You don't have to worry where you're going to live or what you're going to do from now on. In fact, you can live right here, if you want to." I patted Hazel Marie's back with one hand and put my other arm around Little Lloyd's shoulders, trying to comfort them in their joy.

"Right here?" Little Lloyd's face glowed at the thought. "With you? And Miss Lillian? Mama, hear that? Miz Springer wants us to live here with her."

"Oh, child." I sighed, thinking my heart might break.

I glanced at Lillian, who had thrown her head back against her chair. Her eyes were closed and her mouth moved in what I hoped was fervent prayer for us all. Me, especially, because I was the one who needed it.

"Miss Julia," Pastor Ledbetter said, "I am so sorry." He dropped into a chair and leaned his elbows on his knees. Then he wiped his face with both hands, frowning and slowly shaking his head. "Nobody could've foreseen such an outcome. You don't suppose," he said, looking hopefully at Dr. Fowler, "that we could help Miss Julia break this new will?"

"Unlikely," he snapped, as if he were fed up with the whole situation, "if it's as authentic as it appears to be. Besides, if we supported her in breaking it, how would it

appear to the court if you then made application to have her declared incompetent?"

"Good point," Binkie said.

"Well," Pastor Ledbetter said, "I don't
suppose anybody will believe this, but I am
truly concerned for Miss Julia. What will
she do, in her condition, if this will has
made her destitute? Sam, what can the
church do to help?"

"Maybe the best thing," Sam told him qui-
etly, "is to give Julia a chance to absorb
this. It comes as a shock, you know. There
are a few options she can consider, so why
don't you and the good doctor, or whatever
he is, give her some time. Then if she needs
the church's help, she'll let you know."

"Yes, that's good advice." He rose to his
full height and came over to me. "I am so
sorry about all of this, Miss Julia. Maybe I
was wrong to proceed as I did, but I want
you to know it was from the best of intentions."

"I know, Pastor, and I appreciate those
good intentions. And I'd appreciate it even
more if you'd call off Leonard before he
does some major damage."

He nodded, murmuring something about
the Lord issuing a call to a new ministry.

We're told to forgive those who trespass against us, but I declare it was a bitter pill to swallow to keep my mouth shut about his current ministry.

After Pastor Ledbetter and Dr. Fowler took their leave, Brother Vern seemed to expand to fill the space. "Let me add my deep concern to theirs for your misfortune, Miz Springer," he said, hardly able to suppress the smile that pulled at the corners of his mouth. "Now, Hazel Marie, pull yourself together, girl, and let's let these lawyers tell us about this child's inheritance. Maybe we ought to decide right quick how it'll be managed; you can't get slack on these matters, you know."

Hazel Marie took her tear-stained face from my shoulder and looked around. "Brother Vern, there's no we involved in this. Deputy Bates, I want to swear out a peace warrant on this man. Can you do that for me?"

"Yes, ma'am," he said. "We'll have to go to the magistrate's office, but for now, Brother Vern, I'd advise you to keep your distance from these people. Are you understanding me?"

"Why, Hazel Marie, I'm your own kin, and

your nearest male relative," Brother Vern implored. "Nearest that's grown, I mean. But if that don't mean nothing to you, remember that I can have you declared an unfit mother and have myself appointed the boy's guardian. I don't want to do that, 'cause it'll be a long, drawn-out mess, but I will if you push me to it."

Sam said, "Maybe you better look this over before you make any plans to go to court." He held the will out so Brother Vern could read it, but he didn't let go of it.

Brother Vern took enough time to read it two or three times, his face growing longer and sadder as he read. "Hazel Marie's not the guardian?" he finally asked.

"No," Sam said. "I am."

Hazel Marie's body vibrated with tension at this new turn of events. "Does he mean," she asked me, "that he wants to take my boy, too?"

"No, that's not what it means," Sam assured her. "All the will specifies is that I am the executor of the will and the boy's financial guardian. The court will assign me to oversee the boy's general welfare, his education, and to manage his affairs until he's old enough to do it himself. You are his mother and primary caregiver, and it'll be up to me to see that you both live comfortably. And," he said firmly to Brother Vern, "having Miss Puckett declared unfit will not change my responsibility to the estate in any way and it would not benefit any other member of the boy's family. On top of that, my opinion of Miss Puckett's fitness will weigh heavily in any court in the land and, from what I've seen, she's doing a fine job with this boy."

Brother Vern's face darkened as Sam laid it out for him. He didn't linger after that, leaving with an ill grace and a show of bad manners, like letting the screen door slam behind him. You can always tell when somebody's not been raised right.

"I still can't believe all this," Hazel Marie said, tears threatening again. "And I still don't think it's right. Miz Springer, what does all this mean for you?"

"Well," I said, taking a deep breath and trying to accept my fate more gracefully than Brother Vern. "It means that I'm destitute. It means that Wesley Lloyd didn't care whether I had a roof over my head or not."

"I care, Miz Springer!" Little Lloyd cried. "You can live with us, can't she, Mama?"

"She sure can." Hazel Marie smiled her closed-mouth smile. I hoped the first thing she did with Wesley Lloyd's money was to get her teeth fixed. And the second thing, a pair of glasses for his son that fit. "Why don't you do that, Miz Springer? I'd really like you to."

"No, it wouldn't do at all. I can't accept charity, though I thank you for offering. No, what I have to do is submit to the Lord's will, or to Wesley Lloyd's, whichever is responsible for this. The Lord giveth, and the Lord taketh away," I added, striving for a piety I was neither familiar with nor presently feeling.

"Wel-l-l," Sam said, eyes twinkling as he smiled broadly. "He hasn't quite taken everything away."

Binkie laughed out loud and snuggled up against Deputy Bates, right there in my living room. Except it wasn't mine any longer, so I didn't care if she did snuggle.

"I don't see a thing funny about an old woman with no place to lay her head and with nothing to eat," I told them. "It seems to me that you two would have a little more sympathy, or at least wait to laugh at me when I'm gone."

"Don't you worry, Miz Springer," Hazel Marie said. "You'll never be without as long as I have a nickel to my name."

Binkie and Sam couldn't control their laughter, both of them sputtering and carrying on until my feelings were hurting so bad I wanted to bawl out loud.

"Tell her, Sam," Binkie said, finally coming up for air.

"Julia, Julia, Julia," Sam said. "Sorry to carry on this way, but I think we've put over a big one on all those who wanted to get a hand in your pocket. Fact of the matter is," he said, coming over beside me, "in this state, a spouse always has a share in an estate. No matter what Wesley Lloyd intended, and he may well have known this, as his widow you are entitled to half of his estate. And half of the Springer estate is not to be sneezed at. We'll have to file a dissent to the will, but that'll be pretty cut and dried."

I had to sit down. Then I had to get my breath back. And I didn't want Sam too close to me, not knowing what I'd do in my weakened state. I had a powerful urge to throw my arms around him.

"That mean," Lillian asked, "that bof' Miss

Julia and this baby gets Mr. Springer's financials?"

"Yep," Sam said, still grinning. "That's what it means."

"Thank you, Jesus!"

"And thank the state of North Carolina," I said, giving credit where it was due. Then, squinching my eyes at both of them, I said, "Sam, did you and Binkie know this all along?"

"Sure we did," Binkie said. "But I was afraid Dr. Fowler or somebody else might've known it, too."

"Well, this beats all," Deputy Bates said, his arm firmly around Binkie by now. He seemed almost as happy as I was beginning to feel.

"But, Julia," Sam said, "you weren't really concerned about anything, were you? You could always come live with me, you know."

"I know no such thing." And he wouldn't offer such a thing if he'd known my suspected condition.

"Aw, you know I'd take care of you."

"Sam Murdoch, let me tell you something right now. I don't need you or any other man to take care of me. I can do that well enough by myself. And I can do it even better with the help of Little Lloyd and Hazel Marie, if they're willing. I think this house is big enough for the three of us. And Deputy Bates, and Binkie, too, if she wants."

"An' me, too," Lillian said.

"Yes, you, too, Miss Lillian," Little Lloyd said, so happy I was afraid he was going to start flailing those skinny arms around again.

"Praise God," Hazel Marie said, smiling so wide that the two-toothed gap was open for viewing.

We'd have to get that fixed, along with several other things before too long. One of the first things, in case Pastor Ledbetter'd been halfway right, would have to be getting myself straightened out. Even if it meant going to Switzerland or Sweden or wherever they have those quick-change clinics. I'd make a list of all we needed to do, and Hazel Marie and I could spend some time spending Wesley Lloyd's money. He'd always thought he'd take it with him, but it was ours now and I knew we'd put it to better use than he ever had. And enjoy it more, too.

———

Spending his money and enjoying it is mostly what we've been doing for some time now. Lillian still comes by the day, and Binkie's in and out, although Deputy Bates spends a lot of time at her place. They ought to be thinking about making it legal, and I aim to tell them so if they don't soon come to it themselves.

We haven't heard from Brother Vern, but he's still feeding the flame on television. I sent him twenty dollars a few weeks ago, and got back a book he'd written about the end of the world. I couldn't fathom it, since it was all about the Book of Daniel and Russia and Revelation and blowing hot and cold.

Pastor Ledbetter doesn't visit much. His time's mostly taken up with his retirement-home ministry now, and he's over there most days ministering to the sick, the demented, and the dying, none of which applies to me. He's very solicitous of me, though, greeting me mournfully each and every Sunday, like he understands how hard I'm having it. He's still leery of Hazel Marie, as she is of him. Or rather of the Presbyterian way of worshiping. She's not used to our sedate ways, but she goes with me and holds her head up high.

LuAnne Conover still can't get over our living arrangements. She told me that she could never bring herself to be friends with a woman Leonard took up with. I thought to myself it was unlikely that any woman would ever take up with Leonard, but I didn't say anything. She's visiting a little more now since Hazel Marie showed her how to backcomb her hair.

I've adjusted to living with a house full of people better than you might think. I moved my bedroom downstairs to what used to be Wesley Lloyd's study, and gave what used to be our bedroom to Hazel Marie. I threw out the bed I'd shared with him, and bought new ones for her and for myself. I'm cutting off as many untoward associations as I can.

This house is big enough to have privacy when we want it, and when Deputy Bates moves on we'll fix up that area as a sitting room for Hazel Marie and Little Lloyd. With the back staircase, she can entertain privately if she wants to. So far, she's shown no inclination toward entertaining anyone, in spite of one or two widowers in the church casting their eyes in her direction. I think she's like me, once burned, twice shy—especially since it was a man like Wesley Lloyd Springer doing the burning.

But for now, she's good company to me, and I'm learning a lot from her. She's going to do my colors as soon as the scarves come.

Sam is Sam, and I like him that way, which is all I'm going to say on that subject.

On second thought, I might as well say one more thing. Sam asked me not long ago if there was anything I wanted to tell him.

"Like what?" I asked, wondering if he'd guessed or heard something about my awful secret. I thought I had my problem pretty much under control, if I had a problem at all, since with all the men I'd been around recently, not one had created any inner disturbances.

Well, to be honest, I'd felt the condition stir around a little whenever Sam smiled at me.

"Ledbetter kept hinting that something was wrong with you. Are you sick, Julia?"

He put both hands on my arms and said, "If anything's wrong, I want to know about it."

I shook my head, feeling the tears well up at his concern. "No, you don't," I whispered. "It's too awful."

"Tell me. And let me help you with it."

"It's incurable, Sam, at least that's what the pastor said." All the secrets and shame that I'd locked up inside seemed to rush out on his shoulder as I leaned against him. "He said it's a sin I have to guard against all the time, and I don't know whether he was right about it or not. And, Sam, I'm so tired of praying about it, I don't know what to do."

"I can't imagine you having a sin that bad, sweetheart." He put his arms around me and pulled me close, not realizing what danger he might be in.

"You better turn me loose, Sam," I said, unable to leave him under my own steam. "Pastor Ledbetter and Dr. Fowler said I'm suffering from"—I lowered my voice, hardly daring to say the word but wanting to protect Sam from the consequences—*"nymphomania."*

"Wha-at?" He started laughing and he laughed so hard, I tried to pull away from him so I could run hide in a dark corner somewhere. "Oh, Julia, why didn't you tell me you were suffering from this condition?" He ran a finger down the side of my face and said, "Don't you know I've got the cure for that?"

And he does, and that's really all I'm going to say on the subject.

The rest of us have been getting along fine together, too. Little Lloyd has filled out some and he's taken on more of his mother's looks and, Lillian tells me, some of my ways. Which will undoubtedly be of help to him in the future. Sam opened a small checking account for him, and I'm teaching him to write checks and reconcile his bank statement. I must say, he's taken to it right smartly and does it well. You're never too young to learn to handle your money. Or too old, either, as I'm living proof of.

I've learned a lot through all these ups and downs, and the greatest of these is not to live a lie. Wesley Lloyd did, and look what it got him: a heart attack brought on by the stress of it and two women who hardly ever give him a thought. I was tempted to live a lie, almost did it, and look what not doing it got me: a real, though unrelated, family and a conscience that's as clear as a bell. I declare, that's worth half of Wesley Lloyd's estate any day of the week.